ABRACADAVER

**Mysteries by Peter Lovesey
in Perennial Library:**

ABRACADAVER

PETER LOVESEY

PERENNIAL LIBRARY

Harper & Row, Publishers, New York
Grand Rapids, Philadelphia, St. Louis
San Francisco, London, Singapore
Sydney, Tokyo, Toronto

ONE

She burst into Number 4 dressing-room at the Middlesex and wrenched down her spangled bodice to the waist. 'You see that?' she demanded, in case anyone was not riveted by the spectacle. 'A bruise like a set of Crimea medals! The hussy! The stupid, fumbling baggage!'

Jason Buckmaster, rhetorician, elocutionist to Royalty and privileged at that moment to be in the female dressing-room, raised a disciplined eyebrow. 'An abrasion, Miss Lola? How damnably inconvenient. Does one gather that the sisterly *rapport* was a little less than perfect on the high trapeze tonight?'

'Bloody near killed me, that's all!' responded Lola with quivering indignation. 'In me death-defying leap, too. You've seen the end of the act when she swings out to meet me as I dive for her ankles? Well, the silly bitch went too soon and caught me full in the chest with her great feet. I found meself in agony, dangling over the bloody audience with me arms round — if you'll forgive the expression — her thighs, and precious near dragging off her tights to hold on. Me eyes was watering with pain and I must have been pink with the shame of it. We hung there for two minutes before Mr Winter thought of pulling us in with a windowpole. Like two perishing trout on a line. It ain't dignified for a serious artiste.' She glanced down at the strawberry-coloured blotch. 'And it don't do nothing for a girl's prospects.'

From deep in Buckmaster's vocal organs came an unmistakable purring. 'Prospects?' He smiled. ' "For wheresoe'er I turn my ravished eyes, Gay gilded scenes and shining prospects rise." '

'What?'

'Nothing, my dear. A snatch of Addison, and in a different context. Forgive me. I have nothing but concern for your disfiguration. If it were any consolation at all I would observe that your — er — prospects are unimpaired. I shall leave you now, before Miss Bella returns. The disclosure of a second set of injuries might affect me profoundly.'

A vast man, he flitted away with the unobtrusiveness of a veteran haunter of dressing-rooms.

'Barmy,' decided Lola.

The only others present, a mother and daughter from Marseilles who spoke no English and spent up to an hour before each performance applying rouge and powder in order to shout 'Allez!' and lift their right arms as Papa performed feats of equilibrium, ignored Lola. She, clicking her tongue in exasperation, gave her full attention to the blemish, presenting it to the mirror from an assortment of angles. Then she ran some water into the basin in front of her and plunged her hands in to clean off the resin.

The door opened. Lola's double, blonde, spangled, pretty as a case of butterflies, tiptoed in and peeped across her sister's shoulder into the mirror. 'Makes a change to have a *foot*print on your chest, don't it darling? That's original! My, when the word gets round in Leicester Square—'

The wet sponge flew safely over Bella's head as she ducked, but the rain of articles that followed — nailbrush, soaps, cream-jars, powder-bowl — bounced off a screen behind her and scored several sharp impacts on her arched back.

'Dollymop!' screamed Lola. 'Blundering great jade!' She had picked up a weighty mother-of-pearl clothesbrush and was about to hurl it after the rest when a cry of 'Non!' from the end of the room arrested her. Made heroic by the threat to her property, the tightrope walker's daughter rushed forward to retrieve her brush, and Bella used the diversion to find cover from the bombardment behind the screen.

'Now listen to me, Lo,' she appealed from her temporary refuge. 'I'm the one with reason to complain, not you. If you was hurt it's your own fault—'

'Me own fault!' shrieked her sister. 'What do you mean, you stinking haybag? Your swing was all wrong. You went off too bloody soon. Nearly kicked me blinking head off, that's what you did. I count meself lucky to finish with a bruise like a map of all the Russias across me front. Otherwise I might be dead!'

It was a pity Bella was behind the screen, because she missed the impact of all the Russias bobbing emphatically with the force of Lola's invective. 'I went off perfect,' she insisted. 'You'd better admit it, Lo — you swung too far. That's the plain truth, and calling me names can't change it, you dotty old goose.'

Lola swept the screen aside. 'Swung too far? When have I ever swung too far? I suppose you didn't have a nip of something before you went up tonight, did you?'

This was too much for Bella. She straightened from her cowering stance and faced her accuser, bruised and brazen as she was. 'You know very well I've worn the blue ribbon now for seven months, Lo, and I haven't broken out once! Before you start throwing the blame on others, *darling,* I suggest you make sure of your own little weakness. By the time *you* got back to the diggings after walking out with your fancy soldier-boy last night I knew it wasn't walking you'd been doing. With the life you lead, it's a wonder you haven't muffed the act before tonight!'

Lola erupted. 'You foul-mouthed mot! I shan't take that from anyone!'

She had grabbed her sister's hair, forced her against the wall and was poised with her hand on her costume to exact vengeance, when there was a shout from behind.

'Ladies, ladies, ladies!' piped Buckmaster. 'In

4

Heaven's name desist! You can't know how the sight of such talent exposed to danger affects me. I have news for you. Look!'

He held out two pieces of rope, each about eighteen inches in length. The sisters were so mystified that they relaxed their holds.

'What the hell are those?' demanded Lola.

'Those, my dear, are the lengths of rope cut from your sister's trapeze. I found them among the props on the O.P. side of the stage. Someone very neatly shortened the length of your trapeze, Miss Lola. Your accident tonight was planned in cold blood. You are fortunate to be alive.'

A twice-weekly ordeal was taking place in a back room of Paradise Street Police Station, Rotherhithe. Edward Thackeray, as experienced a constable as you would find in M Division, stabbed the blunt end of his pencil distractedly through his beard as he neared the point of decision. Eight fellow-sufferers watched him gather himself. There was a shuffling of large boots and a tensing of bulky shoulders. A clearing of the throat, a forward lean and he rose irrevocably from his chair, the ridiculous desk in front of him nudging forward with a squeak as his knees straightened.

'Well, Constable?'

A deep breath. 'An adjective, sir.' Spoken with absolute assurance.

The Educational Inspector winced. 'What did you say?'

'Adverb. That is to say . . . adverbial pronoun, sir.'

An indrawn hiss from the inspector. 'Perhaps you should try spelling the word instead.'

Thackeray considered this and decided in the circumstances it was wiser not to make the attempt. He assumed as knowing an expression as he could muster, and smiled.

There was no answering smile. 'I should have remembered, Constable, of course. It is your practice to avoid spelling any word of more than two syllables. That is why, in the exercise I shall shortly return, you avoided the pitfalls of the word "misdemeanour" and substituted the alternative phrase "minor offence." An ingenious stratagem, you will concede, gentlemen. The pity is that Constable Thackeray's spelling is not equal to his ingenuity. His "minor" is a toiler beneath the ground, and "offence" when Thackeray spells it is a wooden enclosure.' Dramatically, the inspector assumed the pose of a man plagued past endurance, bowing his head and drawing a set of chalky fingers through his hair. Then he rose to face Thackeray, slowly shaking his head. 'Constable, I have no doubt that in your way you are a most loyal and painstaking member of the Force. If a certificate of efficiency were awarded for qualities such as these, you and I would probably never have crossed paths. Unfortunately, for both of us, the Civil Service Commissioners require evidence of other attainments before they will confer a higher rank upon a constable. That is why, to our mutual discomfort, we have faced each other in this situation twice weekly for four years at various stations throughout the Metropolitan area.'

Thackeray nodded gloomily. He needed no reminding. Twopence a month was compulsorily diverted from his pay into the Educational Inspector's salary. Twopence a month! A dozen pints of Kop's ale a year!

'What depresses me most profoundly,' continued the inspector, now turning his eyes towards the ceiling, as though making an appeal to a Higher Authority, 'is that wherever my duties take me — and in four years I have given classes in four widely-separated Divisions — I can be confident that before many weeks have passed I shall walk into a room and find Constable Thackeray sitting at the front desk like a more substantial manifestation of Banquo's ghost. He haunts me, gentlemen, and his spelling is a continuing torment. He has pursued me from Whitechapel to Islington to Hampstead and now to Rotherhithe.' He produced a handkerchief and mopped his brow. 'However, I have never altogether despaired of a man, and I shall endeavour, if Providence allows me the time—'

The knock, entry and salute of the duty constable provided a merciful intervention. 'Pardon me, sir. An urgent message just come on the despatch cart.'

' "Came", Constable.' The inspector examined the note. 'Extraordinary. It seems, Constable Thackeray, that someone is *asking* me to release you from my class. I shall not refuse. Since the finer points of orthography have eluded you for so long, I am sure that they can wait another week. You are required to report to Sergeant Cribb — whoever he may be — at Great Scotland Yard as soon as possible.'

For once in his career Thackeray sincerely blessed Sergeant Cribb.

A cab-drive and thirty minutes later he was seated in an ante-room at Scotland Yard. In the centre was an island of faded carpet with two chairs, a desk, a hat-stand and a wastepaper basket. Around the island, with never a foot on the carpet, intermittently moved a parade of clerks in tall collars, oblivious of the occupants, intent only on passing between two doors on opposite sides of the room. Sergeant Cribb jerked his thumb towards the door behind him.

'Statistical Branch. All the charge-sheets you've ever written have gone through there. Diaries, station calendars, morning reports of crimes. Keeps a small army of pen-pushers out of mischief, so I don't underrate it. And once in a while they come up with something interesting.'

Thackeray prepared to be interested. Cribb, he knew, demanded complete attention. Foot-shuffling and beard-scratching might do for an Educational Inspector; not for Sergeant Cribb.

'Spend much of your time at the music halls?' the sergeant asked unexpectedly. It could have been the beginning of a polite conversation, except that Cribb was rarely polite and no conversationalist.

'Not usually, Sarge,' admitted Thackeray. 'I'm more of a melodrama man myself.' He added knowledgeably, 'Irving at the Lyceum or Wilson Barrett at the Princess's.'

'Pity. You've been *inside* a music hall, I hope?'

'Oh indeed, Sarge. I did a duty quite regular when I was in E Division. It's just that music hall ain't my—'

'From now on it will be,' Cribb told him. 'Take a look at these.' He handed a sheaf of papers to the constable and then braced his thighs to rock his chair on its back legs as he waited without much patience for the information to be digested.

'Reports of accidents,' Thackeray hazarded, in a few moments. 'From several different Divisions.'

Scornful silence greeted the observation. He returned to his reading.

Cribb got up to look out of the window at the hansoms drawn up outside the Public Carriage Office in the court below. He was a tall, gaunt man, decisive in his movements and unused to periods of inactivity, but it was vital to his purpose that Thackeray fully examined the reports. He waited like a hooded falcon.

'I see the point, Sarge!' Thackeray announced after some minutes.

'Capital!' Cribb almost swooped back to the chair. 'What conclusion d'you draw?'

'Well, Sarge, if I read any one of these on its own I'd pass it over as pure accident, but six in four weeks is uncommon hard to credit. You can't really put 'em all down to coincidence.'

9

Cribb nodded. 'There may have been more, of course. These have all been reported by sharp-eyed constables on duty. Others may have nodded off at the crucial time, or just not bothered to report what they saw. In one police-district a single incident wouldn't seem rum at all. Put together here in Statistics Branch they form a pattern, and not a pretty one.'

'D'you mean one person's behind all of these, Sarge?'

'Could be. Could well be. Put 'em in sequence, will you?'

Thackeray arranged the papers chronologically.

'It seems to have begun on September 15th with the Pinkus sisters on the trapeze at the Middlesex.'

'Ah. The old Mo.'

'What, Sarge?'

'The Middlesex,' snapped Cribb. 'The old Mo. Wake up, man. It's built on to the Mogul Tavern in Drury Lane.'

Thackeray smiled sheepishly. 'Yes, I should have known, Sarge. Well that's where the Pinkus girls complained to Sergeant Woodwright that someone had tampered with their trapeze. It could have had a very ugly consequence, I should think. As it turned out, though, the young ladies was lucky. The sergeant mentions Miss Lola Pinkus showing him a prominent bruise — "somewhat below the left shoulder," he says, but that seems to be as far as the injuries went.'

'Hm. Far enough for the likes of Woodwright. Injuries to young women are best taken on trust.

10

I've heard of more than one sprained ankle that lost a good sergeant his stripes. What's the second report you've got there?'

Thackeray scrutinised the sheet. 'Bellotti the barrel-dancer, Sarge, on September 17th at the Metropolitan in the Edgware Road. He finishes his act with a kind of sailor's horn-pipe on three barrels. As soon as he stepped on the centre one he fell flat on his face, broke his arm and set light to his hair on the footlights. Not surprising with the macassar some of these foreigners use. Inflammable stuff, I believe. Well, the surprise was that they found a line of axle-grease smeared right round one of the barrels. As soon as Bellotti's foot touched that he was sure to come a cropper.'

'Shabby little episode,' commented Cribb with a sniff. 'Then there was this fight at the Oxford. Wasn't that on the next night?'

'Yes, the 18th. A comedian by the name of Sam Fagan broke a stage-hand's jaw after the curtain went down on his act. Constable Barton, who was on the spot, did him for assault right away, of course, but the magistrate at Bow Street dismissed the case next morning. It says here "Fagan acted rashly, but he had been subjected to excessive prov . . . er . . . prov—" '

'Provocation. That's the part we're interested in. Read out Barton's account of what happened on the stage.'

'Right, Sarge. He says here "nothing untoward was noticed until Sam Fagan's third and final song *Take it from me she likes it,* when he invites the members of the audience to sing with him. For convenience, he has the words of the song written on a large sheet wound on to a roller. This evening he unrolled the sheet as usual and called on the customers to sing up. The first line was the proper one, *I wish I could tell you what I've seen,* but the rest of the song had been shamefully altered by some unknown person and contained certain references to a Gracious Personage I cannot as a loyal subject repeat in an open report. I committed them to my notebook, which Inspector Fredericks has secured in a sealed envelope in the station safe. Unfortunately the eighteen hundred members of the audience had sung three-quarters of the song before they realised the appalling significance of the words. Fagan was thereupon showered with fruit and booed from the stage. It was then that the assault on the stage-hand took place." What do you think the words said, Sarge?'

'Better not speculate, Constable,' warned Cribb, 'but if it's what I suppose, you can take it from me she *wouldn't* like it.'

Thackeray thought it prudent to turn to the next report.

'This was on the following Monday, Sarge, September 20th. The sword-swallower, if you recall. I think this was downright mean. It must be painful enough pushing a blade down your throat to earn a living, without someone smearing a line of mustard halfway up the blade. The poor cove must have coughed something dreadful.'

Cribb's hand stole to his own throat in sympathy. 'Bad enough when a fishbone goes astray,' he said. 'Where did this happen? The Tivoli Garden, wasn't it? Near enough to Charing Cross Hospital, anyway. Now, what reports are left?'

'The other incidents happened two weeks later, at the beginning of October, Sergeant. There was this — er — misfortune to Miss Penelope Tring, the Voice on the Swing. What a predicament! The constable on duty seems to have been quite well-placed to report it all so accurate.'

'Damn it, Thackeray, you're looking wistful. You weren't at the Royal that night and we can't stage it all again for your benefit.'

'D'you think it could have been a pure accident, Sarge, not connected with the other happenings?' He saw at once that Cribb did not.

'I can see you got no further than the account of what happened to Miss Tring,' Cribb admonished him. 'If you'll read on, you'll see that the garment had been tampered with in three places. As soon as it came under pressure—'

'Unspeakable!' murmured Thackeray.

'Quite so. It ain't surprising she chose to jump off her swing. Landed in the stalls, broke her arm in two places and knocked out one of the audience. Don't suppose she even felt the pain, though.'

There was a moment's pause while each detective lamented the mishap to Miss Tring. Cribb made a clicking sound with his tongue and Thackeray contemplatively straightened his shirt-cuffs. Then he cleared his throat. 'Last of all there's the accident at the Canterbury on October 9th. If *this* was deliberate I think we're after a lunatic, Sarge. The girl in the box could have died. D'you really think it's connected with the other incidents?'

Cribb shrugged. 'Can't say. But if it is, we're holding the wrong man in Newgate jail.' His off-hand manner came a shade too readily. Thackeray had a sharp ear for deception.

'There's something else, ain't there, Sarge? You wouldn't trouble yourself with penny gaff per-formers getting blushes and broken limbs here and there unless something else was bothering you.'

Cribb responded with a glare, and then pro-duced a folded sheet of paper. 'This was delivered to Stones End Police Station this morning.'

Thackeray unfolded the paper, a tattered music hall bill for the Grampian in Blackfriars Road. Twenty or more acts were listed, none of any dis-tinction, so far as he could tell.

'D'you see the rings?' Cribb asked.

He examined the bill again. The second turn listed was 'Gleaming Blade — Sensational Redskin Hatchet-Thrower.' 'Sensational' was ringed in black ink. Lower down, the word 'Tragedy' was similarly marked in a reference to 'Jason Buck-master, Tragedy Actor and Rhetorician.' A third ring had been drawn around the single word 'To-night', which appeared in heavy ornate type at the foot of the sheet.

Thackeray spoke the three words aloud. 'It sounds like a boast, Sarge. He's a madman, for sure, this one. What do we do?'

'Could be just a crank,' said Cribb, 'but I can't

take the chance. I'm having everything in the Hall checked for safety, and you and I and four plain-clothes men from Stones End will be there tonight to watch every movement on that stage, from the Japanese gyrist to the transformation dancer. But right now we're going to see that man in Newgate — if you think I've got a case, of course.'

Thackeray thumbed through the reports again, trying to establish a connexion between them. Strange things happened in the theatre; odd coincidences. He scratched his beard.

'You'll be detached from all duties at Paradise Street,' promised Cribb.

'Educational classes, Sarge?'

Cribb winked, and in a few minutes they left Scotland Yard together.

TWO

The two detectives, well-wrapped in ulsters and bowler-hats, watched the L.G.O.C. knifeboard bus recede in the direction of Cheapside. Then they crossed Newgate Street to the corner of the Old Bailey, too busy finding a route between copious horse-droppings to give much attention to the sombre exterior of the prison.

'Been inside before, Constable?'

'No, Sarge.'

'You'll find these walls are like a hat-box — all for effect. Inside, it's built like any of your London hospitals. It's not the inmates they want to impress, you see. It's the likes of that solicitor's clerk over there that shudders at the mention of Newgate. All he sees is a fortress with walls forty feet high. Capital way of keeping a man honest.'

Thackeray looked along the grim facade of rusticated blocks and recesses and recalled a bleak Monday morning fifteen years before, when duty had brought him to that same street. It had been jammed by a crowd of twenty thousand and he had stood among them from first light until St Sepulchre's chimed eight o'clock. 'Hats off!' the cry

16

had gone up. 'Down in front,' as the condemned man was escorted to the scaffold from a door in the prison wall. Times had changed; public executions had been discontinued for a dozen or more years, and now Newgate was a hat-box to Sergeant Cribb. But that door remained.

'This'll be a routine visit,' Cribb explained as they approached the governor's house. 'I volunteered the two of us for identification duty. The only prisoners in Newgate now are men on remand or awaiting trial. We have to check 'em for previous convictions. Strictly it's a sergeant's job, but there aren't many sergeants with an eye like yours for a jail-bird.'

Thackeray was flattered. Sergeants often complained about the burden of identification parades at Newgate and Clerkenwell. But their boasting when they had spotted an old lag was something to be heard. The lower ranks were encouraged to think sergeants alone were capable of such feats of recognition.

'You'll need your own identification,' Cribb cautioned, as he knocked at the door of the governor's office. It was opened by a uniformed prison officer, who glanced formally at their papers and admitted them. They waited inside with a clerk who took one hard look at each of them and then returned to his work of sealing envelopes. Above him a clock of a type issued and withdrawn by the Home Office a decade earlier ticked with an occasional snuffle.

In a few minutes the officer returned with two

black-uniformed attendants. 'Warders Rose and Whittle will accompany you, gentlemen. Would you kindly sign the book first?'

They were then escorted through the lodge, which served as a macabre museum, with death-masks of some of Newgate's more notorious former guests and a wall-display of body irons. A turnkey unbarred an iron-studded oak door and they were led down stone steps into a cavernous passage that Thackeray estimated ran parallel with the Old Bailey. Their steps echoed ahead of them.

The warders, accustomed to this ritual, which took place with different police and prison officers three times a week, were disinclined to talk. They walked a few yards ahead of the two detectives, unlocking gates at frequent intervals and slamming them closed when the party had passed through. Once or twice there was a barred window on the left wall, through which Thackeray saw paved yards and the grey walls of the main prison-block beyond.

'Ten years ago we were told this performance could stop,' reflected Cribb. 'Prevention of Crime Act, 1871. Photography, they said! That's the way to spot your felon. Put every blasted criminal there is in a studio like a maharajah and immortalise him in half-profile. Bravo for science! And what happened?'

'It cost too much,' said Thackeray.

'Dear me, yes. In his enthusiasm the Home Secretary hadn't done his arithmetic. In no time at all the photographing was restricted to convicts and habitual criminals, and now you need a special application to the Governor to take a camera anywhere near an old lag. Progress, Thackeray! So three times a week the gentlemen of Clerkenwell and Newgate still show their precious monikers to the Law, and the Law scratches its head and goes through its inventory of eyes and mouths and noses and tries to spot its old acquaintances. Sounds like a parlour-game and ain't so far from being one.'

Another door was unlocked by a bored turnkey and they emerged blinking into daylight, and crossed a deserted exercise yard, where a circular track of polished pavement had been worn by generations of shuffling boots. The walls bordering the yard looked massive and impossible to scale, but as a precaution iron spikes projected inwards from the top.

The warders approached the building at the top end of the yard, mounted its stone steps and knocked at the entrance. Before joining them, Cribb drew Thackeray's attention to the gigantic drumlike contraption built on to the top of the block. 'Revolving fan,' he explained. 'Put there by Mr Howard, the reformer. Ventilates the whole interior of the jail.' His eyes travelled slowly up the full height of the building. 'Not many windows, you see.'

The unlocking and unbarring completed, they mounted narrow stone stairs and were greeted unexpectedly at the top with, 'Damn my eyes, it's Sergeant Cribb!' from a uniformed warder with a style and presence that wanted only a row of medals and a yard of gold braid to be worthy of the doorman at the Cafe Royal.

'Cyril Blade!' responded Cribb. 'Now where was it last? Don't speak.' His fingers snapped. 'Got it! Holloway, the year before last.' He turned to Thackeray. 'If you think Irving's got a voice, listen to this. What did they inscribe on the foundation-stone at Holloway, Cyril?'

Mr Blade drew a deep breath. 'May God preserve the City of London, and make this place a *terror* to evil doers.'

'Carries conviction, eh?' said Cribb, savouring the performance. 'No treadmill here, though, Cyril. Your vocal powers are wasted.'

Mr Blade disagreed. 'I carry the sound of that blasted shin-scraper in me head to this day, Sergeant. Uncommon cruel, subjecting a man's ears to that racket twelve hours a day. I asked for a move to the oakum-shed in the end, but they sent me here instead. And the shock I got, Sergeant!'

'Not so harsh as Holloway?' suggested Cribb.

Mr Blade clenched his fist eloquently. 'This is a better home than my old mother made for me, Sergeant. They're in clover here, I tell you. In clover.'

'They should be, Cyril. They're not convicted yet. Are they lined up?'

'Like a guard of honour!'

'Good. We'll see who you've got, then.'

Mr Blade ushered them through an open door into a whitewashed room the size and shape of a hospital ward. The difference was clear in the positioning of the beds: sets of bunks in tiers of five were ranged head to foot along the length of the wall facing them. A row of well-scrubbed deal tables and benches had been pushed against the parallel wall to make room for the inspection.

Thackeray realised with misgivings that the hundred and twenty prisoners parading before them in three motionless ranks must have heard everything that was said. They were sized and spaced with military precision, but the effect was spoiled by the uniform: each wore the clothes in which he had been brought to Newgate, so a shooting-coat stood between a greasy spencer and a fustian jacket, and well-shod highlows lined up with clogs and naked feet. Yet there was a uniformity in the eyes of the prisoners, a glassy indifference, a torpor that had brutalised all but a handful.

'All yours, Sergeant,' said Cyril expansively. 'Nobbiest parade in London after the Lord Mayor's. Cracksmen, sharpers, screevers, macers, murderers and a few doubtful parties that might just be honest gentlemen, or might be as bent as bicycle-wheels. Take a long squint at 'em, and if you can't find two or three you know, why Lord bless you.' As Cribb started along the line, Mr Blade added confidentially to Thackeray, ''E's a very knowing card, is Sergeant Cribb.'

Thackeray followed a yard or two behind Cribb, conscious that the inspection was not the main purpose of the visit. The sergeant stopped briefly three times, putting questions to men he knew well

21

enough to name. Satisfied, he completed the formality and thanked Mr Blade, adding in an undertone, 'The red-haired customer in the last row wants watching. What does he call himself?'

'The tall 'un? That's Percy Crichton-Jones. Arrived this morning.'

'Is it now? I'll lay a guinea to a shilling it's Albert Figg and if it is he'll be working the three-card trick before the gas goes out tonight. There's not a smarter broadsman in London. Anyone else arrive this week?'

Mr Blade reviewed his platoon in a parade-ground voice. 'Them two in the front row came in together: pickpocket and his stall. Him in the second row, four along, is the Bethnal Green killer. That one moving his head — stand up there! — is a blooming magician, if you please. We have to watch him real sharp in the exercise yard in case the bugger flies over the wall.'

'Magician? What's the name — Woolston?'

'I believe it is, Sergeant, though what he calls himself on the stage—'

'I want to talk with him.'

'You do?' Mr Blade quite superfluously raised his voice. 'Woolston! Two steps forward, march!'

'In private,' said Cribb.

'You shall have a cell to yourselves, Sergeant. Woolston! Step out here at once and fall in behind me. And if anyone else stirs a sinew . . .'

Cribb fell in smartly behind Woolston, and Thackeray behind Cribb, leaving Warders Rose and Whittle facing the ranks. The quartet marched

22

the length of the ward and into a narrow passage flanked by the open doors of a dozen small cells.

'This one,' indicated Mr Blade. 'Sit yourself there, Sergeant. I'll fetch another chair for your companion.' When Thackeray was seated, the warder gave Woolston a threatening look, and added, 'I'll leave you with him, gentlemen. If he gives trouble, I'm within call.'

The potential source of trouble stood before them in a once-white tie and dusty tails, an expression of mild bewilderment on his face. A slight man in every sense, he was impossible to imagine working miracles at the Royal, in spite of his conjurer's costume. Possibly the witchery of limelight might have transformed him, but in the harsh illumination of a whitewashed cell he was pallid, pinch-cheeked and about as mysterious as the asphalt floor.

'On your feet, Thackeray,' ordered Cribb. 'Mr Woolston needs the chair more than you.'

The prisoner thanked Thackeray in a thin voice and sat facing Cribb across a small hinged table, supported in drawbridge fashion by two chains attached to the wall. The impedimenta of prison life — Bible, prayer-book and hymn-book, gaspipe, basin and mug, tin panikin and wooden spoon — were ranged on shelves around them. With some difficulty Thackeray edged into a comfortable standing position at the cell's end.

'Mind your elbow!' cautioned Cribb. 'If that bedding's disturbed, Mr Woolston will have the job of folding it all again.'

Thackeray jerked his arm away from a pile of folded matting, rugs and mattress. The cell-beds at Newgate took the form of hammocks slung between rings projecting from the walls. It was a matter of deep concern to warders that the beds were unhooked each morning and folded in the only acceptable manner, square as postage stamps, with straps and hooks arranged 'Newgate-style'. This and other practical hints on prison life were explained in the Sheriffs' Code of Discipline on the back of the door.

'D'you sleep here?' Cribb asked without much interest. You couldn't really begin a conversation with a prisoner by talking about the weather.

'No. In the ward. I spent the first night here, but I got cold. It's warmer in there with the others.'

'Says in the Code here that you can regulate the temperature of your cell.'

'Yes,' said Woolston. 'That's the ventilator on your left. You get three grades of temperature — cold, very cold and who's for skating?' The music hall patter, unfunny and expressionless, drew a timely smile from Cribb. There was a momentary flicker of gratification in Woolston's eyes.

'Now listen to me,' Cribb said, the formalities over. 'I'm a detective. That needn't mean trouble, though.'

Woolston shook his head. 'No good. I've given all the money I brought to the warders.'

'Damn you, man, I'm not asking for bribes,' ejaculated Cribb. 'I want you to tell me what brought you here.'

24

'A police-van.' Cruelly on cue. The conversation was fast becoming a double act.

'Very well,' said Cribb. 'Let's begin again. I don't think you're a jail-bird.'

Woolston turned his eyes to the wall, like a cow uninterested in the attentions of its milker.

'Put your hands on the table!' Cribb ordered. The prisoner obeyed, conditioned to respond to that tone of address. Thackeray looked on in mystification. 'Neat set of fingers,' Cribb continued, keeping his temper well in check. 'I dare say there's a few miracles you can work manipulating them. What do you call it — legerdemain, ain't it? I wonder what sort of legerdemain you'll be doing in Wandsworth if they convict you. Might see what you can do with a pump-handle, of course. Most men manage about five thousand revolutions a day — before the blisters slow 'em down, that is. Then they get a turn at oakum-picking by way of variation. Now *there's* an occupation for a man with supple fingers! The blisters you get in the pump-house'll heal beautiful. It's your nails and finger-tips that go in the oakum-shed. I remember a violinist. Wonderful player. Had a touch like Paganini—'

'What do you want to know, for God's sake?' blurted out Woolston.

Cribb changed tack at once. 'What went wrong with your trick at the Royal?'

'A mechanical failure, pure and simple,' admitted Woolston. 'Have you ever seen the trick? It's a perfectly simple idea.' As though a spark had

25

been fanned, Woolston's vitality was kindled as he spoke. His features became animated, his voice earnest and expressive. 'The woman in the box, you know. You show the audience a large empty box standing on its end. Then you invite your shapely assistant to stand inside. There are openings at the top and the bottom for her neck and feet, so that the audience can study her reactions. You close the box and show them a set of half a dozen or more sharpened swords, weapons that chill their spines just to see them. You then proceed to plunge these vigorously through a number of small holes in the front of the box. It seems impossible that you have not harmed your assistant. One sword would appear to have penetrated her chest, another her middle, another her upper legs and so on. But she does not scream or show any pain whatsoever. So you withdraw the swords and open the box and out she steps as exquisite as when she went in.' He almost took a bow in the cell.

'I think I've seen the trick, Sarge,' said Thackeray.

'Probably you have, my dear fellow,' Woolston said, now almost gushing in his volubility. 'It is not original. I've seen it done by the famous Dr Lynn and by John Nevil Maskelyne, but they don't use my method. And of course there are scores of provincial performers using rubber swords or girl contortionists.'

'Really?' said Cribb. 'What's *your* method then?

You'll have to explain it in court, so you might as well tell us now.'

Woolston hesitated. An illusionist likes to preserve his illusions, but Cribb's logic was irresistible. So was the invitation to expound his genius. 'Very well, gentlemen. My trick is worked this way. You will understand that the audience sees the face of my assistant and her feet and presumes therefore that she is occupying the central part of the box, and that her body too is facing them, and so is exposed to the swords which I plunge through the front.'

'I would think so.'

The conjurer leaned forward confidentially. 'Now suppose, Sergeant, that what you believe to be my assistant's feet protruding beneath the box are in fact only her empty boots. She has withdrawn her feet from the boots — which are several sizes larger, for this purpose — and now she can move her body freely inside the box. It is a simple matter to make a turn to the left without moving the head, so that the body is in profile, as it were, while the head remains facing the audience.'

'Ingenious!' said Cribb.

Woolston beamed. 'However that is not all of the deception. If you will kindly remove your elbows from the table . . .' Cribb obeyed, half-recollecting Mr Blade's promise of help in case of trouble. 'Now, gentlemen, I shall demonstrate. You will see that this table is no more than a flap on hinges fixed to the wall. When it is down as it is now it forms a kind of ledge supported by the two chains. But when I push it up . . . thus . . . it lies against the wall almost on a plane with it. This simple idea was incorporated in my box. Once she was free of the boots, my assistant released a secret flap on her right. She then turned her body — but not her head — and seated herself on the small ledge thus formed. It was not comfortable, you understand, but it gave her the support that lifted her body clear of the points where the swords penetrated. When the trick was done and the swords withdrawn it was a simple matter to replace the flap and slip her feet into the boots. I then opened the box and showed the girl unharmed.' He straightened his bow tie.

'Marvellous,' said Thackeray.

'What went wrong?' said Cribb.

Woolston shook his head. 'The flap collapsed as soon as Lettice rested her weight on it. My first sword missed her by good fortune, but the second went straight through the thick part of her leg, you understand.'

'Didn't she warn you?'

'She may have tried, Sergeant, but it is a feature of the performance that she looks alarmed as I thrust the swords home. If she shouted I could not have heard her for the drum-roll that accompanies the climax of the illusion. Of course, I realised what had happened when the second sword met some resistance inside the box.'

'So I imagine. What happened then?'

'Confusion, Sergeant. Deplorable confusion!

The curtain was rung down and then rung up again immediately. A policeman climbed on to the stage and a doctor appeared from nowhere. Nobody would open the box for fear of aggravating Lettice's injury. In my own distress I failed to appreciate that to everyone but me it appeared that she had been penetrated through the stomach. We turned the box into a horizontal position and you would not believe the screams from the audience when one of the boots became detached and fell on to the stage. How they imagined I had severed a leg I cannot fathom. Fortunately, someone had the sense to lower the front cloth and soon a comedian had them singing patriotic songs, while a carpenter sawed open the box backstage. Lettice, of course, was discovered with her leg pinned, and the doctor withdrew the sword and took her in a brougham to Charing Cross Hospital.'

'Then you were arrested?'

'Yes!' said Woolston in a shocked voice. 'In her discomfort the wretched girl became positively vindictive towards me, and several times accused me of deliberately arranging the injury. It was just too preposterous! I thought nobody would believe such a thing! She wasn't her normal self at all.'

'Had you known her a long time?'

'Eighteen months — which is a confounded long time in the theatre, Sergeant.'

'Had you quarrelled recently?'

'Quarrelled? Well, hardly quarrelled. Earlier that evening we had a few wry words together, you might say.'

'What about?'

'Her figure, Sergeant. I told her she was putting on too much weight, and she was, damn it. Chocolates and gingerbread, you know. One has no business being overweight when one's in a box trying to avoid being skewered by half a dozen swords.'

'Did she object to being told about her figure?'

'Without going into details, yes. I was right, though, wasn't I? It seems she was too blasted heavy for that secret flap. It's odd, though. I thought it would have taken much more weight than that. I check the hinges and supports regularly.'

'Did you check 'em that evening?'

'Well, not that evening, Sergeant.'

'I see. How many people knew the secret of your trick?'

'Very few,' said Woolston. 'The carpenter who made it for me. A stage-hand or two. And Lettice.'

'And the girl before Lettice?'

'Oh yes, Hetty. And Patty before her, now you mention it.'

Cribb sighed. 'Did you examine the flap after the accident?'

'In the confusion, no.'

'Pity.'

'You won't be able to find it now, Sergeant. No stage-manager keeps useless wood backstage. The whole trick will be firewood by now.'

'Evidence shouldn't be destroyed,' commented

Cribb. 'It's probably saved. What were you charged with?'

'Assault. Didn't you know? But I was told that other charges are to be preferred. The damned girl's not in any danger, is she?' he added on an impulse.

'I believe not,' said Cribb. He studied Woolston's face. 'You wouldn't have wanted to hurt her, would you?'

The conjurer considered the point. 'Not at that moment, and in those circumstances.'

Cribb lifted an eyebrow. 'In other circumstances, perhaps?'

Woolston paused, wary of a trap. 'Now listen to me, Sergeant. I am a professional illusionist, known throughout the London halls, and that girl was a first-class assistant — magnificent proportions, a wonderful suffering expression and legs she wasn't coy about displaying. But you have to train a girl, and training's a matter of discipline, like any form of schooling. Without me, she'd still be just a figurante at the Alhambra on ten shillings a week, taking drinks from soldiers between dances.'

'She was in the ballet, was she?'

'Until I rescued her, yes. She has a lot to be grateful for. I lavished hours of my time teaching her to move in that box. Hours, gentlemen.' He scanned both his listeners for a glimmer of sympathy. Cribb was expressionless; Thackeray plainly regarded packing young women in boxes as no hardship. 'In the end,' continued Woolston, unabashed, 'she knew that movement better than any dance-step she'd ever executed.'

'More's the pity she put on weight,' commented Cribb, nudging the conversation in the direction he wanted.

'Feckless female! Yes.'

'Wouldn't put it beyond a man of your application to teach a girl like that a sharp lesson.'

'By Jove, yes!' exclaimed Woolston enthusiastically. 'A scolding's no use at all.' Then, recovering himself, 'I wouldn't do anything on stage, though. You don't think I'd destroy the act for a silly little slut that can't keep her hands out of a chocolate-box?'

'What I think ain't of any consequence,' said Cribb, who had heard all he wanted, 'but I'm grateful for your plain-speaking.' He got to his feet. 'Well now, Thackeray, we won't detain Mr Woolston any longer. I'm not much of a sorcerer myself, but if my nose is any guide there's a pot of Newgate stew being cooked not far from here, and I wasn't planning to stay for lunch.'

THREE

Sergeant Cribb, in opera hat and Inverness cape, whistled a music hall tune to the rhythm of the cab-horse's canter along Southwark Street, while Constable Thackeray, equally dazzling beside him, wrestled with insubordinate thoughts. The plain clothes allowance for detective-constables was a shilling a day: generous on the face of it, even allowing that there were long intervals of uniformed duty. Indeed, his total allowances for this year must have come close to Cribb's statutory ten pounds. But plain clothes, in Thackeray's opinion, were plain clothes. When a man spent a week's wages on a swallow-tail suit for an occasional evening's melodrama at the Lyceum he did not expect to be ordered to wear it to a common music hall. Scotland Yard might own you body and soul, but it was a confounded liberty to assume they owned your best suit as well.

He was not comforted by the spectacle of the crowds along the approach to the Grampian. Each Saturday evening the unwashed of south London converged there in hundreds for threepenny gallery

33

tickets. On a wet evening like this one, when they huddled together under the gaslamps, you could positively see a noxious yellow vapour rising from their clothes. It was all very well for Cribb to make a lofty promise to book a stage-box. What was that worth against a jostling from a coal-bargee's corduroys as you struggled through the lobby? For Thackeray at that moment, in his tailor-made twill, it was very nearly a resignation issue.

At the entrance, an enormous Corinthian portico, quite outrageous in the architecture of Blackfriars Road, you had to pass a phalanx of salespeople before you even joined the throng struggling to obtain tickets. The cabman had scarcely reined in when a barefoot boy jumped on to the step, wrenched open the door and demanded a tip. Behind him converged match-girls, and walnut-men, beggar-boys and a troupe of young women who gave Thackeray sufficient grounds for arresting them at once. Instead, he observed a studied indifference, nonchalantly stroking his beard while Cribb paid the fare.

At what cost to his suit Thackeray dared not contemplate, he edged towards the first-class box-office behind Cribb, grimly clutching the brim of his hat. The stench of the crowd brought water to his eyes; he was ready to abandon the sergeant altogether if they were unable to book a box, where the fumes rising from the footlights usually obliterated all other odours. At length they arrived at a hole in the wall and Cribb pushed a florin forward. An oddly-illuminated face inside creased into a grimace. Perhaps for a small consideration the two gentlemen might like the management to arrange for a pair of dainty companions to share their box? Cribb turned and lifted a wicked eyebrow. Thackeray shook his head so emphatically that he felt his hat slip round. He hoped to Heaven Cribb was joking.

Taking the numbered tin disc which served as a ticket, an old crone, their boxkeeper, led them through a darkened passage not unlike the corridors of Newgate, except that this one was lined with unaccompanied young ladies. The detectives marched resolutely past, their feet crunching on a carpet of walnut- and filbert-shells. They mounted some stairs, paid the old woman her due and entered their box.

'Now *there's* a high old scene!' said Cribb with undisguised relish. The position of their box, some ten feet above stage-level and actually built on to the forestage, gave a view of the entire auditorium, brilliantly lit by six huge sun-burners turned fully on. Nine rows of tables extended from the orchestra pit along the length of the sanded floor into shadow and smoke beneath the circle. There, shopmen and clerks sat in hundreds, in snowy shirts and dress-suits with recklessly cut-down waistcoats and protruding crimson handkerchiefs — the swells of Southwark that night for two shillings and the price of a buttonhole. A barrage of gin-born good humour passed between tables, punctuated by occasional sharp reports and cheers as somebody collapsed an opera hat or withdrew a cork. Women with cigarettes and painted eyes sat bonnet to bonnet with respectable wives and saucer-eyed children. At intervals the chorus of a music hall song rose and died somewhere in the hall to a measure of stamping feet. At the sides of the seated area beyond the railings and the promenades were the bars, glittering with brass and pewter, polished beer-pumps and gilded mirrors, where overworked waiters urged barmaids to hurry with their orders. Even when their trays were loaded, they still faced the frustration of struggling for a passage between the press of promenaders to reach the tables.

Corinthian columns sprouted here and there as supports for the sixpenny gallery, which was fronted by an army of plaster and gilt cherubs pursuing buxom nymphs among the gas-brackets. Less lavishly, the bowler-hatted customers above were ranged on plank-seats without cushions. In the cheapest gallery above that, where up to a thousand of the lower orders massed, there were no seats provided — only crowd barriers to prevent a disaster.

'Seeing it from this viewpoint,' remarked Thackeray, 'I'm uncommon thankful I don't have to give a performance.'

'At a wage of ten pounds or more I'd sing a couple of songs all right,' said Cribb. 'That's more than the Chief Superintendent himself takes home. They say the Vital Spark — Miss Jenny Hill — is booked for more than fifty a week.'

'I think they earn every penny of it, Sarge, skedaddling across London in cabs to fit in three or four halls a night.'

Cribb sniffed. 'I suppose you think you're better off padding your hoof round Bermondsey all night for thirty-five bob a week, after thirty years' service.'

The opening of the door behind them stifled Thackeray's reply.

'Now 'ere's two 'andsome gentlemen what look the sort to 'ave one of me kidney-pies,' said the fat woman. 'You won't? They're 'ot and fresh, I warrant you, gents. No? Perhaps I could fetch you up a plate of natives, then? Swill 'em down with your fizz.'

Cribb glanced towards Thackeray, who had a weakness for oysters.

'Not on thirty-five bob,' the constable said with a smile.

Action below, the arrival of the orchestra, was greeted with hoots and cheering from the auditorium. The sun-burners were turned low and the footlights flickered into tall, yellowish flames. The conductor took his stance among the instrumentalists and bowed with great seriousness. This evoked a storm of good-natured abuse, which he summarily quelled with the overture to 'Carmen'.

A waiter arrived in the box and was sent for two pints of Bass East India, 'But don't for a moment forget you're on duty,' Cribb warned Thackeray, shouting to compete with the orchestra. 'At the first sign of an accident you're going down on to that stage.'

The constable nodded, and peered over the drop to the boards. He was no coward, but he had a shrewd idea that fourteen stone descending ten feet that way would add another name to the casualty-list. Fortunately the moulding on the front of the box suggested a safer route. By taking a hand-hold on a cupid's upturned rump he could reach the curtain of the box below. From there, if nothing gave way, a sliding descent would bring him smoothly to stage-level.

'Sometimes they make something look like a mishap to give the audience a thrill, Sarge. Like a trapeze-artiste dropping off his trapeze and then being caught by his partner. I wouldn't want to make a—'

'What are you saying?' bawled Cribb.

'It don't matter,' said Thackeray, philosophically.

The overture ended with a clash of cymbals, and a beam of limelight from the circle picked out a small table at the front of the hall. The chairman, a hulk of unbelievable girth, doffed his hat.

'On your feet!' demanded the audience.

He shook his head. His chins quivered like a freshly turned-out blancmange.

'Up! Up! Up!'

Unperturbed, he lit a cigar, and the chanting rose to a frenzy.

He placed his hands on the edge of the table, leaned forward slowly, flexed, strained and then subsided, shaking his head.

'Lord bless you, Billy,' somebody shouted. 'You

can't manage it no more!' Half the audience doubled up laughing.

Three knocks from Billy's gavel restored order. 'Stow your jaws!' he commanded in a voice that brooked no nonsense. 'And watch this.'

He handed the gavel and his cigar to one of the guests at his table and another cleared its surface of tankards. With profound concentration, Billy placed his palms flat on the table like a medium, took a huge breath, and commenced rocking slowly forward from his chair-back. Then with a decisive grunt he projected himself suddenly forward and up from the seat. There was an agonising second of uncertainty as his arms took the strain, before his legs straightened and he stood erect, his small eyes darting contemptuously over the audience. Thunderous applause revived his good humour. Again he sounded the gavel.

'Well, you merciless rabble, since I 'appen to be on my feet I might as well tell you what you've got in store tonight. It's a regular jamboree of delights — a bill that'll touch your 'earts while it's ticklin' your fancies at the same time.' (Exaggerated groans from the regulars and shrieks of scandalised laughter from the pit.) 'And not a word nor a sight to offend even the most delicate-minded females among you.' ('Shame!') 'You think so, madam? So do I. Meet me after the show and I'll remedy that deficiency.' ('Oy! Oy!' from the gallery.) 'But now without more ado to the first delicacy of the evening. Fresh from 'er successes at the London Pavilion' (an awed shout of 'Ooh!') 'the

Metropolitan' ('Ooh!') 'and the Tivoli Garden,' (a prolonged, suggestive 'Ah!') 'here to charm you with her ditties,' ('Lovely!') 'Miss Ellen Blake!'

A flurry of violin-bows; the strains of *Fresh as the New-Mown Hay;* the irresistible chink of curtain-rings; and Miss Blake was revealed in a long satin dress with broad white and lilac stripes, palms extended across the safety-rail and head thrust back to catch the glow of the footlights on her neck and chin. Wayward wisps of blonde hair fluttered against her bonnet in the upsurge of warm air. Constable Thackeray found himself reconsidering a spectacular leap to the rescue.

'She's a stunner, ain't she, Sarge?'

'Keep yourself in check, man. Lord, you're foaming at the mouth.'

'That's the head on the ale, Sarge,' protested Thackeray, wiping his beard with a large chequered handkerchief.

Miss Blake's assault upon *Fresh as the New-Mown Hay* may have lacked somewhat in gusto, but the rapid transition after that to 'Moonlight Promenade' was executed with undoubted professionalism. This was a stronger melody, and involved a few mincing steps to right and left in which the emphasis was diverted from her voice to her figure, to the general satisfaction of the audience. Even so, she was having to compete with pockets of conversation from the galleries and open lack of interest at some of the tables. And when the opening bars of a third song were played, there were blatant groans.

'Take a hold on yourself, Thackeray, for God's sake,' said Cribb. 'You look as solemn as a blasted tombstone. She's getting a damned good hearing. Wasn't many years ago they covered the orchestra with netting to protect them from rotten fruit that fell short of duff performers.'

The sprinkle of applause at the end was more in relief than enthusiasm, but Miss Blake seemed satisfied, took her curtseys, blew kisses to someone still enthusiastic enough to whistle, and left the stage.

'And now to chill your precious 'earts,' announced the chairman from his seated position, 'we 'ave a visitor from the wilds of North America. You've 'eard of 'Iawatha? Yes, my friends, a genuine Red Indian. What do you think 'e calls 'imself? Not Runnin' Water — no-one cares for that 'ere. Not Bleedin' Wolf — there's enough of them about already. No, ladies, it's your 'eart-throb, the man with the 'atchets — Gleamin' Blade!'

Cymbals crashed, the front-cloth was lifted up into the flies, and the mediums, sets of coloured glass worked on the lever principle, filtered the footlight flames, to immerse the stage in Satanic crimson. A prancing Red Indian, with a toma-hawk in each hand, dominated the centre, whooping and chanting. Upstage was a board the size of a door, surmounted with a totem-like carved head. The redskin momentarily interrupted his war-dance to hurl a tomahawk in that direction. It cut into the wood with a fearful thud. The audience's unified gasp died in their throats as the second

41

tomahawk was buried deep beside the first. With a shriek, the Indian retrieved both weapons and leapt round to face the audience. Thackeray tensed. Cribb's restraining hand touched his arm.

A drum-roll promised fresh horrors.

'My God, Sarge! Look over there!'

Waiting out of sight of the rest of the audience in the wings opposite was a young woman in fleshings and a skimpy bodice and breech-clout. A single vertical feather was attached to her head. The hatchet-thrower now ran to the side of the stage, grabbed her wrist and pulled her, apparently struggling to escape, towards the board. There were screams from several parts of the hall.

'Be ready, then,' said Cribb, 'but wait for the word from me!'

Thackeray leaned forward, poised for sudden movement, like the survivor in a game of musical chairs. On the stage below, the girl was being secured by rope to the totem. The Indian spoke a few words to her and then backed some twelve feet away. She waited, helplessly spreadeagled, as the drum-roll began again.

'Not yet,' muttered Cribb.

At the Indian's feet were six tomahawks, glinting in the sinister illumination. He stooped for the first two. The drums reached their climax. His arm swung back behind his head and with a fiendish shriek he flung the first weapon. It hit the board, shuddering, six inches to the left of her waist.

'One!' shouted those of the audience able to speak.

The second tomahawk matched the first on the right.

'Two!'

He picked up two more. The first came perilously close to her left knee.

'Three!'

'Four!'

The last two. They would have to be aimed at each side of her head. The Indian sighted his throw and, with awful menace, slowly drew back the weapon. A yell!

'Five!' Within two inches of the ear.

A final drum-roll.

The hurtling blade shimmered in flight.

'Six!' Shouted in huge relief, and topped with a storm of clapping and stamping.

'Sometimes they try it again blindfold,' suggested Cribb to Thackeray, who was paler than the Indian maiden.

Then — surprise — normal gaslight was restored and there were two unmistakably European performers removing their head-dresses to receive their salute from the enraptured audience.

'Capital act!' said Cribb, applauding energetically.

'It's left me feeling like a glass of beer gone flat.'

A large 3 was already in place on the frame to their right where the order of the acts was charted. Nobody appeared to have a programme, so the information was valuable only to the chairman. 'If that last act 'orrified the ladies a little too much, I've got some news to set your minds at rest, girls.

We 'ave with us tonight two outstandin' guardians of the peace. Yes, the boys in blue are with us tonight . . .'

'Blimey, Sarge. We've been spotted.'

'Steady, Constable.'

'. . .Those two favourite myrmidons of the Law, P.C.s Salt and Battree!'

The act-drop had been lowered during the announcement, and now two performers dressed as uniformed police officers marched in step to the centre of the stage, the second ludicrously close behind the first. Predictably, there was a collision when they stopped in mid-stage, emphasised with cymbals.

'Lord save us!' said Cribb. 'Not one of these lunatic displays!'

'Watch yerselves!' shouted one of the performers. 'I'm watching you!'

'Guying the Force is just about the favourite occupation of your fair-minded British general public,' grumbled Cribb. 'There ain't been a pantomime since Grimaldi without a flatfooted constable blundering about with a string of sausages. And there's more bluebottles on the music halls than there is in the Metropolitan: Vance, Stead, Arthur Lloyd, Edward Marshall — even Gilbert and Sullivan are up to it now. Blasted scandal, it is. Home Secretary wants to look into it, in my opinion.'

I'm the man wot takes to pris'n
He who steals wot isn't his'n

X yer know is my Division
Number ninety-two,' sang P.C. Salt.

Both artistes now produced authentic police-rattles, which they sprang, to the delight of the audience.

'We could take 'em in for having police property, Sarge,' suggested Thackeray.

'It ain't the night for it,' growled Cribb, hunched over the box-front, with his hands over his face, watching the performance between his fingers.

Another song got under way:

They gave us an 'elmet and a greatcoat
And armlets to wear upon our sleeve
An 'andsome tunic too
In regulation blue
But now we've rattled our rattles we want to
* leave—*
All together now — But now we've rattled our
* rattles we want to leave.'*

'Damned disgrace!' said Cribb.

'Watch yerselves!' shouted P.C. Battree, 'I'm watching you!'

'These buffoons earn more for five minutes of this rubbish than you and I would get for a week's beat-bashing,' continued the sergeant. 'And here we are protecting 'em. If this pair suffer an attack, you and I are taking the long way down to the stage, Thackeray.'

Whistles from the audience greeted a pretty

45

young woman who had joined the officers on the stage. Her dress had a certain theatricality about it, but it was her mode of walking — characterised by a singular mobility in the region of the hips — that left no-one in any doubt as to the class of person she represented. After several exaggerated backward glances, P.C.s Salt and Battree began their final chorus:

'Poor old feet
Out on the beat
Pursuin' the enforcement of the Law.
But you gets a saucy wink
And the offer of a drink
And that prevents yer feet from gettin' sore—
Once more now — And that prevents yer feet
   from gettin' sore!'

Then, with arch nods and pointing, to leave the audience in no doubt of their intention, they trotted off in pursuit of their assistant, shortly afterwards returning with her to take their bow.

'At least we didn't have to go to their aid,' said Thackeray, conscious of the fury in Cribb's silence.

'If I ever meet 'em in the course of duty, they'll need aid all right.'

The curtain descended and the limelight returned to the chairman's table. 'And now, my friends, after that rare entertainment, not being a temperance-observer, I shall enjoy a tipple of fizz generously subscribed by the table on my right. The show proceeds with a redoubtable display of manly vigour from that sovereign of strong men, the 'Ercules of Rotherhithe, the great Albert.'

Albert's props were the most interesting so far. He stood like some eccentric costermonger behind a substantial platform on wheels, neatly stacked with an extraordinary array of articles: books, folded clothes, the plinth for a statue, a top-hat, flags, a picnic-hamper and three sets of bar-bells. With a nod to the conductor, a cue for the Anvil Chorus, Albert mounted his platform and stood with legs apart, chest inflated and head in profile to the auditorium, and then clasped his hands so that his biceps bobbed up like ferrets in a sack. He was wearing a one-piece costume of the type introduced by Leotard, the original Daring Young Man on the Flying Trapeze. Generous applause greeted this display of muscularity, so Albert climbed on to his plinth, leaned forward, positioned his legs carefully, and assumed the classic stance of the Discobolus.

'*Pose Plastique,*' explained Cribb authoritatively. 'The man's got a fine body. Pity about the moustache, though. Don't look like ancient Greece to me.'

Albert now descended and progressed to a series of lifts with the bar-bells, accompanied by intermittent chords from the brass section and exhortations from the gallery. Just as the interest was threatening to flag, a novelty was introduced, in the person of an extremely stout, florid-faced woman in long white robes and a hat with red, white and blue ostrich feathers.

'Blimey!' shouted someone from the gallery. 'Keep away from Albert, missus. You'll rupture 'im.'

The lady's contribution to the performance was soon made clear, however. While Albert ducked behind his platform to change his costume, she curtseyed and made the following announcement: 'Now, ladies and gentlemen, in a tribute to a most distinguished member of our race, my son Albert gives his unique portrayal of the bard, Shakespeare!'

There, leaning against his plinth in the pose of the monument in Westminster Abbey, was Albert, with legs crossed, one arm resting on a pile of volumes on the plinth, the other holding an unfurled scroll. He wore breeches, doublet and cloak and a false beard. When the impact of this tableau was fully appreciated, he placed both hands on the edge of the plinth and gracefully upended himself into a slow handstand, the cloak draping itself elegantly over the back of the plinth. Then to a drum-roll and a powerful gesture from his mother's right arm, Albert removed one of his hands from the plinth and remained poised on the other. The audience broke into open cheering. Theatres like Drury Lane and the Lyceum might have their Shakespeare; only the Grampian had him upside down on one hand!

'Had me worried for a moment,' admitted Cribb,

when the strong man had righted himself. 'There was the makings of a nasty little accident there. What are they doing now?'

Albert had disappeared behind the platform again for a change of costume while his mother occupied the centre of the stage with a Union Jack. To the strains of a patriotic tune, she began singing in a strong contralto,

> 'O'er all the mighty world by British sons
>   unfurled
> The red and white and blue!
> But to drag it in the mire now seems the sole
>   desire
> Of Gladstone and his crew.'

Unshaken by the mixed reception this got, she proceeded to:

> 'Oh England, who shall shield thee from the
>   shame?
> And thy sons and thy daughters who shall
>   save?
> But we cherish in our hearts that one undying
>   name—
> Lord Beaconsfield, now lying in his grave!

Ladies and gentlemen, my son Albert now portrays the Greatness of Britain and her Empire!'

From the dangerous area of political controversy, the limelight made a timely return to Albert, now standing on the platform, which had been

49

cleared of everything but a huge bar-bell and the picnic-basket. He was dressed convincingly as John Bull. A portentous thrumming from the orchestra-pit promised something even more spectacular than Shakespeare upside down.

John Bull spat into each hand and crouched at the bar-bell as the drumming slowly increased in volume. He braced, strained and began to lift, his veins protruding with the effort. The bar itself bowed impressively as it took the weight of the massive iron balls. He hauled it to the level of his knees. His hips. The Union Jack on his chest. His chin. His top-hat. Finally the lift was complete, his arms fully extended above his head, his legs vibrating with the colossal strain.

The role of the picnic-basket was now ex-plained. While Albert bravely held his stance, his mother began unstrapping the lid.

'Fancy bothering to strap it up, Sarge,' mur-mured Thackeray. 'The poor cove has to stand holding that lot above his head while she — Good Lord!'

One second of action transformed the scene. From the basket struggled a large white bulldog with a Union Jack tied about its middle. Snarling ferociously, it sank its teeth into the nearest of Albert's quivering calves. His howl of pain echoed through the theatre, even after the crash of the bar-bell descending straight through the platform. Man and dog, still attached, disappeared in a mass of splintered wood.

'That's it, Thackeray!' shouted Cribb. 'Get the dog!'

Whether Thackeray used the route he had planned he could not remember afterwards; his descent was a four-second fumbling confusion among gilt bosoms and bottoms and torn curtains. But his debut on the stage was impeccable. The great Irving could not have moved with more despatch to the battered structure at the centre of the stage, pulled the debris aside with more vigour or seized the collar of the bulldog with more resolve. So surprised was the animal that it relaxed its grip on Albert and found itself hoisted by collar and tail-stump and clapped into the basket before uttering another growl.

FOUR

'Sergeant likes to take a look
For anarchists and spies
Down the basement-stairs when cook
Bakes her rabbit pies,'

chorused the singing policemen, Salt and Battree, on special duty. In the best theatrical traditions, they had volunteered to return to the footlights and divert the audience until order was restored backstage. So in front of a hastily lowered act-drop of mountain scenery they padded the beat with truncheons drawn, singing hilariously about life in the Force.

On the other side of the cloth the great Albert lay in the ruins of his dais emitting heart-rending groans. Around him stood the interested group who could be counted on to materialise around any unfortunate, from a lost child to a broken-down cabhorse.

'Animals on the stage are always the next thing to disaster,' a small cigar-smoker in a dress-suit was informing the group. He was evidently the stage-manager. 'I've had 'em all here — dogs, monkeys, mules and baby elephants. Perfectly docile off-stage. Put 'em in front of an audience and you're in no end of trouble. If they don't bite you they're liable to knock the scenery down and if they don't do that there's ways of drawing attention to 'emselves I won't go into. You wouldn't believe the jobs I've had to tell my stage-hands to do.'

'Right now you can tell 'em to lift the lumber off this poor cove,' barked Sergeant Cribb. 'Where's the medical chest? He'll need attention.'

'Keep your voice down, sir,' appealed the manager. 'No need for panic. We're professionals here.'

'The medical chest,' hissed Cribb.

'Yes. Now I'm not entirely certain where . . . No matter. You props over there! Start removing these battens, will you? You may need tools from the carpenter's room. And you in the purple weskit, fetch some salt quick from the nearest bar. We'll bathe his leg in salt water as soon as we've cleared the stage. You all right, Albert?'

A sonorous groan from the centre of the debris caused some pessimistic head-shaking among the rescue-party. Murmurs of concern rose in the ranks behind — for most of the company had abandoned the dressing-rooms at Albert's first yell of pain, and now stood about the stage in what they were wearing (or not wearing) at the moment of crisis. Constable Thackeray, seated on the basket containing the bulldog, had given all his attention to fastening the straps securely. He was dimly conscious of a group clustered near him, but not that they were ballet-girls. When he raised his face it was within a yard of a surface normally concealed by a tutu. A veritable outrage on decency! He dipped his head instantly, like a bargee just seeing a low bridge. Then by degrees, and strictly in the cause of duty, he mastered his modesty and raised his eyes.

Then someone arrived with a crowbar. A sudden commotion, the intervention of a young woman in lilac and white crying shrilly, 'Don't you dare go near Albert with that!' so alarmed the man that he dropped the implement with a clatter. The bulldog barked ferociously inside its basket and the unseeing audience exploded with laughter, 'Watch yerselves!' shouted the resourceful P.C. Battree, 'I'm watchin' you!'

Albert's protector was Miss Ellen Blake, the first act that evening. She now crouched by the shattered platform in a singularly affecting manner and put her hand comfortingly through a gap in the side. She withdrew it at once with a cry of horror. 'His arm! It's deathly cold!'

'If you'll stand up, miss, and look through here,' suggested Cribb, 'you'll see that his head's at the other end. You've just put your hand on the crosspiece of Albert's bar-bell. Now stand back and let's get him out.'

Two more planks were prised up. Cribb borrowed a lamp and peered in with the air of an Egyptologist uncovering his first mummy. 'He's not

54

in bad shape. Two more boards and we can drag him out at this end.'

Miss Blake came forward again and to everyone's relief a pale hand rose from inside to meet hers.

'He's quite all right now!' announced the manager, clapping his hands. 'Back to the dressing-rooms everyone except the ten-minute calls. The show goes on as billed.' He added in an afterthought, 'We'd better hurry. There can't be many songs about policemen left.'

Cribb looked up at the gigantic prancing shadows of Salt and Battree projected through the act-drop. 'Wouldn't hurt those two to get the bird. Deuced poor impersonation they give of the police, anyway.'

The manager snapped his fingers. 'I say, you're not . . . ? I *thought* you had an air of authority. How did you happen—'

'Never mind,' said Cribb. 'Where can we take Albert?'

'The property-room's the nearest.'

'Very good.'

Still clutching Miss Blake's hand as she walked beside him, Albert was borne off the stage and deposited on a dusty chaise-longue in the property-room. Thackeray followed, dragging after him the basket and its growling occupant.

'Does that animal have to be here?' were Albert's first comprehensible words.

'The dog is the evidence, blast it. A pukka investigator never lets the evidence out of his sight.

You can't trust a confounded soul,' announced a new speaker from the doorway behind. He was the stage-hand in the purple waistcoat who had gone for salt: a man of slight build and soft, boyish skin, quite eclipsed by fierce blue eyes under a shock of upthrusting grey hair. 'There's been an uncommon demand for pies and baked potatoes in the hall tonight, and salt's as scarce in there as upright women. So I borrowed this from the photographer's studio next door.' He held up a large brown bottle. 'Iodine — the unfailing remedy for a dog-bite. It does a deuced fine job of disinfection, and if you pour it liberally over the wound it has a rare capacity for enlivening a dazed man.'

The manager beamed his admiration. 'Good Lord, Major Chick, you're the right man to have in an emergency. Allow me to introduce you to this gentleman. He is a policeman.'

'Really? Wouldn't have thought it — looks too blasted intelligent.'

'Sergeant Cribb, sir.' They shook hands. 'And that's Constable Thackeray on the dog-basket. What was your name, sir?'

'Chick. Percival Chick. Major, retired. Late Adjutant of the 8th Hussars. Perhaps you have heard of me. I'm not, as you realise, a common scenery-remover. That was a mere subterfuge. Like you, Sergeant. I'm a detective now. But my investigations are limited to the private sphere.'

A private detective! Cribb inwardly snarled with a ferocity equal to the bulldog's at the instant it sank its teeth into Albert. What an evening! Music hall policemen, and now a private detective! It was his first contact with one of the species, though he had seen their newspaper advertisements often enough, and the brass plates on their doors. Anyone who spoke with a plum in his mouth and could afford the price of lodgings in one of the nobbier areas of London could set up in business and derive a tidy income from it. You filled your rooms with barrowloads of old books and obsolete chemical apparatus and soon there was a stream of wealthy callers with fantasies of blackmail, kidnap and family scandals. So you fed their fears with a few quite spurious discoveries, pinned a crime on some wretched servant and claimed your fee in guineas, with a few choice remarks about the impotence of Scotland Yard. 'Interested to make your acquaintance, sir. What's your business here, if I may inquire?'

Major Chick looked cautiously around him. Only the manager, Miss Blake and the Scotland Yard men remained there, besides Albert. 'I rather think my client, Mr Goodly, should explain.'

'Why, of course,' said the manager. 'A series of unfortunate accidents in the London music halls led me to engage a detective. You see, I doubted whether they were, indeed, accidents. Almost every hall of any reputation has suffered in this way in the last month or two — except the Grampian. Our turn seemed inevitable before long. So Major Chick has been disguised as a stage-hand for the past week in readiness to investigate just such an occurrence as this — even though it appears most improbable that tonight's small embarrassment was deliberately provoked. You can't put a bull-dog's fickle behaviour down to Anarchists, now can you? However, I gather from your swift arrival on the scene that you were on the watch for trouble too.'

'Never mind that,' said Cribb. 'Let's attend to Albert. Hand me the iodine, Major.' His voice bore the authority of a colonel at the very least and the Major almost clicked his heels as he obeyed the order. From that moment there was no question of who was in charge of the inquiries. 'Your pocket-handkerchief, if you please, Thackeray.'

Among the bric-a-brac of the property-room was a card-table on which Cribb placed his jacket, before rolling back his shirt-cuffs like a conjuror. 'Perhaps you will support the leg, Major, and you, Miss Blake, try to keep Albert from becoming distressed. Now, I shall remove this torn section of the tights and expose the wound . . . Capital! An ugly little bite, that. Not a lot of blood, but those teeth sank in a bit, eh Albert? I'll just wipe the surface clean now, like that. Then I form a pad with the handkerchief, saturate it with iodine and apply it firmly—'

Albert drew in breath through his clenched teeth and made a sound like a sky-rocket ascending. Everyone grabbed and held down a limb as his muscles tensed. His eyes first shut tight, then opened wide, streaming with tears. His hand gripped Miss Blake's so tightly that she squeaked with pain.

'Beautiful job,' Major Chick told Cribb. 'You could make a living as an army-surgeon, you know. Dammit man, you're wasting your time at Scotland Yard.'

Cribb surveyed his patient. 'You'll find it smarts a bit at first. Wounds need cleaning, though. Any other injuries?' He held the iodine bottle in readiness.

Albert shook his head decisively. 'Just the merest grazing where I fell through the platform. I'm sure the iodine won't be necessary. It's my ankle that hurts. I twisted it when I fell.'

'You'll be out of work for a week or two then,' said the manager, without much sympathy. 'And you can thank your dog for the lost wages. If you'll take my advice you'll have nothing to do with animals in the future. Just listen to the snarling brute! If you were mine, you ugly hound, I'd know what to do with you.'

Albert sat up. 'But that *isn't* my dog! That one's white with brown patches. Beaconsfield is strictly black and white. Surely someone noticed — I've been doing the act for three weeks or more. Some blackguard put that vicious animal into Beaconsfield's basket, knowing it would attack me as soon as it was released.'

'Do I understand you right?' asked the manager. 'Are you sure that the bulldog in that basket isn't yours?'

'Beaconsfield wouldn't attack me,' said Albert, shocked by the suggestion. 'He hasn't got the energy. It's all he can do to stand up on his four legs

59

while I'm holding up the bar-bell, and then he sometimes needs prodding. I tell you he's black and white, anyway.'

'Shall I lift him out for you to have a closer look, Sarge?' suggested Thackeray.

'That isn't necessary, Sergeant,' Miss Blake interposed. 'I know Beaconsfield and that is not him. If you look through the basket you can see a large brown patch where the Union Jack has ridden up on this dog's back.'

'A substitution, by Jove!' exclaimed Major Chick. 'Ingenious! Ah, the vagaries of the criminal mind! We're on to a cunning enemy here, Sergeant.'

Cribb ignored the assumption that the Major was now a party to the investigation. 'If *that* ain't Beaconsfield, Albert, then where *is* his Lordship? When did you last see him?'

'During the overture, when I brought him down here and put him in the wings in his basket. I like to watch Ellen's — Miss Blake's — act from the promenade, so I prepare everything for my own act first.'

'Then the dogs could have been exchanged at any time during the first three acts?'

'The first two, to be precise. I'm waiting with Mother in the wings from the beginning of the policemen's act.'

'It was done while Miss Blake or the Red Indians were performing then. Who would have been in the wings at that time, Mr Goodly?'

The manager smiled. 'It's not as simple as that, Sergeant. Music hall isn't like the legitimate theatre, where everyone's movements are planned and known. I'm managing a three and a half hour show with twenty-seven acts including dancers. I often have to change the order at very short notice to fit in with the commitments of the star billings. Tonight, for example, I've got Miss Jenny Hill on at eight o'clock. Nothing must alter that, because she's appearing at the Royal Aquarium at nine and the London Pavilion at a quarter past ten. So I shall change the order of the acts to ensure that she goes on in time to make a cab journey across to Tothill Street. No two nights in the music hall are the same, you see.'

'But you must have some notion who was in the wings at that time,' insisted Cribb.

'Very well,' said the manager acidly. 'Let's make an inventory, if that's the way Scotland Yard would like it. There would be the Red Indians, Henry and Cissie Greenbaum, waiting while Miss Blake was on, and the singing policemen, the Dalton brothers, and their assistant Vicky. Then there are up to nine stage-hands and scene-shifters dispersed on either side of the stage, two female dressers and one male, three fly-men looking after the curtain and the act-drops, two lime-boys on their perches in the flies, two call-boys, the gasman at the index-plate, my assistant, myself and any one of the other twenty-four acts who cared to look in. I would say almost a hundred people had a right to be there, Sergeant.'

'In that case someone must surely have seen the dogs being changed over.'

'I doubt it. Most of us are far too occupied with our own duties to notice anything like that. Moreover, the wings are in semi-darkness for the whole of the Red Indian act, to achieve the special lighting effect onstage. That's when the basket was opened, in my opinion.'

A murmur of assent on Cribb's left provided him with a sudden thought. 'Where were you positioned, Major?'

Major Chick coloured noticeably. 'Why — er — in the gallery on the side-wall above the stage, where the ropes and so forth are controlled.'

'The flies,' explained the manager.

'Didn't you see anything?'

The Major pulled at his moustache. 'I was observing the stage, dammit.'

'But of course.' Cribb placed a reassuring hand on Chick's shoulder. 'Well now, Major, I'm really uncommon fortunate having you here to advise me — a professional investigator on the scene of the crime a full week before it was committed. That's a gift from Providence, wouldn't you say?'

The Major nodded guardedly. He was plainly not used to being thought of in that way.

'You've had time to meet the staff and performers and form an estimate of 'em,' continued Cribb, 'and you'll have noted down anything irregular that happened this last week.'

It was plain from the Major's expression that he

had not. 'Fact of the matter is, Sergeant, that there's nothing regular at all in the music hall life, so far as I can see. You can't even count on seeing the same faces from day to day. There are stage-hands being hired and sacked in the same week, stage-door Johnnies by the dozen wandering about backstage, out-of-work performers arriving for auditions—'

An unexpected outburst of barking from the picnicbasket halted the Major's flow. To everyone's amazement it was answered by a submissive whining from the doorway. Albert's mother, still dressed in her white robe and ostrich feathers, filled the lower three-quarters of the door-frame. Cradled in her arms was a black and white bulldog that from its generally lethargic attitude had to be Beaconsfield.

'Keep your animal quiet, Thackeray!' ordered Cribb. 'Push it behind the piano, for Heaven's sake!'

'He was shut away in the dark, weren't you, my poor busy little Dizzie?' crooned Albert's mother, planting herself heavily on the chaise-longue, perilously close to her son's injury. Beaconsfield slumped over her knees with lolling tongue, accepting the banalities impassively. 'Shut in that horrid quickchange room without even a saucer of water. If Miss Charity Finch-Hatton hadn't needed to repair her garter we might not have found you for hours and hours. Why the silly little baggage made such a scene when you jumped up to be rescued I cannot understand.'

'Perhaps like the rest of us she thought Beaconsfield was a savage animal,' suggested Cribb. 'I'm a police officer, Ma'am, and I should like to take the liberty of asking you two questions.'

'We shall answer them if we can,' she said, caressing Beaconsfield's dewlap with her fingertip.

'Thank you. Could you tell me, then, why you didn't notice before the act that the dog in the basket wasn't Beaconsfield?'

She did not look up. 'I never venture near the basket until the moment comes to release Dizzie. I wouldn't want him to suppose me a traitor. It pains me to see him imprisoned there night after night. All that I noticed tonight was that a dog — and I presumed that it was my Beaconsfield — was in the basket and wearing the flag.'

'Who do you think could be responsible for tonight's mishap?'

'If I knew that, Inspector, I should have repaid the scoundrel by now and you would be arresting me. I have a powerful pair of arms, you know, and I'm not afraid to use them when anyone is inconsiderate to my little pet.'

'I'll remember that, Ma'am — but I really think someone must attend to your son. Albert will need helping home tonight.'

'Will he?' said the fat woman in surprise, for the first time turning towards her son. 'What's wrong with you then? A dog-bite won't stop you from walking a couple of streets, will it?'

'I twisted my ankle when I fell,' explained Albert.

'Oh, congratulations, my son!' she said sardonically. 'So the strong man must take a rest for two weeks on account of his weak ankle, while his mother is forced to return to serio-comic singing to keep Beaconsfield and herself out of the workhouse. Kindly explain what I am supposed to do to get you to the lodgings — carry you on my back?'

'We'll see to him,' said Cribb. 'Miss Blake, perhaps you'll be so obliging as to fetch his clothes.'

Major Chick rounded on Cribb in amazement. 'But there are suspects to be interviewed — a case to investigate. You can't leave the theatre, Sergeant.'

'Who's going to stop me?' asked Cribb. 'You're a competent detective, ain't you, Major?'

'Indubitably, but—'

'You've been here for a week, so you know everyone concerned?'

'Yes—'

'You understand, of course, that if you learn anything important from your inquiries you have a duty to pass it on to me?'

'Naturally, Sergeant, but—'

'Excellent!' The matter was settled so far as Cribb was concerned. 'Thackeray, whistle up a cab and have it wait at the stage-door, will you? We'll have you home in half an hour, Albert. Oh — and don't forget our four-legged friend in the hamper, Major. I leave him in your good care. We may need him later. Evidence, you know.'

FIVE

'Is this the house?' Cribb inquired. The four-wheeler had drawn up in an ill-lit cul-de-sac off the Kennington Road. The walls of Bethlehem Lunatic Hospital loomed higher on one side than a row of mean terraced houses on the other, built of the same grey bricks with an eye to harmony of appearance. Barefoot boys abandoned their pitch and toss under the street-lamp at the end, and scrambled for the privilege of opening the cab-door.

Albert nodded. 'Just one small room upstairs. It's not Grosvenor Square — but then I'm not George Leybourne or the Great Vance. Leybourne once treated me to a drink and told me that lifting weights would never get me a top billing. "What you need in the halls is a *voice* that carries," he said. "Humping weights about is hotel-porters' work." '

With the last remark fresh in his mind, Thackeray supported the strong man as he descended. Cribb paid the cabman and tossed a halfpenny to the nearest urchin.

'Can you climb the stairs with your arm over

Thackeray's shoulder or would you like him to carry you pick-a-back style?' asked the sergeant when they were inside, ready, as always, to volunteer his constable's services. Albert accepted the first suggestion. Thackeray was no small man himself, and the addition of Albert's considerable breadth as he supported him made for a laborious ascent up the narrow, uncarpeted staircase. Cribb followed, straightening the pictures knocked aslant by his assistant's shoulder. On the landing Albert pushed open the first door.

'Matches?' asked Cribb.

'On the tallboy to your right.'

The gaslight revealed a room of modest size, dominated by a suite of grotesque lacquered bedroom furniture, obviously designed half a century earlier for a room three times as large. How it had got up the stairs was a mystery.

Thackeray guided Albert towards the bed, thankfully deposited him there and began brushing the mildew from his cape at the points where it had touched the wall on the way up. 'You're a good weight, sir,' he said breathlessly. 'You haven't got a dumb-bell in your pocket, have you?'

Albert grinned. 'I'm wondering whether my landlady saw anything. She'll be suspicious, I can tell you. She's very particular on temperance.'

'Don't worry about that,' Cribb grandly assured him. 'I'll tell her who we are.'

'I'd rather you didn't, Sergeant. Coming home with two policemen is even more certain to get me a week's notice than an evening at the pub.'

Thackeray concealed his smile from Cribb by finding a sudden interest in a Landseer canine study on the wall behind him. Albert identified it. ' "Dignity and Impudence." The landlady's as partial to dogs as my mother, but only in the pictorial form. You can turn it over.'

Thackeray did so. The hooks supporting the frame were screwed into the top so that it was reversible. Pasted on the back was a photo-engraving of a young woman with a narrow length of muslin over one shoulder, standing beside a Greek column.

'Now I'm at home, you see,' said Albert with a laugh. 'That's my single contribution to the decorations. Sit down, gentlemen, if you can find a chair. You won't object to my reclining on the bed, I trust.'

Thackeray settled into a wicker chair by the window and regarded Albert's impressive physique, now constricted by the inadequate brass bedstead. This strong man was a queer sort of cove, with his public school accent and his waxed moustache. How did a man of that class fit into a shabby lodging-house like this, pasting doubtful figure-studies on the backs of Landseers and living in fear of a Lambeth landlady?

'We won't detain you long,' said Cribb, 'but I'll thank you for a few moments of your time. You probably gathered from the conversation at the Grampian that your injury tonight was one of a series in recent weeks suffered by music hall artistes. I want to discover if yours has anything in common with the others. You'll forgive me, I hope, if I put some questions to you that may seem unduly personal.'

'You can ask whatever you like,' said Albert.

'I'm obliged to you.' The sergeant moved an upright chair to the bedside, its back facing the bed. Then he swung his leg across it to sit astride, with arms folded along the back, and chin resting on them a yard from Albert's face. 'Now it's crystal-clear, ain't it, that someone went to a deal of trouble to arrange what happened on the stage tonight? Stray bulldogs aren't six a penny on the streets of London, as any bobby who's done dog-pound duty will tell you. Nor is it easy to exchange two dogs in the wings of a music hall when the show's in progress. Ah, I know all about your traditions of practical joking — silk hats coated with soot, and the like — but this was in a different class, wasn't it? Whoever arranged it knew very well that he was putting you out of work for a week or more.'

Albert shook his head. 'Longer than that, I fear. Who is going to hire me in a London music hall as a serious artiste after tonight's absurd exhibition? You'll see a report of the incident in next week's *Era* and that'll be the last notice I get as a strong man.'

Cribb nodded gravely. 'Who would have done such a thing, then — another strong man, perhaps?'

'Absolutely not. There aren't more than two dozen of us who lift weights professionally in London, and there are over a hundred halls, you know. We're not in competition with each other.'

'You don't have any enemies among the other acts at the Grampian?'

'Not really, Sergeant. People don't stay long enough to become jealous of each other. You might get a booking for three weeks and then you move on — unless you're Champagne Charlie or The Vital Spark and you're hired for a three-month engagement.'

'Let's look outside the music halls then,' said Cribb. 'Who do you meet in your spare time? Is there some acquaintance who might have turned sour on you?'

Albert laughed. 'Spare time? But there isn't any! From Monday morning's band-call to Sunday night's training with the bells my life is wholly given over to the music hall. Why, even my mother and my donah are part of it.'

'Miss Blake?'

'Ellen. She's a real beauty, you must admit. When her singing is in the same class as her face and figure she'll be the rage of the halls.'

'I don't doubt it.' Miss Blake's voice required a miracle, but Cribb spoke with conviction. 'She has other admirers, I expect.'

'Scores, I'm sure. Every night there are bunches of flowers and chocolate boxes delivered to her dressing-room.' Albert seemed naively proud of it.

'Then you have rivals.'

'Ah, but she gives them no encouragement. She doesn't even eat the chocolates. The other girls share them out after Ellen has gone home. She is entirely loyal to me, Sergeant . . . Yes, smile to yourself if you like, but I know Ellen. She is singularly strong-willed. I shouldn't want to be the masher who tried forcing his attentions on her.'

'Perhaps just such a gent arranged your downfall tonight,' suggested Cribb.

'I'm doubtful of that. Whoever took Beaconsfield out of his basket knows a rare amount about my act. Anyone knowing so much must also know that making overtures to Ellen is a waste of time.'

Cribb paused in his questioning, scratching speculatively at his side-whiskers. Thackeray, who disliked silences, lowered his eyes and slowly rotated the brim of the silk hat in his lap. He had a strong intuition that Cribb was about to move into a sensitive area of questioning.

'Then we seem to have eliminated everyone but your mother, Albert. I can't believe she would play a trick like this.'

There was a guffaw from the bed. 'Mama? There's not much she hasn't stooped to in her time, Sergeant, believe me! But I can't think why she would want to ruin the act. Besides, she wouldn't do anything to upset Beaconsfield. She dotes on that animal.'

'Has she always been a part of your act? I wouldn't think her contribution is indispensable.'

Albert laughed again. 'She's left four or five times to get her hooks into some unfortunate fellow with tin to spare, but she always comes back. I'm too soft-hearted to turn her away. It's the blood-tie, I suppose. She was once quite a celebrated figure in the halls — you won't believe this — as a *coryphee* in the ballet. That was how Papa met her. He was the chairman at Moy's Music Hall in Pimlico, right back in the fifties before it became the Royal Standard. He gave dramatic monologues on occasions, too. Oh, the hours he devoted to teaching me the vowel sounds — perhaps he knew I might need to follow in his footsteps some day. Well, about fifteen years ago he told Mama she ought to give up her dancing because she was already overweight and past forty. She took offence, there was a terrible argument, Papa walked out of our lives and Mama bought Beaconsfield. Oddly enough, she gave up ballet and took to singing, with me in a sailor-suit and Beaconsfield walking on to distract the audience a bit. She isn't a bad singer, you know. I tried to persuade her to pass on some hints to Ellen, but she wouldn't. Unless you've got bow legs and a wet, black nose, Mama isn't interested in the way you do anything.'

'But you're quite certain that she isn't responsible for what happened tonight?'

'Well, you saw the state she was in after she had rescued Beaconsfield, Sergeant.'

'Quite so.' Cribb got to his feet. 'We'll leave you to get some rest now. You'll be feeling the effects of tonight's experience. There's nothing we can do for you before we go? Very good. There's just one thing I want you to do for me, then. Whatever happens in the next day or two — and I suspect that something may — avoid violence. Scotland Yard won't be far behind you.'

With that, Cribb picked up his hat and cane and quit the room. Thackeray hauled himself out of his comfortable chair, mystified by the sergeant's last remark. Violence? He looked hard at Albert; what kind of violence was a bed-ridden man capable of, even if he *was* the Hercules of Rotherhithe? He followed, shaking his head.

There was a tap at the door of the interview room at Kennington Road Police Station. Sergeant Cribb rubbed his hands in anticipation. 'It had better be Cadbury's,' he told Thackeray. 'Come in!'

A bright-eyed constable in full uniform with helmet, greatcoat and armlet, made his entrance.

'Lord, they get younger and younger,' muttered Cribb. 'You can put the tray down here, lad. What's your name?'

'Oliver, Sergeant.'

'And how long have you been in the Force?'

'Four months, Sergeant.'

'Is that so? That's a fine new uniform you're wearing, Oliver, but there's no need to dress up to bring us a cup of cocoa, you know.'

'I'm on night duty, Sergeant, and Sergeant Flaxman insists—'

'Does he now? It's not for me to interfere, then. You're on till six tomorrow morning, are you?'

'Yes, Sergeant.'

'And you're the man whose beat takes in Little Moors Place?'

'Yes, Sergeant.'

'Then listen to me, young Oliver. I want you to keep a special watch on that road tonight — number nine in particular. You may know it — theatrical lodging-house. Just as soon as anyone enters there, it's your job to hare back here and let Constable Thackeray know. You can stand at the end of the road: it's a one-ender, you know, so you should be able to keep out of sight. Pity you're not a plain-clothes man, but we'll have to make do with you. Keep your lantern out; there's nothing like a bull's-eye for giving a bobby away. And take that armlet off when you get there.'

'But Sergeant—'

Cribb put up his hand. 'I'll square it with Harry Flaxman. This is a chance for you to make a name for yourself, lad, so don't disappoint me. Here, let's have a look at that armlet of yours. See that, Thackeray. What do you make of that?'

'Soda, Sarge, without a doubt.'

'Unmistakable. Never wash your armlet in soda, young Oliver. Makes the colour run like you're going to run back here from Little Moors Place as soon as you've got any news for us. That'll do, then. Fine cup of cocoa!' He turned back to Thackeray, as P.C. Oliver left to begin his vigil. 'You can relieve him at six. I don't think anything'll happen before then, but I can't take the chance. Well, Thackeray, I know the symptoms. Your face has been as long as Big Ben all evening. You want to speak your mind to me. Very well. Now's the time. Just wipe the cocoa-skin off your moustache and I'll give you my complete attention.'

'Well, Sarge,' said Thackeray a moment later, 'I suppose it's just that I can't take all this music hall stuff seriously. It don't seem nothing like your class of investigation to me. It's not really worthy of you, Sarge. A blooming bogus bulldog in a basket and a strong man with a twisted ankle — that don't seem worth losing a night's sleep over. We've taken on some odd cases, I know, but there's always been a corpse to make the whole thing worth while.'

'You might have got one tonight if that dog had rabies,' said Cribb. 'I understand you, though. On the face of it, tonight's affair at the Grampian seems pretty small beer. But look at it as the latest episode in this string of accidents on the stage — and remember we had a warning that something would happen tonight — and it becomes a deal more sinister. What we saw at the Grampian certainly wasn't murder, Thackeray, but from Albert's viewpoint it was professional assassination. You heard him yourself saying he was finished as a strong man. We heard Woolston saying something similar in Newgate. That's serious enough for me, Constable.'

Thackeray admitted that it was.

'Let's recall the incidents,' continued Cribb, reaching for a sheet of paper. 'I'll list them here. First there was the collision of the Pinkus sisters on their shortened trapezes; then Bellotti's tumble from the greasy barrel; the shameful alterations to

Sam Fagan's song-sheet; the accident to the sword-swallower; the unspeakable calamity suffered by Miss Tring; and the sword through the leg of Woolston's assistant. And now Albert's attack by a fraudulent bulldog. What do they have in common, would you say?' He handed the list to Thackeray and returned to his cocoa.

'I've given this a lot of thought, Sarge, because I expected you to ask me sooner or later.'

'Good. What conclusions d'you draw, then?'

Thackeray drew a deep breath. 'I haven't been able to conclude anything, Sarge. The more I think about it, the more ridiculous it all seems.'

To his amazement Cribb pitched forward, laughing. 'Thackeray, you're incomparable! I knew you wouldn't fail me. Of course it seems ridiculous, man! That's the point of it all!'

'The point?'

'Damn my eyes, you still don't see it! The common element, Thackeray, is ridicule. Absurdity. There's no better way to ruin a serious performance on the stage. Imagine your precious Irving falling through the stage-trap in the last act of *The Bells*. He'd be finished! Just as Albert was finished when the bulldog bit him tonight. Can you see a music hall audience ever taking him seriously again? Of course they won't. As soon as he appears anywhere you'll hear barking and growling all over the theatre. Ridicule, Thackeray — it's a devastating weapon.'

Thackeray agreed, drawing comfort from the private thought that a man of Cribb's stamp ought to know more about the offensive use of ridicule than he did. 'So somebody plans to make laughing-stocks of all these performers, Sarge. Then we're looking for someone with a grudge against each one of them. Shouldn't we interview 'em all to find out who they've fallen out with in recent months?'

'And find one common name? That's what I thought until I tried tracing them. Do you know, Thackeray, they've all quit their lodgings and dis-appeared except Woolston? At least he won't find it easy to do a flit from Newgate.'

'Why should they all do that, Sarge?'

'Could be they can't afford the rent any more, being out of work,' said Cribb. 'It's cheaper in a common lodging-house. That's where half the missing persons in London are, in my opinion. It's no use asking the keepers who they've got under their roofs, when their only obligation is to report infectious diseases and limewash the walls and ceilings twice a year. Yes, that's where they could very well be. For all the spangles and champagne, your music-hall artiste is just a step from the poor-house.'

'Didn't they leave forwarding-addresses?' suggested Thackeray, on an inspiration.

'I had the same thought,' said Cribb, 'but it seems you don't do that in the theatre. You move around so much that you use your agent's office as your official address, and collect your letters from him periodically. Inquiries were made this morning at five different agents in York Road — just up the street from here — "Poverty Corner" they call it in the halls. Well, *none* of our accident-prone friends have visited their agents. There's a pile of letters as tall as your hat waiting for the Pinkus sisters, and *they* weren't badly hurt, by Sergeant Woodwright's account. It's a rum business, Constable.'

'We could list them among the missing persons in the *Police Gazette*.'

'Already arranged. But the fact remains that six people have come to grief on the stage, lost their jobs and disappeared in the space of four weeks. With Woolston it could have been seven. D'you see now why I want to keep a watch on Albert?'

Thackeray was on his feet. 'Blimey yes, Sarge! We can't leave a job like this to that young cub who brought in the cocoa. I'll get round there straight away!'

Cribb raised his hand. 'And a precious fine plain clothes man you'll be, standing in a Lambeth street all night in your opera hat and cape. Better leave it to young Oliver and get yourself some sleep. Ask Sergeant Flaxman if there's a section house with a spare bed. And borrow a set of clothes for the morning. What's the time?'

'Just above your head, Sarge. Ten minutes past midnight.'

'Capital! I'll snatch a quiet glass of rum and shrub before they close. Look out for me in the morning.'

SIX

For the second time in five minutes Thackeray eased a forefinger between his neck and the collar of Sergeant Flaxman's shirt. Borrowed clothes! If they didn't chafe you because they were so tight, they constricted your circulation somewhere. What was the matter with the Kennington Road Constabulary, that they couldn't produce a set of toggery to fit an average — well, slightly larger than average — man? Were they all stunted, or worn thin by beat-bashing, or something? You would almost think they had got together to produce the least comfortable set of 'plain clothes' possible. They *couldn't* have known he had tender skin in the area of his neck when they gave him the coarse flannel shirt. But knickerbocker tweeds! He *had,* on rare occasions, seen Londoners wearing such things; only in parks, though, never the seedier backstreets of Lambeth. Yet when the moment of choice came in the mess-room, and he stood in his underwear with a pile of discarded, undersized clothes behind him, there were just two survivors; the knickerbockers and a red velvet smoking-suit. Lord! What a picture that presented of the off-duty hours at Kennington Road! Knickerbockers it had to be, then, with a deerstalker and elastic-sided boots to match. And now he shrank into the shadows of the asylum wall, half-expecting some nervous passer-by to suppose he had just climbed over.

About twenty past six. Too early, perhaps, for anything dramatic to happen, but he could not afford to relax. There was a hint of October mist in the air, but from where he was, sheltering against a buttress formed by two rows of bricks, he could already see lights appearing at windows in the terrace opposite. No sign of life from Albert's room yet; being a theatrical, he would be accustomed to a later start than most working men. The poor beggar was going to wake up stiff this morning, too; there wasn't much to tempt him from a warm bed.

Activity at the end of Little Moors Place: three cats came running from the shadows to meet the milk-cart. The milkwoman hitched two large cans to the wooden yoke slung across her shoulders and moved to the first house to fill the jugs on the doorstep from her tin measure. The cats waited, mewing, for some to be spilt.

She was the first person he had seen in the road since he relieved P.C. Oliver on the stroke of six. A promising member of the Force, young Oliver. Hadn't batted an eyelid at the deerstalker and knickerbockers. Recognised who it was straight away; perhaps the beard was the clue. Thackeray hoped it was nothing else. Section 11 of the *Police*

Code was constantly in his mind: *It is highly un-desirable for detectives to proclaim their official character to strangers by walking in step with each other or in a drilled style, or by wearing very striking clothing or police regulation boots or by openly recognising constables in uniform or saluting superior officers.* Just as well young Oliver himself had spent the night in uniform; Section 11 called for a rare amount of concentration. Years of experience. Even so, the lad might make a detective one day. He certainly had sharp powers of observation.

A postman now started at number one. What was that he was whistling? The fellow most have been at the Grampian the night before. *'And that prevents yer feet from gettin' sore'* indeed! A fine tune for a postman to be whistling. Why was it always the bobby who was a public laughing-stock? The song was in damned poor taste, too. Bad enough being prone to corns and blisters, without being reminded about them by damned-fool postmen. He shook his head indignantly, chafed his neck on the collar and swore to himself.

Not long after, he detected something distinctly odd in the postman's behaviour. Having passed up the street, making his delivery as the milkwoman had done, the fellow marched back to number one and commenced his round again! And when Thackeray observed more closely, he saw that although the postman was carrying a letter in his right hand he did not deliver it. Instead he paused at the door, tapped the envelope against his chin, turned and moved on to the next house. The performance was repeated at each house in the street, and then the whole process began again at number one.

Decidedly irregular! Thackeray was contemplating casually crossing the road to scrutinise the postman more closely, when another figure appeared from the shadows, carrying a pole: the lamplighter. Best, in the circumstances, to wait till he had attended to the single lamp-post in the road, and gone. But would you believe it, instead of getting on with his work, the wretched man was leaning against the lamp-post and lighting a cigarette. Infuriating!

Then there was a most singular development: the postman abandoned his fourth sterile tour of the front doors and crossed to speak to the lamplighter. They were too far away for their conversation to be audible, but if only they would turn a fraction under the light it might be possible to see . . . Good Lord! The postman had removed his cap to reveal an unmistakable shock of upstanding grey hair. Major Chick. What the devil!

Thackeray pressed himself back behind the buttress, wrestling with the significance of what he had seen. A private detective masquerading as a postman? And in Albert's road at half past six on a Sunday morning? Was this the way investigations were conducted in the private sphere? Really, some people would stop at nothing. What was the Major doing talking to a lamplighter, anyway? Was it even conceivable that Major Chick was no

Major, but a postman masquerading as a detective masquerading as a Major? Or one of the criminal class masquerading as a postman masquerading . . . ? Diabolical to contemplate!

Footsteps unexpectedly invaded his deductions, a heavy, regular tread approaching on his side of the road. What on earth now? Little Moors Place was busier than the ruddy Strand. He was certain to be seen this time. Couldn't avoid it. Damn the knickerbocker suit! If only there were some notice on the wall he could appear to be reading. He felt so infernally awkward, standing there in eccentric clothes, facing a row of houses where people were putting on their lights and getting dressed. Why, anyone could put the most appalling construction on his presence there. And — Heavens above! — it was a uniformed police officer approaching.

'No action yet, Mr Thackeray?'

Jerusalem! Young Oliver again.

'What the devil have you come back for?'

'Me, Mr Thackeray? I'm on my way home. I live at number thirteen, you see, across the road. You can knock if you want any help. I'll bring you over a cup of tea shortly.'

God help the Metropolitan Police! That lad had seemed so promising. 'Just move on,' Thackeray hissed, 'and don't stop until you're inside your house with the door bolted and if you so much as *think* of putting a foot outside, I'll . . .'

P.C. Oliver was gone. And so, curse it, was the light. Seconds later the lamplighter passed with his pole and turned into Brook Drive. Major Chick was presumably back delivering mythical letters; you couldn't see a blessed thing with the gas off.

Perhaps an hour later his nostrils began to twitch. A delicious aroma was being carried towards him by the breeze. Kidneys and bacon, he was certain. Devilish cruel to an empty stomach, tantalizing it with the smell of other men's breakfasts. How long would he have to endure this?

Several of Albert's neighbours had emerged before full daylight and started for work; no Sabbath for them. But the curtains remained drawn at the upper window of number nine. The better light brought one bounty: the sight of Major Chick, exhausted by letter-delivering, standing at the end of the road making a lengthy inspection of his bag, which was plainly empty. Interesting to see where *he* would go when the genuine postman arrived.

With dramatic suddenness Thackeray was alerted to the arrival in the street of a black four-wheeler that was driven the length of the cul-de-sac, turned with a grating of wheel-tread that raised sparks, and brought back to rein outside number nine, with enough noise to bring the whole road to the windows. A black-coated figure in a tall hat got out, glanced along the street, and turned back to say something to somebody still in the cab. While he talked, he was drawing on a pair of black kid gloves, smoothing the wrinkles fastidiously over unusually long fingers. He turned, and his face was in sharp profile: hawklike, the features taut with purpose. Presently he knocked at the door of Albert's lodging and was admitted.

What now? Approaching any closer to the carriage would certainly give Thackeray away. His instructions were to observe, not to become involved. He wished Cribb were there and had seen that face for himself, as odious a set of features as any in Newgate.

A movement caught his attention. Albert's curtains were drawn back, confirmation that the visitor was, indeed, for him. Thackeray gazed at the windows, abstractedly twisting a button on his jacket until the tweed itself was screwed out of shape. Of course intervention was out of the question. The caller might be a doctor, or Albert's agent, or someone with a perfectly legitimate reason for being there. Patient observation was the only possible course.

Some ten minutes passed, and the visitor emerged alone and walked briskly to the waiting cab. Was his business with Albert done, then? Apparently not, for he called his companion, a smaller, bearded man, from inside the cab. They waited while the cabman unstrapped an item of luggage from the cab-roof and lowered it to them. It was a large, black trunk, empty from the way they handled it. Between them they carried it to the door of number nine and were admitted.

Thackeray frowned, baffled. An empty trunk. What on earth could Albert want with such a thing? And why should it be delivered by two men in top hats and kid gloves arriving in a cab on a Sunday morning? He waited in growing disquiet.

Farther up the road Major Chalk waited, mak-

85

ing notes on the back of a letter. And the cabman, after descending to fit a nosebag to his horse, lit a pipe, leaned against his cab, and waited too. Three small boys came from one of the houses, walked up the road, looked hard at the Major, strolled back in Thackeray's direction, stopped to study him too, stared speculatively at the asylum wall and then stationed themselves by the carriage.

At length the door of number nine opened. A man backed out cautiously, feeling for the step with his foot. He was supporting one end of the trunk as before, but now his movements were ponderous. His companion stumbled after him, clearly feeling the effects of descending the stairs. No doubt about it: that trunk now contained something of quite considerable weight. One of the watching boys solemnly removed his cap.

'Under our very eyes, eh Constable?'

Thackeray started in surprise. Major Chick was at his shoulder. 'Lor' lummee—'

'No need for hysterics, man. I spotted your cover two hours ago. Thought I was a postman, eh? Never take a blasted thing for granted, Constable, least of all the Postal Service. Now, look here, I don't know what Scotland Yard's planning to do about this infamous affair. Personally, I'm ready to pursue the scoundrels all the way to the Continent, if necessary. One of my orderlies, the lamplighter — surprised you again, eh? — has lined up a cab round the corner in Brook Drive. I've room for you if you want it.'

Thackeray decided at once. 'I'm greatly obliged.'

'Very good. I'll be aboard. We must be prepared in case the blighters separate, though. Basic strategy. If either of 'em makes a break for it on foot you'd better give chase, and I'll follow the four-wheeler. Otherwise, you can meet me at the end of the road. Agreed?'

'Er — yes.' He was almost constrained to salute.

The Major moved off at a gait unlike any postman's, but the men with the trunk were occupied raising it on to the cab-roof and could not have noticed. Thackeray leaned heavily against the wall, assimilating the developments of the last few seconds. Perhaps he was staking too much on the Major's co-operation. Could the man be trusted? But really, when he considered it, he had no choice. The sight of that trunk being slowly manhandled out of the house and on to the waiting cab had made a profound impression on him. There was an awful possibility that he shrank from accepting. All he was certain about was that it was now his duty to follow the cab and its load wherever it was driven.

Then to his amazement and unbounded relief the door of the house opened again and Albert appeared, walking with a stick and supported by a small, grey-haired woman, undoubtedly his landlady. With the cabman's help he was man-oeuvred up the step of the cab, not resisting in the least. Then the horse was deprived of its nosebag, the two trunk-bearers joined Albert inside, the cabman flicked his reins and the carriage moved away. The landlady stood at her door fluttering a handkerchief.

Thackeray felt an overwhelming sense of deliverance at Albert's appearance in one piece. In spirit he was beside the landlady waving his deerstalker. Only when the cab was turning the corner did sentiment give way to more practical considerations. Heavens! Albert had been abducted in front of him!

'Just one moment!' He ran over to the landlady, knickerbockers flapping. 'I am a police officer. Your lodger—'

'Not my lodger no more, duck. He just left.'

'Yes, I know that. Did he tell you where he was going?'

'Sorry, love. He just paid his rent and went off with his two friends. What's he done then? Got himself inebriated? It don't surprise me, you know. They're all like that in the theatre. Well, did you ever?'

The constable was already pounding up the road towards the waiting hansom. Major Chick leaned forward to help him aboard and they set off at a canter in the direction of the river. 'Tickle him with the whip, cabby!' the Major shouted through the aperture in the roof. 'I've never known a hansom that couldn't catch a growler. Give the beast a tickle and we'll soon have 'em in sight again.' He turned to Thackeray. 'Nothing like a chase, Constable. Gets the old claret coursing through the veins, what? Got your bracelets with you? We'll need 'em when we've run this lot to earth.'

'My what?' inquired Thackeray.

'Bracelets, man. Handcuffs. You can't take chances with a pair of assassins.'

So the Major had been deceived by the trunk, too.

'I think I should explain something, sir. Albert is on board that four-wheeler.'

The Major laughed grimly. 'At the twopenny rate on the roof, eh? And we have to pay a shilling. Of course I know he's on board, Constable. I didn't imagine those scoundrels had packed their trunk for a week at Brighton, not the way they carried it. Why, I've been a pall-bearer myself, a dozen times—'

Thackeray broke in. 'Albert's alive and well, sir. He walked out to the cab himself.'

The Major received the good news in silence, pursing his lips and staring past Thackeray towards the gaunt exterior of St Thomas's. As the cab started across Westminster Bridge he removed his Post Office cap and buried his right fist in its centre. 'Alive and well, you say. Would have been my first murder case, you know, and dammit, I had it solved.'

'I'm sorry,' said Thackeray. 'I hadn't thought of it that way, sir. Perhaps we're on to a case of kidnapping, though.'

The Major was dubious. 'There's nothing to compare with a murder, Constable. It would have been in *The Times*. Very good for business, a mention in *The Times*. You're quite sure it *was* Albert? Easy to impersonate a limping man, you know.'

'I'm quite sure.'

The cab raced under the shadow of Big Ben, weaving a devious passage through a line of almost stationary buses and vans. Occasionally a pedestrian or a bicyclist appeared unexpectedly in front of them. Not for the first time, Thackeray was conscious of the vulnerable position of passengers in hansoms, with traffic hazards almost within touch, while the driver sat secure and aloft in charge of their safety. Any mishap now could result in a most embarrassing situation, Westminster being B Division and Scotland Yard so near.

'Do you really ask us to believe, sir, that you are a detective constable wearing a borrowed knickerbocker suit, travelling in the company of a private detective at a reckless speed through a Division not your own in pursuit of three innocent men and a trunk?' A nightmare.

'I can see them, I think,' said the Major as they turned past the Guildhall into Broad Sanctuary. 'If we get a clear run in Victoria Street we'll catch 'em.'

'I wasn't instructed to do that, sir — unless they committed a serious crime, of course. My orders was to keep an eye on Albert. I'd be obliged if we could keep 'em in sight without overtaking 'em.'

The Major seemed satisfied. He gave instructions to the cabman and then turned back to Thackeray. 'Very proper, too. Give 'em enough

90

rope and they'll hang 'emselves, eh? I might see my name in *The Times* yet.'

'It would be my duty to intervene if I judged the young man's life to be in danger, sir,' said Thackeray. 'You'll pardon me for asking: how did you come to be in Little Moors Place this morning?'

'Another surprise, eh?' said the Major, recovering his spirit. 'Well, I questioned scores of people at the Grampian last night. Heard some damned disquieting rumours. Performers unaccountably missing after they'd had one of those accidents we've been so troubled about. I may tell you that I had my doubts about you and your sergeant when I heard that. Dammit, man, you spirited Albert away pretty sharply last night, didn't you? Well, as a consequence of all these stories, I decided to keep a watch on our friend Albert. His mother gave me the address.'

'Did your questioning produce any information I should pass on to Sergeant Cribb, sir?'

The Major shook his head. 'Deuced disappointing. You know, the class of person you get in music halls doesn't impress me much, Constable. Very narrow existence. Ask 'em a civil question and they're liable to become positively abusive. Precious little concern among 'em for their fellow artistes' misfortunes, I can tell you. Hello! Enemy in sight. Not too close, driver!'

Four-wheelers were less common than hansoms in Victoria Street, but there must have been a dozen in the line of traffic that stretched ahead from the Army and Navy Stores to Victoria Station. Fortunately that trunk on the roof was as sure a sighting-point as a top-hat in church. The Major's hansom pulled smartly into the main stream behind a phaeton. 'Nice-actioned horses,' he commented with a nod. 'Making for Hyde Park, I dare say. Better class of person on this side of London.'

Past the station the traffic became less dense and moved at more of a canter as they approached Hyde Park Corner along Grosvenor Place. 'Wouldn't mind a turn along Rotten Row myself this morning,' said the Major, but Thackeray was looking towards St George's Hospital on his left. The journey continued through Knightsbridge and the Kensington Road. Here a certain tension was detectable in the Major. He smoothed the front of his uniform and fastened a button, replaced the cap on his head and arranged the strap of the post-bag symmetrically across his chest. Thackeray straightened his deerstalker, uncertain of the reason. It was made clear seconds later when the Major stiffened in his seat and executed a smart eyes right towards the Albert Memorial.

The cab with the trunk turned right in High Street, Kensington, into Kensington Palace Gardens. 'This is a private road, postman,' the cabman called down to the Major. 'Shall I follow?'

'If you please, but if they stop I want you to drive past slowly.'

As the hansom sedately pursued its quarry down the elegant avenue, Thackeray mopped his forehead with a large handkerchief. Where *was* the logic in this case? It would take a smarter detective than he to trace a connexion between these fine houses, neighbours of a royal residence, and Newgate jail. There wasn't one without wrought-iron gates and gravel drive and steps up to the front entrance.

About two hundred yards from the Bayswater end, the four-wheeler turned into the drive of a mansion fronted by a white wall with eagle-topped pilasters.

'Slowly past, and then halt fifty yards along the road,' ordered the Major.

Thackeray thought he glimpsed Albert standing at the foot of the steps watching the trunk being unloaded, but it was difficult to observe anything in more than a flash between thickly planted conifers at the front of the house.

'Philbeach House,' read the Major aloud. 'Means nothing to me.' When the hansom was stationary he turned to Thackeray. 'You won't do much more observing unless you climb a pine-tree, Constable, and I don't recommend that. What does Scotland Yard do now?'

Thackeray pushed open the door. 'I noticed a gardener in the place next door. I'll try to have a word with him.'

The knickerbockers were exactly right for Kensington Palace Gardens. The gardener actually doffed his cap. 'Ah yes, sir,' he replied. 'That's Philbeach House all right.'

'And who is the owner?'

'Why, Sir Douglas Butterleigh, the gin manufacturer. A millionaire, they say, and a very decent gentleman too, however he came by his money. He doesn't live there, you know. Were you looking for him?'

'As a matter of fact, no,' said Thackeray. 'Who is the resident there, then?'

The gardener cackled. 'Now you're asking! I'd say there's twenty or more residents in Philbeach, by the comings and goings I see while I'm clipping my roses here. And very odd some of 'em are, sir. But that's part and parcel of life in the theatre, so I understand.'

'Theatre?'

'Well, the music hall, Sir Douglas maintains a home for music hall performers who've come upon hard times. A very decent man.'

SEVEN

'Scotland Yard ain't the Bank of England,' grumbled Sergeant Cribb. '*Four* shillings! That's what I pay for a week's rent in married men's quarters. I don't know what came over you, Constable, lording it across London in a hansom. How can I put that down as reasonable expenses? You might at least have taken a bus back.'

Thackeray accepted the rebuke. Better to be shamed by the rough edge of Cribb's tongue than by a bus journey in knickerbockers. He would never disclose the real reason for that expensive return-journey. Confidences of that nature were best kept from Cribb.

Comfortable now in bowler and flannels, Thackeray led the way along Kensington Palace Gardens to Philbeach House. A perfect autumn afternoon, the leaves flashing unbelievably crimson in their twisting descent. Really no occasion for Cribb to niggle over cab-fares. A uniformed nanny passed, pushing a three-wheeled pram. Thackeray raised his bowler, and she almost ran over the infant toddling in front.

'I'm damned if you're listening,' said Cribb.

'Where is this rest-home then? Time we get there, I'll need somewhere to put my own feet up.'

Thackeray gave an artificial cough. 'Told you it was a long way from the bus stop, Sarge.' Privately he recalled Cribb's dramatic statement at the beginning of the afternoon. 'The Yard has watched and waited long enough. An immediate entry to this house is imperative. Time for action, Constable.' So they set off at once to Westminster Bridge Road. And waited twenty minutes to take a threepenny bus ride to Kensington.

But the moment came when they stood importantly at the front door of Philbeach House and Cribb pulled the bell-handle. 'Police,' he announced to the manservant who fractionally opened the door. 'Kindly inform the tenant, would you?'

The face had the scarred and brutalised look of an ex-pugilist. Comprehension dawned on it slowly. Dumbly it withdrew.

'D'you hear anything?' Cribb asked.

Thackeray removed his hat and put an ear to the door. 'Sounds like singing, Sarge. Hymns, I expect. Sunday afternoon.'

Cribb disagreed. '*Tommy Make Room for Your Uncle* ain't in my hymn-book.'

The face reappeared: 'Mistress says come in.'

'Mistress?' Cribb mouthed the word, arched his eyebrows, snatched off his bowler and stepped forward. They were ushered ungraciously through a tiled hall, flanked by rows of wilting shrubs in brass pots polished to inspection standard. Framed music hall posters lined the walls like reward bills at Scotland Yard. From somewhere ahead of them the singing swelled into a chorus, emphatically not ecclesiastical. In another part of the house someone was hammering.

The servant shambled to a stop, leaned against a door and mumbled, 'Them two coppers,' as it opened. Then he turned about, shouldered the detectives aside as though they were baize drapes, and slouched away. If *he* was a former star of the halls he kept his talents well-hidden.

Cribb pushed the door further open and they entered a remarkable room. The obligatory drawing-room furniture was there: sideboard, table and chairs in ebonized mahogany; velveteen-covered arm-chairs and couches; piano, display-cabinet and screen. But the ornamentation was so unexpected that they stopped, momentarily stunned. Where there should have been some unobtrusive flock paper, the walls were hand-decorated with hundreds of individualised human faces staring expectantly inwards, a dazzling parade of pink and orange blotches, broken by shadowy patches representing hats, cravats and whiskers, and all becoming smaller and less prominent towards the ceiling to give the effect of depth. It was like straying on to a stage in front of a packed auditorium.

After that sensation came others. More faces, white, expressionless faces, a row of plaster death-masks under glass domes, ranged on the sideboard, one grotesquely decked in a crepe wig, another topped with an old silk hat. Each labelled in gilt with the name of a deceased star of the halls. The piano-top supporting a small army of egg-shells painted to represent yet more faces, miniatures of comedians and clowns in full make-up, with bits of horse-hair glued on for realism. And the cabinets cluttered with puppets and ventriloquists' dummies, bolt-eyed, staring blankly ahead with the rest.

One face among the hundreds stirred. 'Please step in. It is a little unnerving, I believe, if you are not a theatrical. Most of us are, at Philbeach, you see. My name is Body. Widowed, seven years. What is yours?' She spoke from the centre of a large winged arm-chair, a doll-like figure enveloped in a black shawl, with the legs tucked out of sight on the chair-seat. The face was precise, finely moulded, radiant, though what was rouge and what the glow of firelight was impossible to tell. Hair too blonde to be natural framed the features in a profusion of curls, like a child-study by Reynolds.

'Cribb, Ma'am. Sergeant Cribb and Constable Thackeray. Checking on missing persons. I understand that this is a home for destitute music hall performers.'

'That is correct.' Mrs Body's elocution, like her hair, was a fraction too fussy. 'The singing you can hear is part of an entertainment they are rehearsing. One never really retires from the theatre, you know. The banging is not part of the performance. I have the gasman here.'

'On Sunday, Ma'am? That's irregular.'

'Yes, but leaks of gas are no respecters of Lord's Day observance. The gasman tells me it could be dangerous if neglected. Now please sit down and tell me how I can help you.'

Thackeray selected an upright chair to the side of the arm-chair Cribb took. Upholstered furniture seemed inappropriate to the rank of constable when solid woodwork was available. Mrs Body addressed him: 'You are sitting on one of our most precious relics, Mr Thackeray. No, it is quite in order for you to use it. Do not get up. That is the very chair W. G. Ross used to sit on in the forties when he sang the *Ballad of Sam Hall* at the Cider Cellars.'

'The condemned sweep,' said Cribb.

'You remember it! Splendid! Mr Cribb, you are a connoisseur of the variety stage, I declare!'

'That would be overstating it, Ma'am. My interest in Sam Hall is more for his criminal record than his legend in song. It's a fine collection of music hall items that you have, even so. Would that be a lime-tank doing service as a coal-scuttle in the grate, there?'

She clapped her hands. 'You *are* knowledgeable! They must have sent you specially. I do hope I can help you find some of your missing persons and then you can keep coming back to talk to me.'

The Sergeant's interrogations rarely took such a

personal turn. Was that a touch of colour rising to his cheeks? Thackeray forbore from peering too closely. Firelight, surely.

Applause broke out in the room next door, strikingly raucous for Sunday afternoon, even among music hall performers. But this gave way to a rich bass-baritone rendering of one of John Orlando Parry's most popular polite comic songs. *'Wanted a governess, fitted to fill—'* when, inexplicably, an outbreak of giggling interrupted the soloist. He managed to sing *'The post of tuition with competent skill'* and was again forced to stop for the noisy reaction of his audience. *'In a gentleman's family highly genteel,'* he began again, *'Where 'tis hoped that the lady will try to conceal—'* when ungovernable laughter made it impossible to continue. How a simple ballad gave rise to such guffaws defied the imagination.

'Excuse me.' Mrs Body got up decisively from her chair, crossed the room to the connecting door and marched into the uproar, which stopped almost at once. Only the hammering from a room on the opposite side continued.

'Look at the gasman quick!' ordered Cribb, striding to the door Mrs Body had used. 'I'll stand watch.'

Thackeray reacted instantly, almost upending W. G. Ross's chair in the process. He opened the door, and looked into a long, panelled dining-room. Several tables were laid for dinner. Silver candelabra stood among the table-ornaments. At the near end, in a fine mist of dust, was the gasman, in overalls, standing knee-deep in the foundations, half-a-dozen floor-boards prised open around him. He turned, hammer in hand, and winked. Major Chick!

'Slap bang in the enemy camp, eh?' said the Major in a stage-whisper. 'I'm full of surprises, Constable.' Thackeray closed the door and gave a long-suffering nod in answer to Cribb's uplifted eyebrows.

'You *will* excuse me, rushing out like that?' said Mrs Body, re-entering. 'They were quite unaware that their little concert was disturbing us.'

'Are your guests exclusively masculine?' asked Cribb, fingering a pair of ballet-shoes that were attached to the side of the mantelpiece with several others, reminiscent of shot rats on a barn door.

'No, no. I take anyone who is temporarily incommoded. As it happens, I have nine ladies in residence at present. But there has never been a breath of anything improper at Philbeach House, you understand.'

'That goes without saying,' said Cribb.

Thackeray nodded too.

'How charming. You know, Mr Cribb, you remind me so strikingly of Mr Body, my late-lamented husband, except that he was not so tall as you and wore spectacles. Your sight is quite in order, is it?'

'I believe so, Ma'am.'

'Do not count on it. *Nusquam tuta fides,* as Mr Body used to tell me often. "Our confidence is nowhere safe" — and he lost his spectacles in Hyde

Park, and drowned in the Serpentine. How can I help you, Mr Cribb?'

'Do you keep a register of your guests, Ma'am?'

'A register? Nothing so formal, I am afraid. I can tell you who they are, however.'

'Very good. Thackeray, you'll need your notebook. Perhaps you would begin with the ladies, Mrs Body?'

She clapped her hands to her cheeks. 'Oh dear, a notebook! That is enough to make me forget my own name, quite apart from the names of guests.'

'Just forget Thackeray's here, Ma'am,' suggested Cribb. 'Think of him as one more painted face on the wall. You can remember the names for *me*, can't you?'

She wriggled with pleasure in her large chair. 'Now that you put it that way, I think I can. Well, there are my longest residents, Beatrice and Alexandra. They are singers, you know.'

'Surnames, Ma'am?' requested Thackeray.

Cribb glared at him. 'When did they arrive?'

'Oh, eighteen months ago, at least,' said Mrs Body. 'They are sisters, you know. Their name is Dartington. I have two sets of sisters here at present. The others are trapeze artistes, Lola and Bella Pinkus. If it were not making an old music hall joke I would describe them as highly strung. Decent girls, but spirited, you know. I think they miss the exercise they used to get.'

'They're out of work, then?'

'Yes, poor waifs. One small mishap at the Middlesex and they were asked to leave. They couldn't pay their rent or find other work so we offered to let them come here. It was the same with most of the others — Miss Goodbody, Miss Archer, Miss Tring—'

'The Voice on the Swing?' said Cribb.

'But yes! How thrilled Penelope will be when I tell her you know her name! She was in a dreadful state when she arrived here — an unendurable experience on her swing, you know — but we are trying to laugh her out of it in our cheerful fashion.'

'I'm sure you are,' said Cribb. The noise in the next room, already reasserting itself, was evidence of that. 'That makes seven ladies. Who are the others?'

Mrs Body made a rapid inventory of her guests on her fingers. 'Ah! Miss Harriett Morris, the song and dance artiste — such deplorable misfortunes that poor child has suffered — and then there is my latest guest who arrived after lunch, and I must confess that I don't yet know her name. She is the mother of a strong man who was savaged by a dog and brought here this morning.'

'The great Albert,' said Cribb. 'Who brought him to you, then?'

'Why, the Undertakers! I haven't surprised you, have I gentlemen? You must have heard of the Undertakers, George and Bertie Smee, one of the most whimsical comic turns in London until their accident two months ago? They're frightfully good

103

company and so helpful. They went all the way to Lambeth in a cab to persuade Albert to come here and convalesce.'

'Really? And how did you come to hear of Albert's injury?'

Mrs Body produced a beatific smile. 'There are more Good Samaritans in the music halls than you would believe, Mr Cribb. When an artiste suffers an injury, you may be sure that someone in the same company or in the audience will have heard of Philbeach House. In this case it happened to be a personal acquaintance of Sir Douglas Butterleigh.'

'Your benefactor?'

'The very same. We see very little of Sir Douglas, but he has many friends, and some of them like to associate with our philanthropy. They prefer to remain anonymous.'

Cribb nodded in a way that showed he had expected as much. 'Did your informant give you Albert's address as well? You got him here uncommon fast.'

There was a pause while Mrs Body twisted one of her curls around her left forefinger. 'Mr Cribb, you ask such suspicious questions. Do you think that you will trap me into saying something indiscreet? I believe I rather relish the prospect of being trapped by a real policeman. What would you like me to say?'

Thackeray's pencil slipped from his fingers and rolled across the floor. He muttered an apology and recovered it. How could you behave like a wall-painting when your superior was being subjected to moral danger?

'I merely inquired how you got Albert's address, Ma'am,' said Cribb.

'From his agent, of course,' said Mrs Body. 'Every artiste makes sure that his agent has his latest address. Do you know, Mr Cribb, I have something upstairs that would interest you, as a lover of the variety stage. You must have visited the old Alhambra in Leicester Square before it lost its music and dancing licence? Well I have a small sitting-room furnished as a perfect replica of a box at the Alhambra, complete with hangings and chairs that I bought from the owner.'

'I don't know that I've time today, Ma'am—' began Cribb.

'Perhaps on a future occasion, when you desire to interrogate me further,' ventured Mrs Body. 'You can understand my wish to escape from my responsibilities from time to time. That is when I retreat to my little box upstairs.'

Thackeray blew his nose stridently.

'But you will want to know the names of my male guests,' Mrs Body said, her thoughts evidently deflected by the interruption. 'I doubt whether I can remember all of them. I accommodate most of the old Alhambra orchestra, you see.'

'I understand you, Ma'am,' said Cribb, with conviction. 'But they wouldn't feature on my list. Would you have an Italian barrel-dancer — name of Bellotti?'

'Yes, yes!' She opened her arms expansively.

'How splendid! You can cross him off your list! He is a missing person no longer.'

'And a comedian named Fagan?'

'Sam Fagan! That is Sam's voice you can hear in the next room.'

'That's very good news,' said Cribb. 'Could we go in?'

Mrs Body lifted a hand. 'Not this afternoon. Rehearsal, you know. They insist on private rehearsals.'

'What are they rehearsing for, Ma'am?'

Momentarily Mrs Body seemed confused. 'What for, Mr Cribb? Why, for their return to the footlights, when they are quite restored. Some of them may never be hired again, but it would be cruel indeed if we denied them their slim hope.'

This somewhat pathetic view of the guests was difficult to reconcile with what was now issuing from next door. A voice, presumably Sam Fagan's, was endeavouring to articulate a poem by the late Mr Thackeray. Like the song, it was being most oddly received.

> 'But of all the cheap treasures that garnish my
> nest, (recited Mr Fagan)
> There's one that I love and I cherish the best;
> For the finest of couches that's padded with
> hair
> I never would change thee, my cane-bottom'd
> chair.'

—at which hoots of indecorous laughter held up the rendition. It was impossible to believe that a familiar parlour-poem could be so received.

> "Tis a bandy-legg'd, high-shoulder'd, worm-
>   eaten seat,
> With a creaking old back, and twisted old
>   feet; (persisted the speaker)
> But since the fair morning when Fanny sat
>   there
> I bless thee and love thee, old cane-bottom'd
>   chair.'

'Extraordinary!' declared Cribb, not at the poem, but at the persistent under-current of giggling that accompanied it, women's voices as prominent as the men's. Was some unexplained pantomime being performed in accompaniment?

> 'If chairs have but feeling in holding such
>   charms,
> A thrill must have pass'd through your
>   wither'd old arms!
> I look'd, and I long'd, and I wish'd in despair;
> I wish'd myself turn'd to a cane-bottom'd
>   chair.'

A veritable pandemonium of horse-laughs provoked the expected reaction from Mrs Body. 'Excuse me, gentlemen. They are getting beyond themselves again.'

She had not reached the door when she was halted in her tracks by a shattering explosion from the opposite direction.

'The Major!' said Thackeray, and ran to the dining-room door. Dust billowed out as he opened it. For a moment it was impossible to see anything. Then the results of the blast were revealed: ripped floorboards, upturned tables and broken windows. There was no sign of the Major, but an open window gave grounds for hope.

'Get to the main and turn off the gas!' ordered Cribb to the first startled face to appear from the room next door. The man had the good sense to obey at once. 'Look after Mrs Body, will you?' Cribb asked someone else. The room was rapidly filling with people, blundering into each other in the enveloping dust.

'I've shut the door, Sarge,' said Thackeray, when he had found the sergeant. 'The Major seems to have gone. I don't think it was violent enough to have . . .'

'Blasted him to bits? I doubt it,' said Cribb. 'What's that under your arm?'

Thackeray rearranged the burden he was carrying. 'I think it's Beaconsfield, Sarge. I nearly tripped over him a second ago. The poor brute's quivering like a jelly.'

'Damned ridiculous he looks, too, with that pink ribbon tied round his throat. My guess is that he's shaking with mortification.'

The atmosphere in the room was clearing, though a babble of excited conversation persisted. Two young women in tights were attending to Mrs Body, who lay in her chair in a state of shock.

'Ain't that Albert, Sarge, in that group over there?' said Thackeray.

'Probably. Best not to recognise him openly. There's a lot more we can learn with Albert's help. And watch out for his mother. If she comes this way you'd better drop Beaconsfield and make for the front door. Stupid slobbering animal's liable to ruin everything. Are you partial to bulldogs or something?'

'Not particularly, Sarge. He just seemed to lack confidence in all the confusion.'

Cribb gave the dog a withering look. 'That's his natural condition.'

On the other side of the room Albert had caught Thackeray's eye.

'Albert seems concerned about something, Sarge. D'you think he's all right? I believe he pointed at me. I say, those are the men who were in the cab with him.'

Cribb regarded the group with interest. Messrs Smee, the Undertakers, were difficult to picture as a comedy turn. Albert was standing between them, easing his collar with his forefinger.

'Got some dust down his shirt by the look of things,' said Cribb. 'Don't stare. They all know we're bobbies. Put the dog down and we'll see if we can recognise anyone. Those must be the Pinkus girls.'

A moment later, Thackeray stubbornly returned to the subject of Albert. 'Sarge, he's scratching his neck like a blooming monkey. It ain't natural. He's taking off his collar.'

'His collar?' Cribb jerked round. 'Good Lord! What the hell have you done with Beaconsfield?'

'I set him down as you asked, Sarge,' said Thackeray, bewildered to the point of despair. The dog was not in sight.

'Well find him again quick, for God's sake! Albert's signalling to us. There's got to be something hidden under that ribbon round the bulldog's neck. Where's the ruddy animal gone now?'

Each detective set off on a different route around the room in the ape-like gait customarily adopted by members of the Force when rounding up strays. One of the young women in tights bending over Mrs Body straightened up and gave Thackeray a long, hard look, but otherwise the prevailing confusion deflected interest from the search.

It was Cribb who located Beaconsfield, panting behind a screen. He put a hand towards the ribbon. 'Easy, now. Easy.'

Beaconsfield growled. Cribb withdrew his hand. 'Ah! There you are, Constable! Kindly feel underneath that ribbon at once!'

The dog permitted Thackeray to approach. He removed a scrap of paper from under the ribbon and handed it to Cribb.

'Well, blast his eyes!' said the sergeant when he had read it. 'What do you think of that?'

Thackeray read the message: *Everything in perfect order. Thank you for your interest. Albert.*

EIGHT

Scarcely a civil word was exchanged between constables at Paradise Street police station on Monday mornings. You sensed the atmosphere as soon as you passed under the blue lamp and saw the baleful expression of the duty constable at the desk. From the moment when the First Relief paraded shivering in the yard at a quarter to six and the Station Sergeant sized them and marched them off in single file to their beats, the list of duties was enough to draw a tear of pity from a convict's eye. For by ten o'clock, when the Relief returned complaining at the week-end's accumulation of orange-peel on the pavements (which every constable was under instruction to remove, *'frequent accidents having occurred to passengers slipping therefrom'*), those on station duty were obliged to have checked the charge-sheets, turned out the occupants of the cells and got them to the magistrates, swept the station floor, studied the *Police Gazette,* completed the morning reports of crime in time for the despatch-cart, brought their personal diaries up to date and dealt with an unending flow of trivial public inquiries.

And it was on Mondays that erring officers learned that their names had been entered in the Divisional Defaulters' Book.

That was why Sergeant Cribb was surprised to hear a contented humming from his assistant when he found him in the Criminal Investigation room. He soon put a stop to that. 'Touch of indigestion, Constable?'

Thackeray sat quite still. White crescents appeared on his finger-nails as his grip tightened on his pen. Why should he endure insults? 'No, Sergeant. Sorry if my singing offends you. It's my high spirits, I reckon, with the investigation over and my report three-quarters written.' He wiped the nib carefully and looked up at Cribb. 'If you want the truth, I'll be glad to get back to some serious detective work.'

Cribb's eyebrows jumped in surprise. 'Good gracious! Caught me off guard! Thackeray, there's a streak of malice in you I never knew was there. We'll make a sergeant of you yet.'

'It ain't that I mean to be offensive, Sarge,' Thackeray explained, conscious that his remark had struck home harder than he intended. 'But I can't tell you how relieved I was when we found all them missing persons at Philbeach House yesterday. I'd already been thinking of 'em as corpses. As you know, I look forward to finding a body as much as the next man, but sometimes it bucks you up to discover that things ain't what they appeared. I mean, that message from Albert came like a ray of golden sunshine.'

'In a pink ribbon,' added Cribb.

Thackeray gave him a sharp glance. 'An incident like that, coming so unexpected, restores your faith in your fellow-creatures, or so I think, anyway. "Everything in perfect order." I'm going to finish my report with those words. They'll make a nice change from all the accounts of violence and bloodshed that get sent in to Scotland Yard.'

'Should gladden the hearts of Statistical Branch,' murmured Cribb. He stroked his forefinger around the rim of the table-lamp on Thackeray's desk and examined it for dust. 'So you're planning to return to routine detective work. So far as you're concerned, the music hall investigation ended yesterday.'

Thackeray pointed his pen at Cribb. 'Ah, I know what you're going to ask me, Sarge — how do I explain all those accidents? Well, I thought a lot about that before I got off to sleep last night. I went over the whole case in my mind, one accident after another. It was when I got to thinking about Albert that I suddenly made sense of it all. I remembered that ugly little room he lives in, the worn-out linoleum and the furniture. And the depressing view over the asylum. Then I thought of them silver candlesticks at Philbeach House and the white table-cloths and thick carpets, and I saw why everything's in perfect order now for Albert and all the rest of 'em. They're on velvet over there at Kensington, Sarge. They've never known such circumstances in their lives!'

'I don't doubt it,' admitted Cribb, 'but does that

explain the accidents?'

'Don't you see it?' asked Thackeray, eyes gleaming. 'They staged their own accidents to get admitted to Philbeach House! Albert switched those bulldogs himself — or perhaps his mother did — and he exchanged a sore leg for a few comfortable weeks in Kensington. Ain't it obvious when you think about it? The word's gone round the halls that there's free board and lodging to be had by anyone smart enough to fall on his face on the stage. They even get collected in cabs. That's why there's been such a rash of accidents. When you think about it, they were mostly minor injuries—'

'Woolston running a sword through his assistant?' queried Cribb.

'Well there's always some cove that goes too far,' continued Thackeray with a frown. 'It was obvious he didn't care twopence about the girl. By running the sword through her leg he thought he'd get the pair of 'em a berth at Philbeach House. Instead of that he's had to settle for Newgate. But if you think about any of the others — the Pinkus sisters, Bellotti, Sam Fagan — they all made sure of losing their jobs without causing real danger to their persons. And now they're installed among the silver candlesticks with Mrs Body. If it was a home for out-of-work bobbies, I'd be tempted to take a tumble down the station steps myself.'

'Well I wouldn't,' said Cribb emphatically. 'I felt deuced uncomfortable in the same room as that woman yesterday. And that was with you there as chaperon.'

Thackeray grinned. 'It just hasn't been our kind of case, Sarge. I felt it all along. We're not built for music hall capers. I'll be quite relieved to get back to some straightforward robbery with violence. You do see the drift of my reasoning, don't you?'

Cribb nodded gravely.

'Does that conclude the inquiry, then, Sarge?'

Cribb shrugged. If you want to withdraw.'

'Well since it ain't a murder, Sarge, and false pretences aren't easy to prove—'

'You'd like to leave the rest to me? Very well, Thackeray.' Cribb picked up his hat. 'Sorry you've been troubled. Should have made sure I had a corpse before I interrupted your educational classes. We'll part on good terms, though. Remember past successes, eh?'

Thackeray clutched his beard. Heavens! The educational classes! What had he said? 'Sarge, I'm not giving up! If there's more to be investigated we'll do it together. I just thought that my theory . . .'

Cribb stood looking out of the window. Agonising seconds passed before he spoke. 'Attractive theory, too. Your deductions have improved over the years. You might even be right this time.' He tapped his nose reflectively. Thackeray waited palely. 'Little things bother me still. Questions wanting answers. Who was it that first put us on to this investigation by sending us the Grampian bill with the message marked on it? Someone wanted us to investigate. Then why did all the accidents occur at different theatres on different nights — and no two victims performing similar turns? Why don't the guests at Philbeach House collect their letters from the agents? What was going on there yesterday in the next room — a rehearsal, Mrs. Body said, but for what? Where was the humour in that poem they found so hilarious? Small points, all of 'em. Silly, niggling things.'

'There's still a rare amount to be unravelled, Sarge,' said Thackeray, seizing the first chance to affirm his loyalty.

'Enough to keep *me* occupied a little longer, at any rate,' said Cribb. 'No need for you to stay on the case, though. Just indulging myself, you understand. It's only details that irritate me; I shan't be content till I've got 'em all accounted for. Like a flock of sheep, really.'

Cribb as shepherd was a novel conception, but in spirit Thackeray was already at his side in gaiters and smock. 'I couldn't give up now, Sarge, not when there's work unfinished. Why, the answer to just one of them questions might alter everything, like one move in a game of draughts. How do you think I'd feel if you found something to upset my deductions?'

'Can't say,' said Cribb. 'But if you *are* wrong, and someone else staged those accidents, there's a man in Newgate about to be tried for a crime he didn't commit. I can guess how *he* feels. It ain't no parlour-game to him, poor beggar.'

Thackeray, squashed utterly, made no comment. At such moments he had learned to wait for Cribb to take up the conversation again.

'Made some inquiries of my own last night. Discovered a thing or two about Sir Douglas Butterleigh, the owner of Philbeach House.'

'The gin manufacturer?'

'Yes. Very rich man. Made his money when gin palaces were all the go. Now he's ninety and bedridden and lost his power of speech a year ago. Lives in a nursing-home in Eastbourne.'

'I shouldn't think he can help us much, Sarge. Does he have any family?'

'One son. A missionary in Ethiopia.'

'He'll stand to inherit a large fortune.'

'Three factories,' said Cribb, 'two large houses and more than a hundred pubs.' He paused. 'And a music hall.'

Thackeray whistled. 'Which one, Sarge?'

'I don't think you'll know it. The Paragon, in Victoria. Not one of the larger halls.'

Theories bubbled in Thackeray's brain. 'A music hall! Blimey, Sarge, we ought to look it over!'

'That's what I was proposing to do,' said Cribb. 'That is, if that crowning sentence in your report can stand a small delay.'

Three mature gentlemen in blue satin drawers and zephyrs paraded with chins erect, arms linked and stomachs indrawn as if for a photograph. Not a thigh quivered nor a moustachio twitched as two younger men in white ran, sprang and bounded on to their shoulders from behind, linking their own arms for stability and gingerly straightening to the same elegant stance. Even the unexpected rasp of someone moving the springboard at the rear caused not the slightest upset in the human edifice. There was simply a simultaneous flexing of five sets of knees, a scamper from behind, a resounding thump on the board and a sixth acrobat rose irresistibly aloft. Fittingly, he was dressed in red. The others took the strain, steadied and straightened into a perfect pyramid.

'Smoking-concert stuff!' a voice called from the auditorium. 'Better find yourselves a church hall, my friends. There's no place for you on my stage.' As the pyramid crumbled and slunk to the wings the voice added, 'That's the auditions finished, thank God. Now where's the bloody ballet? I called a rehearsal for ten. Is there anyone in the house at all, dammit?'

In the back row of the pit, Cribb and Thackeray dipped even lower in their seats. From the front only the domes of their bowlers were exposed, like cats on a coalshed. The Paragon was cold and smelt of orange-peel and stale cigars. Besides the stage-manager, who sat with his tankard at one of the tables at the front of the house, there were up to a dozen other solitary figures in overcoats huddled in seats at the back. By Grampian standards the auditorium was small, built for an audience of five or six hundred, but it had the merit of being designed for its purpose, not adapted, as other halls were, from a restaurant or chapel or railway arch. There was no trace of the maligned 'gingerbread' school of architecture in the decorations. The mouldings were based on sweeping lines and curves, ivory-coloured, with gold relief. Maroon plush and velvet had been used for the seat-coverings, hangings and box curtains, and it was easy to imagine the cosy intimacy of a full house at the Paragon, with the gas up and a layer of cigar-smoke keeping down the less pleasant aromas attendant on public gatherings.

'Mr Plunkett, sir!' a voice called from the wings. 'What now?'

'It's inclined to be draughty backstage. The girls are breaking out in goose-pimples. May I be so bold as to suggest that we turn up the floats? I think the dancing might be the better for it.'

'You can inform their ladyships from me,' returned the manager, 'that if they aren't onstage in the next half-minute they can warm themselves up walking to York Road to find new employment. Goose-pimples!'

A pianist at once produced a series of trills, and the *ballet divertissement* took the stage, a row of dancers in crimson tiptoeing from the left to meet a black row from the right. Each girl had one hand on her neighbour's shoulder, the other casually lifting a hem to dazzle the audience with flashes of silken calf in a flurry of lace.

'That's really quite tasteful, ain't it, Sarge?' whispered Thackeray. 'By music hall standards, I mean.'

'I reserve judgement,' said Cribb. 'Unexpected things can happen.'

Thackeray's eyes opened a little wider and swivelled back to the stage, but the variations in the dance were strictly conventional, a series of simple movements producing pleasing alternations of red and black.

'Stop!' bellowed Mr Plunkett. 'Where are the figurantes?'

The lines halted and three chalky faces appeared round the curtain.

'What do you mean by it? You missed your bloody cue.'

'If you please, Mr Plunkett,' one was bold enough to answer, 'it's cold as workhouse cocoa back here and Kate's got cramp something awful.'

'Cramp? Don't talk to me about cramp. I'm getting apoplexy down here. Tell that madam I want her on stage on cue in whatever state she's in. And that's no cause for giggling, the rest of you. A figurante with cramp — I never heard such gammon!'

Thackeray jerked up in his seat. Someone had nudged his left arm: a young man in uniform, with an orange in his hand. 'Would you like one, brother? I've another in my pocket. Old Plunkett's an ogre, ain't he? Bark's worse than his bite, though. I don't care for the language he uses, but that's his nature, I reckon. I'm a Salvationist myself. Never use indelicate words, though I've heard more than most.'

'What are you doing here?' whispered Thackeray.

'There's nowhere the Army won't go, brother. I'm here for every performance and all the rehearsals I can manage. Ah, the opportunities for a man of my calling! You see the black-haired one in red, third from the left? I'm counting on a conversion before Christmas. Stunning, ain't she? You can't see a young creature like that selling herself to perdition, can you? I say, you ain't her father, are you?'

'Good Lord, no,' said Thackeray.

'It wouldn't surprise me. Half these fellows sitting around us are related to the *corps de ballet*. Husbands and fathers, you know. They like to keep a watch on Plunkett, but he's harmless, I tell you. It's family entertainment at the Paragon. Nothing worse than you're watching now. Of course, the hall's in a better-class area than most. The girls in some halls are beyond all hope of redemption. If you'll pardon the expression, I've seen pimps and procurers, men of iniquity, eyeing the chorus at places like the Alhambra. Who's the cove with the sharp nose sitting on your right?'

Thackeray turned to see whether Cribb was listening. He appeared to be absorbed in the dance. 'Just come in to get out of the cold, I think.'

A missionary gleam entered the young man's eye. 'Would he like a soup-ticket, do you think? We look after a lot of his kind at our shelter in the Blackfriars Road.'

'I'm sure you do,' Thackeray said out of the corner of his mouth, 'but he don't look like a soup-drinker to me.' He nudged the sergeant. 'This gentleman was telling me he watches all the performances.'

'Does he?' said Cribb, touching his hat. 'Tell me, do they have a barrel-dancer on the bill here?'

'Barrel-dancer?' repeated the young man. 'Never seen one at the Paragon.'

'Sword-swallower, then?'

'I can't remember one, brother.'

'Trapeze artists?'

'Yes, we had one of them. Called himself the English Leotard. Wasn't much good, though.'

'You don't recall any women performers on the trapeze?'

He gave Cribb a look of distaste. 'No, praise the Lord.'

'I like comedians myself,' said Thackeray, changing tack with unusual skill. 'Comic singers in particular. That Sam Fagan's a real caution!'

'Never seen the bloke here,' said the young man. 'There's always a comic turn, mind you, but he's a new one on me.'

The dance reached its climax. To a *fortissimo* accompaniment each girl in turn made two full revolutions and ended with a low curtsey, the cut of the bodices adding profoundly to the effect. In a crowded hall the forward dips would certainly have been performed to clashes of cymbals and a succession of cheers. Instead, there was just the spirited pounding of a small piano. Even so, the charm of the finale caught the C.I.D. unprepared. Both detectives were too wrapt in the spectacle onstage to observe the approach of Mr Plunkett. He boomed at them from the end of their row, 'Perhaps you gentlemen would kindly replace your eyeballs in their sockets and explain what you're doing in my hall.'

Thackeray blew his nose. Explanations were a sergeant's job.

Cribb stood up. 'We didn't like to interrupt you, sir. My friend and I simply wished to have a word with you. Accordingly we sat down here to wait for a suitable moment to approach you.'

'So you squatted in the back row and had a squint at my girls?' said the manager, with more than a hint of sarcasm. 'Would you like them to perform the dance again, or have you seen enough? Perhaps you would care for a tour of the dressing-rooms?'

Thackeray's indignation rose like sherbert in a glass. Cribb hastily replied, 'That won't be necessary. It's tickets we came for.'

'Then why didn't you go to the ticket-office in the foyer?' snapped Plunket. He turned and clapped his hands. 'You girls can go now,' he shouted. 'Report at six sharp tomorrow.'

Cribb brushed a trace of cigar-ash from the sleeve of his overcoat. 'I have always found,' he said with all the dignity he could muster, 'that a personal approach to the manager is to be recommended. Invariably he can advise you in the matter of selecting tickets. We wouldn't want to see a bill that is less than the best you offer.'

'All my shows are tip-top entertainment,' said Plunkett, his tone more conciliatory. 'What did you want exactly?' He had the build of a navvy, but the speed of his responses suggested a livelier intelligence.

'The best you can offer,' answered Cribb. 'We can pay.'

Plunkett's eyes travelled over Cribb and Thackeray, assessing them. Offers of payment were apparently not enough at the Paragon.

Cribb spoke again: 'You have a show tomorrow—'

'Who told you that?' demanded Plunkett, all aggression again.

'You did,' said Cribb. 'You just told the dancers to report tomorrow evening at six o'clock. That's not for rehearsal, I take it.'

'Six? Ah yes. The overture begins at half past seven. If that's the bill you're wanting tickets for, you'd better see my daughter in the office. I'm a busy man.'

'Thank you,' said Cribb. He raised his bowler. 'We shall look forward to it. They're a handsome line of dancers. My friend here is a fine judge of a figurante.'

Thackeray was uncertain of the allusion, but suspected that in some way Cribb was having his revenge for the reference to Salvation Army soup.

Plunkett sniffed, took one more speculative look at the intruders and stumped back to his table. The detectives nodded to the young Salvationist and made their way to the office in the foyer, where a surprise awaited them. Their knock was answered by a young woman each recognised but momentarily could not place. She was exceedingly pretty. Her hair, fine, the shade of fresh primroses, was dressed high, showing the line of her neck to advantage.

Cribb clapped his hand to his forehead. 'Got it! Miss Blake, of the Grampian!'

'You have the advantage of me—' she began. 'Why, of course! Albert's gallant rescuers! Please come in, gentlemen. What are you doing here?'

'Looking for Mr Plunkett's daughter, Miss. We hope to purchase some tickets. May I ask you the self-same question?'

She laughed. 'Of course you may. Samuel Plunkett is my father. You were looking for me.'

'You, Miss?' Cribb frowned.

'You're confused by my name? It is pure invention, I confess. Blake is my stage-name. Even Papa had to admit I wouldn't get many billings as Ellen Plunkett, romantic vocalist. Now please sit down and tell me why you really came to the Paragon. And *don't* call me Plunkett, will you?'

'Very well, Miss.' Cribb carefully lowered himself on to a battered upright chair, which was evidently a reject from the table-section of the hall. Miss Blake having taken the only other chair,

Thackeray settled on a property-basket. 'But I should like to make it plain,' Cribb went on, 'that it's tickets we came for.'

Ellen Blake shook her head. 'You can't convince me, Sergeant. Great Scotland Yard and its workings are another world to me, but I feel quite sure its officers cannot afford the time to trail round London music halls, without very serious matters being under investigation.'

Thackeray wished he shared Miss Blake's confidence. On the wall behind her was a bill listing the week's entertainment. Not a single name was known to him. None of the turns suggested any connexion with the inmates of Philbeach House. No air-borne sisters, no barrel-dancer, no voice on a swing, no strong man. Not even a bulldog.

Cribb shrugged. 'We get two days' leave a month in the Force, Miss. They try to make sure every man gets one Sunday a month, but his other is liable to be a weekday. If he spends that day buying music hall tickets, it's a tribute to the quality of the entertainment, I say.'

'It couldn't possibly be that he suspects another accident?' said Miss Blake.

Cribb side-stepped her irony. 'Have you heard from your young man, Miss? He seems well content with his new lodgings.'

'Albert?' She coloured. 'What do you mean?'

'Perhaps I shouldn't have spoken, Miss. I thought he would have told you. Albert moved out of Little Moors Place yesterday morning.'

'Moved out? Where to?'

'Kensington, Miss. A retreat for music hall performers. Perhaps you've heard of it. It's a slap-up place.'

Ellen Blake briefly closed her eyes. She whispered, 'Philbeach House.'

'The very same, Miss,' Cribb said, airily. 'There's sure to be a letter on its way to you.'

'But I thought you were—'

'Protecting him, Miss? That's right. Thackeray here followed him all the way to Kensington. We paid him a visit to make sure he's comfortable. Frankly, Miss Blake, he's living like a regular swell. I don't know if you've ever been there but — Good Lord! Thackeray, your handkerchief!'

Miss Blake had tried to hold back tears by biting her lip, but they came nevertheless. 'I beg you to excuse me,' she said, after some attention with the handkerchief. 'It was so unexpected. He told me nothing of this. Nothing.'

'Seems to have been quickly arranged, Miss,' said Cribb by way of consolation. 'Albert ain't the sort to hurt a lady's feelings. But I promise you no harm'll come to him at Philbeach House. Why, he's got his mother and the dog with him. No-one in his right senses would lay a hand on Albert when Beaconsfield's around, I tell you.'

Thackeray shifted uneasily on his basket. Cribb would have to do better than that. The prospect of Beaconsfield going to anyone's defence was remote. It took an explosion to lift that animal off its haunches.

'You wanted tickets?' said Miss Blake, making

127

an effort to recover her composure. 'There are performances three nights a week, on Tuesdays, Thursdays and Saturdays.'

'Does the programme change at all?' Cribb asked.

'It changes very little, unless someone happens to be ill. The turns are as announced on the bill here, whichever night you choose.'

'Then we choose tomorrow,' said Cribb firmly.

'Tuesday.' She hesitated. 'Why Tuesday?'

'Why not?' said Cribb. 'It's a night when both of us can get along. Is there something wrong with Tuesday?'

Miss Blake got up to unlock a metal box. 'No, no. Every night is the same. What price of ticket would you like? There's everything from the sixpenny gallery to a table for a guinea. Boxes are five shillings.'

Five shillings! They had paid two at the Grampian.

'It'll have to be a cheap seat for us, Miss,' said Cribb. 'Have you got any at a shilling downstairs?'

'That would admit you to the promenade, but you'll need another shilling for a seat in the pit.'

'The promenade'll do,' declared the sergeant, producing a florin. 'Shall we see you performing, Miss?'

'Not in my father's hall. I concentrate on the business side of things at the Paragon. My career as a singer is pursued at other halls. I want to make my own way, you see. Here are your promenade tickets. Perhaps I shall see you on Tuesday. I could take you backstage if you would like that.'

'That's uncommon generous of you,' said Cribb, rising. 'We'll look forward to that, won't we, Thackeray?'

'Er — yes, Sarge.' There was not much enthusiasm in Thackeray's reply. He massaged the back of his trousers. The basket-weave pattern was firmly imprinted on his person.

As they prepared to leave, there was a heavy rap on the door. Miss Blake asked Cribb to open it. Two tall men stood there. For the second time that morning, Cribb and Thackeray experienced that sensation of recognising a familiar face but being temporarily unable to identify it. Yet there was something significant in the clothes, the black overcoats, patent leather boots, black kid gloves. Why, the men only wanted crepe hatbands attached to their top hats to look like — what they were! No doubt about it. The Undertakers, from Philbeach House.

Cribb stepped aside to allow them to address themselves to Miss Blake.

'A special delivery, Miss. Mr Plunkett said you would sign for it.'

'Certainly. What have you brought?'

The first Undertaker signalled to his companion. They withdrew, and re-entered, carrying between them a box-shaped object draped with a small Union Jack. There could be no doubt what it was: Beaconsfield's basket.

NINE

Cribb's penny-pinching led to certain complications at the Paragon the following evening. His theory was that two tickets for the promenade fulfilled all the conditions for thorough-going detection. For the modest outlay of two shillings, he and Thackeray could patrol the entire outer gangway of the house throughout the evening. Unfortunately, the facilities were also enjoyed by the better-off ladies of the town. The result was that when the Yard promenaded, the sisterhood converged, and in effect Cribb and Thackeray found themselves penned at the bar on one side of the hall, where further expenditure was necessary to establish themselves as imbibers, rather than seekers of pleasure. Even there, they were several times accosted for 'a glass of gin neat' which they strenuously refused; it was not C.I.D. policy to take on auxiliaries.

The painted promenaders were noticeably better-dressed than the wives and sweethearts of the mechanics and shopkeepers who sat in the place of virtue, within the railing. And they were infinitely smarter than the contingent who paraded in the aisles of the Grampian, across the river. Fallen women they may have been, Formosas every one, but they were decently gloved and fashionably gowned and — one was compelled to admit — not without charm. The men conversing with these women looked to be mostly of good class, and prepared to spend freely. There was talk of late suppers of game and native oysters in the Cafe de l'Europe, washed down with moselle and champagne. Thackeray looked steadfastly into his pint of Kop's ale and promised himself that virtue was rewarded too.

Behind the footlights the entertainers went through their repertoire without attracting much interest from the bar. Conversations animated by gin were altogether too distracting. So, too, were warm waves of perfume, jostlings and giggles. A stiff-lipped ventriloquist and his dummy were no match for a whiff of Paris at one's shoulder and the flutter of eye-lashes brushed with lamp-black. Like everyone around them, the detectives shouted in appreciation whenever the ballet appeared, and crashed their pewter-pots on the bar-counter each time a dancer flung a leg higher than her companions; authenticity demanded it. But by mid-evening the shimmering fumes above the footlights increasingly set the performers apart from the audience. That, at least, was what Thackeray supposed after five pints of Kop's, though the cigar smoke and gin vapours closer to hand may have played a part. Whatever the cause, it was devilishly difficult to concentrate. His memory was unaccountably slow, too. He *knew* the words of all the choruses, but for some reason they came from him a little late. People were beginning to move away from him.

'It's a disappointing show, ain't it, Sarge?' he confided to Cribb. 'We might have paid five bob for a blooming box, too. I wouldn't give twopence for this lot.'

'Music hall's more than a list of performers, Thackeray. It's everything around you,' the sergeant lectured him, wiping the ale from his chin. 'Your kidney-pies and conversation are just as vital to it as that fellow up there making a mess of *Dear Old Pals*. D'you think your gallery boys and their donahs are particular about whether they're watching acrobats or animals or ruddy clog-dancers? They'll pelt 'em with oranges if they're no good, but that's all part of the enjoyment. They're just as pleased to see 'em on the bill next time so they can pelt 'em again. It's participation that counts. Look at 'em in the middle there. Worthy shopmen and clerks decked out in their dress-suits and sitting at the guinea tables. That's what they call "high ton". Next week they'll be back in the gallery, but they've lived like swells tonight. *They're* not disappointed in the show.'

Thackeray sipped his drink in silence. There never was much point in arguing with Cribb, least of all during one of his homilies. Mercifully there was an interruption, a woman's voice from behind them: 'Good evening, gentlemen. I seem to remember an arrangement between us.'

132

'Indeed!' said Cribb, turning about. The sauce of some of these madams left him speechless. That was just as well on this occasion, because the speaker was Miss Ellen Blake. The rebuke on his lips dropped clean away like the Tay Bridge.

'I was merely suggesting that you might like to see behind the scenes' she said, smiling. 'I hope I make myself clear. In half an hour I must leave for the Grampian. I'm no longer first on the bill, you know, so there is just time, if you are still interested.' Wrapped in a black opera-cape trimmed with fur, she had a freshness of appearance that quite eclipsed the perfumed and powdered company around her.

'Nothing would please us better,' said Cribb.

'We will go through the canteen, then.' She led them towards the stage. Thackeray fully in control of his movements, but wishing that the slope of the promenade were not quite so steep. On the stage, a black-faced comedian in an ancient grey hat was talking in monotone, a theatrical plainchant. 'There is nothing like a wife. I say to all of you, young and old, get a wife, anybody's wife. Marry, marry early and marry often. Get a wife, marry and have children. Bring 'em up, bring 'em all up and in your old age they'll repay you by bringing you down.' To the left of the orchestra-pit there was a door. They descended a spiral flight of iron steps and ventured beneath the stage.

After the brilliance upstairs, the canteen was shadowy, illuminated by four feeble gas-burners with orange shades. Drinks were being served from a semi-circular bar to soldiers in uniform, who took them to wooden benches where young women sat.

'It serves as a green-room,' Miss Blake explained. 'Those are the ballet-girls in the grey waterproof cloaks. Do you see their white slippers and tights? They are mostly the figurantes, who can't dance a bit. They're paid about fifteen shillings a week, so they're very pleased to be bought champagne. The soldiers are their friends, nearly all of them officers in the Household troops. The girls come down here between dances. We shall go up the staircase on the opposite side.'

They emerged in the wings in time to see the comedian take his bow to desultory applause. A pale woman with a pair of cockatoos on her arm prepared to take his place. Thackeray was standing directly under the lime-boy's perch, and had to brush down his jacket, which was peppered with white dust.

'If you'll come this way,' said Miss Blake, 'I can show you one of the dressing-rooms. In many small halls they have to manage with two, but Papa has six. The ballet girls are all downstairs, I think, so we can look into their room without embarrassment.'

As they followed Miss Blake along a narrow passage between a scene dock and a collection of property-baskets, Cribb unexpectedly stooped to tie a shoe-lace. Thackeray blundered into him and only avoided pitching forward over Cribb's back by snatching at a dustsheet to his right. 'Well done,' muttered the sergeant. 'Cover 'em up again quick.' Under the sheet a pile of barrels was revealed, freshly varnished. The name 'G. Bellotti' was clearly inscribed on the top one in pink enamel. There was a positive swagger in Cribb's gait as he marched ahead.

Miss Blake approached a door marked *Ladies' Dressing Room. Gentlemen Strictly Not Admitted,* pushed it open fractionally, peered inside and then beckoned conspiratorially. They stepped into a narrow room, some forty feet in length, divided by a clothes-line, over which the day-garments of the ballet were draped, drab gowns of serge and kersey, and cambric chemises, fraying and stained at the hem from use in London streets. Cheap scent lingered in the room; but the reek of clothes was stronger. A row of shelving round the walls at a height of three feet served as dressing-tables, with tarnished pieces of mirror, candles, hair brushes and pots of grease to indicate each girl's territory. A few had beer-crates for stools. Corsets, garters and stockings littered the stone floor. Thackeray cleared his throat.

'Does it surprise you?' Miss Blake asked. 'When you see them on the stage in their tinsel and tissue you probably don't imagine them slinking back to their lodgings in these rags. It surprises their officer-friends at the end of the evening, I can tell you. There isn't much glamour about them then, poor things.'

'You said that the figurantes got fifteen shillings a week,' said Cribb. 'What does your father pay the better dancers?'

'The coryphees? Thirty shillings if they're in the front row, and that's generous by music hall standards. Out of that they provide their own shoes and tights. You can't buy a pair of silk tights for less than ten shillings.' Miss Blake took Cribb's arm. 'Come and see what they use for making up their faces.' She picked up a jar from the shelf. 'Powdered chalk as a base, with rouge. A penny cake of Indian ink. A packet of Armenian blue. Fuller's earth to dust off with.'

'Then what is the burnt newspaper for?' asked Cribb.

'For lining and shading the face. Some of them also burn a candle against a porcelain bowl and use the brown deposit for an eye-shadow. Don't look so shocked, gentlemen. It all comes off afterwards with butcher's lard. It's a cheap recipe for beauty, you must admit. Sometimes I look at the so-called fallen women who parade in the promenade where I met you and I find myself hating them, Sergeant. Hating them for their expensive perfumes and lacquered lips and rows of jewels, while these poor creatures have to darn their tights and patch their clothes and sit downstairs with soldiers if they want to be treated with consideration. Try telling *them* that virtue is rewarded as they stand shivering in the street tonight, watching those Jezebels being handed into carriages.'

Impassioned outbursts from young women

about social matters were becoming fashionable, but one hardly expected such arguments from the singer of *Fresh as the New-Mown Hay*. Even the young Salvationist had not spoken with half the fervour of Ellen Blake.

'There's only one way to change things, Miss,' said Cribb, 'and that's to persuade your father not to admit unaccompanied females to his hall. But in my estimation that's the next step to bankruptcy. They're trying to run the old Victoria across the river on temperance lines, and I hear they're playing to half-empty houses. The fact is that when a hall closes, the ballet-girls lose their jobs, while the women of the other sort simply move on to the Casinos and the Cremorne and such places.'

Miss Blake re-arranged the cosmetics on the shelf. 'There is really no question of my father discouraging such women from the Paragon. If I have a conscience about what happens here, Sergeant, I can assure you I did not inherit it from Papa.'

'Well if it's any consolation, Miss, Thackeray and I see a rare amount of the seamier side of London life in our profession, and there aren't many of your promenaders that'll escape the poorhouse or the river, I can tell you. Remember their faces as they strut up and down in your father's hall. One of these days you'll see the same faces looking down at you from the threepenny gallery at the Grampian—'

'The Grampian!' said Miss Blake. 'Good gracious, I must leave. And there won't be time to show you the wardrobe or the prop-room.'

'That's all right, Miss. We'll make our own way back through the canteen. You'll need to hurry or you'll have Mr Goodly to face. Can we pass on a message to Albert for you?'

'Albert?' Miss Blake was visibly upset at the mention of his name. 'But he is—'

'Laid up at Philbeach House, Miss? Of course. I simply thought that if we should have occasion to visit there — to clear up certain outstanding matters, you know — we might pass on your good wishes for his recovery.'

'Of course. Please do.' She composed herself, shook their hands, said, 'You do know the way?' and left them.

Cribb remained in the attitude of contemplation for several seconds, his left hand supporting his right elbow and his right forefinger poised on the bridge of his nose. At length, he said, 'Wouldn't do to be found in the Ladies' Dressing Room, Constable. Let's proceed with the inspection.'

Thackeray was about to observe that Miss Blake had expected them to return directly to the promenade, and that wandering about backstage unaccompanied might be regarded as a suspicious, not to say improper, practice, when he recognised a particular expression in the sergeant's features, a flexing of the usually quiescent muscles to the fore of his side-whiskers. The twitch of Cribb's cheek was the equivalent of the order to take aim aboard one of Her Majesty's gunboats. Thackeray put on his hat and followed him.

They had not gone many yards along the corridor when Cribb stopped at a door, listened, pushed it open, stepped inside and pulled Thackeray after him. He sniffed in the darkness. 'Carpenter's shop. Shouldn't be disturbed here. I want a good look round this hall. We'll wait till the show's over, and they've all gone. Should be a bench here somewhere. Ah, yes. Careful where you sit. Carpenters are uncommon careless with chisels. Now, Constable, what are your observations?'

A pause, followed by the sound of a beard being scratched.

'Come on, man. You saw Bellotti's barrels, didn't you?'

'Yes, Sarge.'

'And Beaconsfield's basket yesterday? And the Undertakers?'

'Yes.'

'What do you deduce, then?'

More scratching. 'Well, Sarge, I think there could be a connexion with Philbeach House.'

'The devil you do! What other evidence are you hoping for — Mrs Body in a tutu? A copper shouldn't drink on duty if it slows up his thinking, Thackeray. Of course there's a connexion, man. If the barrels are here, Bellotti won't be far behind 'em. They're no good to anyone else, are they?'

'But barrel-dancing ain't on the bill, Sarge.'

Cribb sighed. 'Nor are bulldogs, nor any of Mrs

Body's guest-list. Did you expect to see 'em up there tonight? But I'll lay you a guinea to a shilling that there's a room here somewhere stuffed with their props.'

Inspiration descended on Thackeray in the darkness. 'Maybe they're preparing for a return to the stage, Sarge! Mr Plunkett lets 'em use the hall for rehearsals. It's only in use three nights a week, remember. When they've got their confidence back they can go on the halls again.'

'You're forgetting something, Constable. It's not *their* confidence that matters. They can rehearse as much as they like, but it ain't likely to do much for the confidence of the music hall managers. Performers who've been laughed off the stage aren't going to get another London billing that easily. The best they can hope for is to change their names and their acts and start again in the provinces. Besides, Plunkett doesn't strike me as a charitable man. He won't have his hall cluttered up with down-and-outs and their baggage, unless there's profit in it.'

'He seemed to have *something* to hide, Sarge.'

'That's why we're here, Constable. A man of my standing doesn't risk his reputation parading in music hall promenades without damned good reason. There's things going on this evening that Plunkett doesn't want us to know about. Remember yesterday, when I asked for tickets? Perfectly simple request, yet the fellow's eyebrows jumped like grasshoppers when I mentioned tonight. His daughter was just as nervous, too. Never mind your secret rehearsals, Thackeray. I want to know what's going on tonight.'

'Shouldn't we get back and watch the performance, then, Sarge? There might be another accident while we're hiding here.'

Cribb produced an odd sound of contempt by vibrating his lips. 'Most unlikely, in my opinion. No need for us to be there anyway. There's a perfectly capable man watching for something like that.'

'You didn't tell me, Sarge. Another C.I.D. man?'

'For God's sake, Thackeray. Third violin in the orchestra — didn't you spot him?'

'Not Major—'

'Scraping away like a professional. At least we know he wasn't blown to bits by the gas explosion. I'm surprised you didn't spot him. Too much else to keep an eye on, eh? You're yawning. Thackeray.'

'It's the dark, Sarge.'

'The beer, more like. Look, we're liable to be here an hour. Stretch yourself out on the bench and sleep it off. That's an order. I want you sober, Constable.'

It was all a little humiliating, but Thackeray knew better than to defy orders. He wouldn't actually sleep, but it would be a relief to get the weight off his feet. He groped along the bench, checking for loose nails and chips of wood, and put his hand on something soft, an overall perhaps, folded in the shape of a pillow. He lowered his head thankfully on to it. Not Cribb's overcoat, surely? That was so unlike the man; there wasn't an atom of pity in him, not for constables at any rate. Cribb didn't believe in rests; forty winks any time was dereliction of duty. If he connived at that, he was planning something, you could depend on it.

Thackeray was uncertain how long he had slept when a nudge from Cribb revived him, but his bones ached and his mouth was dry. 'What is it, Sarge?'

'We'll be on the move shortly. It's half an hour since the National Anthem. Plenty of 'em have gone already. You're in better shape, I hope?'

He was shivering and aching all over but he said, 'Sharp as a winkle-pin, Sarge.'

'Good. Hand me my coat, will you?'

'Hurry please, everyone. Mr Plunkett wants you all out in the next five minutes,' called a voice unpleasantly close to the door. Shrieks of protest answered from the ladies' dressing-room up the corridor. 'Five minutes, *whatever* state you're in,' reiterated the voice, and the ballet evidently took the warning seriously, for groups of booted feet clattered past very soon afterwards, and soon there was silence.

After a strategic interval, Cribb eased open the door to the passage, which was still fully lit. Thackeray blinked, looked down at his evening-suit and began brushing off wood-shavings.

'Leave that, blast you,' Cribb hissed, 'and follow me.' Thackeray obeyed, privately noting that his sergeant had reverted to type. They scudded as silently as two large men could along the passage and past the scene dock and Bellotti's barrels to the area of the stage. A movement ahead stopped them short, and they backed into the shadows between some flats stacked in the wings. Groups of men in labouring clothes, corduroys and doe-skin waistcoats or short serge jackets, were talking in groups on the stage side of the lowered curtain. Far from preparing to leave, they seemed to be waiting for something. Several peered up at the battens and perches as though they had never stood on a stage before. More ascended the staircase from the canteen. They were followed by Plunkett.

Someone moved a stool into the centre of the stage and Plunkett stepped on to it and clapped his hands. 'Thank you, gentlemen. If you will all come close I shall not need to shout. Most of you know me, but for those who are new to the Paragon I should explain that I am the theatre manager. You are responsible to me. The work I have for you is not taxing in a physical sense, but it is responsible work and you have been employed because you have the reputation of being responsible working men. The pay, you will know, is generous, to say the least. You will earn it by carrying out your orders with despatch, in silence and without question. Things you may see and hear tonight as you go about your work are not for you to question or comment upon, either tonight or later. I am very particular about loyalty among my staff and there are ways of cutting short loose talk. Do you all understand me?'

Concerted nods and grunts indicated that Plunkett was taken seriously.

'Very well. You will work as teams of three and four under the direction of experienced scene-removers and you will carry out their orders implicitly. I shall be in the audience, but your foremen — to use a term familiar to you — will report fully to me before you are paid at the evening's end. You will now repair to the supers' room, which is on the O.P. side of the stage — behind me. You will find there your uniforms for tonight. You are to be dressed as footmen — ah! Already I see looks of dismay among you, as you imagine the contempt of your fellow-artisans when they learn that you have been seen in stockings and wigs. But allow me to remind you that what happens at the Paragon is not to be the subject of taproom conversations. The memory of your eccentric appearance — which I may say will be perfectly accepted by the audience — will assist you to control your tongues. You have ten minutes then to select a set of clothes that fit, after which you will return here, to be divided into work-teams and to receive your instructions. Look sharp, then.'

Far from that, the recruits looked dumbfounded, but someone made a move towards the O.P. side, and the rest shuffled bleakly after, unprotesting. Plunkett descended from his stool and returned the way he had come.

'Capital!' whispered Cribb. 'First piece of luck we've had, Thackeray. Take off your jacket and trousers.'

Had he heard correctly? 'My—'

'Hurry man. Get 'em off and wait here.'

'Where are you going, Sarge?'

But Cribb was already striding openly across the empty stage, and there was such an air of urgency in his movements that Thackeray was infected with it and found himself actually beginning to carry out the preposterous instruction. He hung his jacket on a convenient nail, unbuttoned his waistcoat and loosened his shoe-laces. There propriety called a halt until a minute or so later when Cribb marched back, a set of garments over his arm. 'Trousers, too, Constable. You can't appear as a flunkey in a satin jacket and black twill bags. You're joining the scene-removing squad. Get these things on quick. Stockings first.'

Good Lord! The Yard in white silk stockings? Was Cribb finally deranged? 'Sarge, I really don't feel it would be fitting to our position as officers. You a sergeant—'

'That's all right, Thackeray. It's only you that's dressing up. I'll be among the audience — watching developments, of course. Try the breeches now. They were the largest I could find. You'll need to adjust the buckles round your calves. There isn't much time, so listen carefully. There's no-one likely to recognise you, but keep your wig on all the time, and if you go on stage try not to show your face to the audience.'

'Would you, dressed like this?' asked Thackeray bitterly, standing up in his yellow satin breeches. 'I can't do it Sarge.'

145

'Nonsense, man. You'll be no different from the others. I collected these things from the room where they're changing. They took me for one of the staff. They're kitted out in yellow just like you, and they're just as sensitive about being made to look like — er — footmen. Don't you see, Thackeray? You'll be perfectly placed to observe what's going on. Tonight could settle this case for us. We're about to get our answers. Now put on the jacket and wig. Your fellow-workers'll be here shortly and I must be gone. Splendid! That's a better fit than the trousers. Push your evening clothes into the corner there. When they assemble, you simply join in as though you're one of the recruits. Carry out your orders like the rest, whatever happens. And Thackeray . . .'

'Sergeant?'

'I feel obliged to warn you that there could be rum goings-on here tonight.'

Thackeray adjusted his wig and stared down at his silken calves and silver-buckled shoes. Cribb was down the canteen stairs before he could respond.

TEN

There were no difficulties over Thackeray's entry to the ranks of the scene-removers. 'You're a sturdy-looking cove,' said the man in charge. 'You can join the heavy contingent.' Nor was there any problem in identifying who the heavy contingent were: three burly figures, a little apart from the others, standing like bears hungry for buns on Mappin Terrace. He joined them.

'It's money for old rope,' one confided in him, when the teams were being dispersed to their duties. 'Just a bit of scene-shiftin' and some hoistin', that's all. There's only one bugger and that's the transformation scene. We never get that right, but what do they expect if they ask four men to move half a dozen of them flats across the stage and back and keep the bloomin' car swingin' in the air at the same time?'

'The car?' repeated Thackeray.

His informant rolled his eyes upwards. High above them in the flies, suspended from two pulley-blocks attached to the gridiron, was a huge basket. 'This is a handworked house, not counterweight, so it's all controlled by us. There's a

147

couple of blokes up there on the fly-floor with lines, but all the muscle-work's done from down here. Harry!'

A voice answered from the fly-gallery above their heads.

'Loosen your guys will you, Harry, and we'll have the car down.' He moved to a winch in the wings and commenced turning the handle vigorously. The basket slowly descended, to rest on the boards.

'I see now,' said Thackeray. 'A balloon car!'

'That's right, mate. It don't look much from here, of course, but when the lights are on and the old scene-drop's glowin' blue you can sit out front there in the hall and believe you're watchin' the aeronauts above the Crystal Palace gardens. There you are! Down now, and ready for her ladyship to step into.'

'Does a lady go in there?'

'Any time now, friend. Then it's our job to winch her up again and there she stays in the flies until we bring her down for the transformation scene. When you see the one we've got tonight you'll understand why we told Mr Plunkett we weren't havin' no sandbags on the side of the car. "Realism demands sandbags," he says. "You can have your sandbags," we told him, "or you can have the lady, but the ropes won't stand both and neither will we." That's realism, ain't it?'

'Indubitably,' said Thackeray. 'How should I employ myself this evening?'

'You'd best help me with the winchin' first, and then we'll put you on props — movin' the heavy stuff into the middle when it's wanted. You can't go wrong there.'

'That's good,' said Thackeray, not really convinced, but the possibility of further explanation was cut short by the arrival, from the opposite side, of the lady balloonist. He saw at once why sandbags were out of the question: she was of sufficient size to warrant an immediate overhaul of the lifting mechanism. Dressed as she was, in a brown *poult-de-soie* taffeta jacket and skirt and a large floral hat secured under her chin with a pink scarf, she might well have presented herself to balloonists in general as a challenge, like the unrideable mule or the caber no-one could toss. But redoubtable as the lady's physique was, Thackeray found his attention drawn to an accessory clamped firmly under her right arm, a white bulldog in a pink ribbon, unquestionably Beaconsfield. The aeronaut was Albert's mother.

Thackeray turned aside at once to shield his face from her. The possibility of being recognised in these circumstances was hideous to contemplate. He tugged the wig forward. Silver curls lolled over his forehead, actually meeting the natural crop of whiskers on the lower half of his face and giving him the shaggy anonymity of an Old English sheepdog.

'You've got the idea, mate,' said his new colleague. 'You'll find a basket down there, a kind of hamper. She wants it in the car for the dog to perch on, so that the audience can see him. Bring it over, will you?'

The last thing he would have volunteered for! He groped in the shadows for Beaconsfield's basket and raised it in front of his face like a shield. Meanwhile the rest of the heavy contingent were assisting Albert's mother over the rim of the balloon car. As Thackeray approached behind the basket, Beaconsfield barked excitedly and struggled in his mistress's arms. The confounded animal had seen its basket — or had it picked up a familiar scent?

'In the corner here, my man,' ordered Albert's mother. 'Place the basket on end. You can sit there and put your little paws over the edge of the car, can't you, Dizzie?' — but Beaconsfield was too occupied licking the hands on the basket to listen to such prattle. Thackeray snatched them away and almost fled to the obscurity of the wings.

'Are you ready, Ma'am?' called his companion. 'Right then. Haul away, everyone!'

Heavens — the relief of bending over the winch-handle to help raise the car and its passenger by squeaking stages to a position where they could no longer identify anyone below! With three men on the handle the job took over a minute. Not once did Thackeray look up; for his part, Albert's mother, basket and dog could continue their ascent indefinitely.

The floral hat appeared over the edge of the car.

'Are we quite secure up here? It seems a long way from the stage.'

'Don't worry lady. It don't take long to come down,' someone cheerfully assured her. Thackeray eyed the winch, now secured by a simple ratchet-mechanism. One kick at the wooden support would bring the balloon-car plunging straight through the boards, the trap-floor and the canteen, to bury itself in the foundations. Anyone wanting to stage an accident here had no need of subtlety.

Then a blare of brass dismissed Albert's mother from all immediate thoughts. The overture! Thackeray was at once assailed by an overwhelming sense of incompetence. The stage-hands in their yellow uniforms were everywhere, pulling at ropes, manhandling scenery across the stage, scaling the ladders to the fly-gallery. It was like being aboard a clipper as she set sail: incomparably thrilling — unless you were trying to pass for one of the crew. What the dickens did a C.I.D. man do in this situation? Certainly not remain where he was, anyway. Observing a large piece of scenery to his right, he backed cautiously around it, and into a situation one must hope is unparalleled in the annals of Scotland Yard.

He found himself in the thick of a close-packed group of almost naked young women. So tightly were they pressed against his person that it was quite impossible to observe what, if anything, they were wearing. He blushed to the roots of his beard. Any further movement was unthinkable. One sim-

151

ply had to stand shoulder to shoulder with them (as he wrote later in his diary) and submit to physical contact. An insupportable experience!

'Careful with your whiskers, my love,' one redheaded member of the group appealed. 'You're brushing the black off me eye-lashes.'

He held his chin high, his eyes closed and his hands firmly to his sides. Nothing could last for ever. Surely enough, he presently found himself still at attention, but quite unaccompanied. Purely in his role as investigator he turned to look at the stage, where the curtain had gone up. His so recent intimates were ranged in two circles and dancing like dervishes.

They were not naked after all, but it was easy to see how he had gained that impression. Gaping areas of undraped flesh gleamed brazenly in the limelight. Skirts recklessly divided from hip to hem revealed not only the black silk hose worn by the dancers, but the means of suspension as well, drawn tight across white expanses of thigh. Above the waist the only substantial garments worn were elbow-length gloves in black kid; flagrant indecency was just averted by short lengths of chiffon and large amounts of luck. 'That's nothing, mate,' said a voice behind Thackeray. 'Just wait for the living statues. If you think this is strong stuff, that'll have you crawling up the blooming scenery. This is just the *hors d'oeuvre,* mate.'

He turned.

'Sam Fagan,' said the speaker, extending a hand. 'Top of the bill in my time, but just a fill-in here.

This class of audience don't take to my brand of humour. It's the spice they've come to sample — the tit-bits you don't get in the penny gaffs. They're all toffs out there, you know. Mr Plunkett don't allow no riff-raff in the midnight house. Members of Parliament, Peers of the Realm, Field-Marshals and Generals. Now what can a cockney comic like me say to a nobby crowd like that? I tell you, they ain't interested. It's no good getting myself up in this toggery, neither. I might as well put on my tartan suit and red nose.' Even so, he checked the angle of his silk hat in a mirror hanging on the wooden framework of the scenery. The strain of years of laughter-seeking showed in his face. He grinned like a gargoyle. 'The poem ought to curl 'em up, though. Listen, if you haven't heard it. Hey ho! Here comes the girls.'

The dancers performed their last shrieking high-kicks, turned, wriggled their hips, blew kisses across the footlights and swaggered to the wings, clustering round Thackeray again, several holding his arms for balance as they loosened their boots. Waves of warmth rose from their glistening bodies. 'What's Plunkett got out there tonight?' the red-headed dancer angrily demanded. 'You show more leg than anyone's seen outside the giraffe house and bob your bristols up and down like buoys at high water and what does the applause sound like? Two wet plaice being dropped on a marble slab. Not a ruddy whistle from anyone. You'd think it was a bleeding temperance meeting. Well wouldn't you?'

No-one answered. Perhaps they were too short of breath. Certainly the response of the audience had been luke-warm. Thackeray surmised that if Fagan were correct and Peers and Parliamentarians really were present, the cool reception was not so remarkable. People of that class were not accustomed to such displays. Some of them had probably walked out in disgust. Plunkett would need to find something more tasteful if he hoped to attract the aristocracy to the Paragon. Sam Fagan, at least, had the wit to see that vulgarities were not in order tonight. He was reciting 'The Cane-bottom'd Chair'.

Nobody seemed to require any heavy props, and Albert's mother was still secure in the flies, so when the dancers had dispersed (not without winks), Thackeray gave his attention to the poem. For a small man, Sam Fagan possessed a good carrying voice. One of the prop-men on the opposite side had brought on a large potted fern and Fagan was standing beside it, addressing his audience, but turning occasionally to direct a limp hand towards the wings. As an elocutionist, he lacked the polish of more practised performers, but it was a spirited rendering, even if the emphasis seemed a little uneven in parts. The disquieting feature of the recitation was the way it was being received. Sections of the audience were openly convulsed with laughter. To Fagan's credit he was not at all discountenanced; perhaps the rehearsal at Philbeach House had steeled him for such an ordeal.

'It was but a moment she sat in this place.
She'd a scarf on her neck and a smile on her
  face.
A smile on her face and a rose in her hair,
And she sat there and bloom'd in my cane-
  bottom'd chair.'

He paused, actually smiling back at the mockers below, who now regrettably seemed the greater part of the audience.

'And so I have valued my chair ever since
Like the shrine of a saint or the throne of a
  prince;
Saint Fanny my patroness sweet I declare,
The queen of my heart and my cane-bottom'd
  chair.'

Where was the humour in that? Thackeray was beginning to believe that the halls were not the place for serious poetry.

Then the lights were lowered, indubitably for effect as the final verse of the poem was recited, but the audience could scarcely contain themselves, whistling and calling out as coarsely as anyone had done at the Grampian. 'He can't find his Fanny!'

Someone tugged Thackeray's sleeve. 'Push this into the middle. Not too fast.'

On to the open stage? Good Lord! Thank heavens the place was in darkness.

He looked down at the prop. Of course — a

cane-bottom'd chair! And in it he could just see a seated young woman, presumably a dramatic representation of Fanny. By George, someone at the Paragon had a genius for scenic effects. He pushed at the chair-back; it was on wheels and moved easily. Fagan was already beginning the verse:

'When the candles burn low, and the
    company's gone,
In the silence of night as I sit here alone—
I sit here alone, but we yet are a pair—
My Fanny I see in my cane-bottom'd chair.'

A spotlight streamed down from the flies, dramatically picking out the chair. Thackeray reacted with as neat a side-step as you could hope to see outside a prize-ring. He smiled in the shadows. Who would have believed it was his first night as a scene-shifter? An instant later the smile froze and he was almost bowled over. Not by the massive and unexpected roar from the audience, but by the sight which provoked it. The young woman in the chair was wearing nothing at all.

Thackeray clapped his hand to his forehead. Thirty years in the Force had to have *some* relevance to this situation. His first impulse was to restore order by snatching the chair back into the darkness, but that involved the considerable risk of ejecting the sitter. That was unthinkable. Then he considered treating the audience like a runaway horse, and leaping protectively in front of the chair with arms outspread and waving. In uniform he could have brought himself to do that; not in yellow satin and white stockings.

Before he could think of another expedient, someone mercifully brought down the curtain. A coat was tossed to the young woman and she got up, put it round her shoulders and walked past Thackeray and off the stage, as unconcerned as if she were shopping in the Strand. He felt a trembling sensation in the region of his knees. What in the name of Robert Peel was he participating in?

'Look alive there!' someone shouted. 'Transformation scene!'

Other liveried figures were already struggling with scenery and scrambling up the fly-ladders. 'Carry out your orders like the rest, whatever happens,' Cribb had said — but could he have envisaged anything so unspeakable as what had just taken place?

'The winch, man!' a voice bellowed. 'You're wanted on the winch!'

In a ferment of scandalised confusion, he reeled to the wings and took his place at the handle, beside another of the heavy contingent.

'All right. She comes down about fifteen turns of the handle till she's nice and central,' explained his companion. 'When I release the catch I want you to take the strain. Hold on as if it's your own mother up there. Right?'

Thackeray nodded. The catch was released. He braced and gripped the handle grimly. The seam down the back of his jacket began to part under the strain. By Jove, it was harder work letting Albert's mother down gently than winching her up. Even before the fifteen turns were made, Harry in the fly-gallery pulled on his guy-rope to produce a lateral swing on the balloon-car. At the same time the curtain went up, the band played and the lime-boys directed a brilliant blue light on to the gauze-cloth suspended across the stage.

Albert's mother, soon oscillating convincingly against an azure background, launched powerfully into Nellie Power's song.

> 'Up in a Balloon, girls, up in a Balloon,
> Sailing through the air on a summer
>   afternoon.
> Up in a Balloon, girls, up in a Balloon,
> What a happy place, now, to spend your
>   honeymoon.'

Unfortunately either the pendulum motion or the awfulness of the lyric had upset the second passenger. As a *pianissimo* passage sought to convey the airy delights of ballooning, a dismal whining was plainly audible from above. Beaconsfield's face peered dolefully over the rim of the car.

'She's secure now,' said Thackeray's companion. 'You can help with the scene-removing. There's no sitting about when the transformation scene's on, you know.'

Behind the gauze-cloth an exotic scene was almost mounted. A drop decorated with a crudely painted skyline of cupolas and minarets was already in place and a border representing Eastern arches had been flown from the grid. Thackeray joined two men struggling with a profile flat, a piece of shaped scenery representing a section of wall surmounted by palm trees. On the other side of the gauze-cloth Albert's mother gamely started the fourth verse of 'Up in a Balloon'.

'That's safely home,' said one of the men, addressing Thackeray. 'Just secure it, will you, while me and my mate get the small props in place? There's all them potted plants to go yet.'

He found himself standing alone behind two pieces of scenery with a length of sashcord in his hand, attached to the left-hand flat. It was a long time since he had felt so inadequate.

'Why, if it ain't the feller with the beaver again,' said a voice behind him. 'Having trouble, are you, Dad?'

It was difficult to look round when one was providing the only support for a large piece of scenery, but he thought he recognised the voice of the red-headed chorus girl. Unless she had found some more clothes he was not inclined to conduct a conversation with *that* young woman anyway.

'You don't know what you're about, do you?' she continued. 'Here. Give the throwline to me.' She wedged herself in front of him, took it from his hand and tossed it neatly over a cleat, high on the right-hand flat. Then she brought the line back across the join and fastened it below, over two cleats, one on either flat. 'You tie it with a slippery-hitch like this, so as it's easy to break when you need to strike the scene.'

'I'm obliged to you.'

'You can step away now. It won't fall down. That is, unless you've a mind to remain here pressing yourself against me.'

The very idea! He backed away like a horse from the halter. He could now see her red hair and a good deal more of her besides. She was dressed in a sequinned waistcoat and diaphanous harem trousers. 'I think I may be wanted on the winch,' he said.

'About time,' said his companion testily, when he got there. 'I can't turn this blooming thing on my own, you know.'

Ahead of them, the swinging motion of the balloon-car had stopped and Albert's mother was completing her final chorus. As the applause — there was not much of it — died away, the blue lights went out and the scene behind the gauze cloth was illuminated. Albert's mother leaned precariously over the edge of the car.

> *'Gentlemen, just look at what my gas-balloon*
> *has caught on—*
> *A palm-tree in Morocco in the harem of a*
> *sultan!'*

'Right. Lift her clear. Fifteen turns!' said the man on the winch.

As Albert's mother ascended into the flies so did the gauze-cloth. Five young women, dressed like the one Thackeray had seen, performed what passed for an Arabesque dance among the props and scenery. Now that the initial shock was over, he could bring himself to look at the scene. The audience, from what he could hear, actually seemed quite friendly-disposed towards the dancers. He supposed that if one had a well-developed imagination — and people of that class unquestionably would have — one might even make a mental journey to Morocco and observe the performance without reference to British standards of decorum. If he tried hard, even a man of his upbringing might manage it. But a nudge in the ribs brought him firmly back to London.

'Unwind her slowly now.'

Albert's mother descended, and so did the gauze. Thackeray remained firmly at the winch; others could change this scene. Unbelievably soon, it was time for another couplet:

'Sometimes, you know, the weather is a
    menace.
A powerful breeze has blown me over —
    Venice!'

'Marvellous!' exclaimed Thackeray, as the floating city was revealed, complete with moving gondolas.

'Just turn the handle, mate, or they won't see anything of it. Blimey, if you think that's a scene, you ought to go to Drury Lane. They run everything from race-horses to railway-engines across that stage.'

'It was the transformation that surprised me,'

panted Thackeray, when the fifteen turns were made.

His companion sniffed. 'Falling flaps. Get a good man up there on the catwalk and you can change a common lodging-house to Buckingham Palace in ten seconds, if you've a mind to. Right! Down she comes again, and then you'll be wanted on the living statues.'

Fifteen turns later, he tottered away to report for his next task. Behind the gauze-cloth, Greece was being constructed, a series of columns secured with stage-braces in front of a cloth depicting the Acropolis.

'Are you one of the heavies?' someone asked him.

'Yes.'

'Good. This one's yours. Aphrodite. Keep your head well down, don't jerk, and watch out for the Thinker coming towards you from the other side.'

'Aphro . . . ?'

'Miss Penelope Tring. Get yourself in position and she'll climb up at once.'

A wooden structure on small wheels, not unlike an upright piano painted white, with two steps on the keyboard side, was waiting for him. Young women with sheets draped about them were standing nearby, ready to go on. He noticed two handles on the back of the structure and gripped them. It moved quite freely. He waited uncertainly.

The last of the footmen quitted the stage and the Grecian maidens arranged themselves behind the gauze-cloth in an arc, leaving free the area ahead of Thackeray. In the opposite wing he could

see another of the heavy contingent crouching behind a similar plinth on wheels, but his already
supported a white statue. The orchestra stopped
playing and Albert's mother made her final intro-
duction, but Thackeray did not hear a word
of it. Miss Penelope Tring was mounting his
plinth . . .

Next moment the stage was bathed in light, the
orchestra were playing some stately melody and
someone was pushing him from behind. Automatically, he began the journey to the other side:
automatically, because his mind refused to accept
the reality of what he had just seen and could continue to see if he turned his eyes that way. It was
manifestly impossible that he, Detective Constable
Edward Thackeray of Scotland Yard, was at that
moment crossing a stage in a satin suit, crouching
behind a conveyance supporting a female person
clothed only in white silk fleshings. Never mind
the disturbingly life-like male figure being wheeled
past on his right; never mind the warmth proceed-
ing from the vaguely rotund areas of whiteness on
his left, a few inches from his cheek. Fantasy, all
of it. Why, Sergeant Cribb, for all his bullying
ways, would never subject a man to such indig-
nities.

'Hold on, mate!' a voice at his elbow cautioned.
'You'll shove the lady through the wall if you don't
put the brake on.'

As they halted, Miss Tring relaxed her pose and
hopped down heavily from the plinth in front of
Thackeray, sufficiently substantial to convince

163

anyone else that she existed. Of course he had heard, over pints of ale, of things that happened across the Channel, of *poses plastiques* and *tableaux vivants* in Parisian theatres. That unquestionably accounted for the trick of his imagination that had produced the present illusion. Why, if he pinched himself or, better still, reached out a thumb and forefinger to Miss Tring, she would certainly vanish. But something restrained him, and presently the apparition accepted a cloak from someone and walked away to the dressing-room.

Above the stage Albert's mother completed a final chorus of 'Up in a Balloon', the curtain was lowered, and so were she and her bulldog, with someone else assisting at the winch. But there was no respite for Thackeray. 'Carry this to the centre,' a bystander told him, 'and place it on the blue spot.' He found himself holding a species of umbrella-stand made of glittering chromium and containing a formidable array of swords. 'For the illusionist,' he was told. 'Get moving, damn you!'

Swords! His thoughts raced back to the unfortunate conjurer languishing in Newgate, and his abortive trick with the girl in the cabinet. Would the perpetrator of these 'accidents' (if there were such a person) have the audacity to repeat his wickedness here? Cribb's words came back to him: 'Carry out your orders . . .' He walked to the middle and found the blue spot. The swords had one good effect on him, anyway: his mind had cleared itself of illusions and was fully alive to the dangers in the present situation. Another order was barked at him: 'Only the table now. On the yellow square.' That looked harmless enough, thank goodness. A silk-covered card-table with conjurer's impedimenta, a silk hat, wand, gloves and a glass containing a red liquid.

The curtain was up again almost before he was back in the wings, and from the other side a performer in white tie and tails had taken the stage. Thackeray recognised him at once as one of the guests at Philbeach House, and it shortly became quite clear why he had been there. The man picked up one of the swords, thrust back his head, opened his mouth wide and slowly inserted the blade until the hilt was six inches from his teeth. The sword-swallower!

He withdrew the blade, and repeated the feat twice, with broader swords, accompanied by drum rolls. In the wings, Thackeray breathed with relief as the weapons came out as clean and shining as they had gone in. Not for long, however. As though sword-swallowing were not spectacular enough, the performer produced a box of matches, lighted a spill and began a demonstration of fire-eating. Really! Did people like that *deserve* police protection?

'My Lords, Ladies and gentlemen, for my final trick,' said the sword-swallower, when the fire-eating was safely completed, 'and for your delectation, I should like to introduce my charming assistant, Miss Lola!'

She ran on to the stage from behind Thackeray, brushing him with her cloak as she passed. Lola

Pinkus, like Miss Tring, had found a new forte in the profession. She curtsied most appealingly, tossing her blonde curls back as she straightened. How refreshing to see at last a young woman decently covered from neck to ankle!

'Take it off!' appealed some philistine in the audience.

'Patience, sir, if you *please,*' remonstrated the sword-swallower. 'You may think, my friends, that you have seen all too little of Miss Lola. Soon you shall see less. In fact, she shall vanish altogether, before your very eyes.' He picked up the glass. 'In here is the most marvellous fluid in the world—'

'Gin!' shouted someone.

'No, sir! Not even gin has the properties of this particular brew. Take one draught of this and within seconds you will disappear completely. And I feel obliged to announce that it may not be purchased afterwards by gentlemen wishing to experiment on their mothers-in-law. Now, Miss Lola, would you care to give me your cloak? Our friends in the audience may wish to be assured that you are, in truth, flesh and blood and no mere illusion.'

Even this act! Thackeray noted a depressing sameness in the entertainment. Whatever their billing, the object of the performances seemed to be to display the fair sex in various degrees of indecency. Lola Pinkus was more adequately covered than Miss Tring, but somewhat less than respectability would have required in, say, a swimming-bath for females only. And the audience were behaving intolerably, whistling and shouting as though they had never seen a half undressed woman before. Perhaps they had not. Thackeray sniffed. There were compensations, after all, in a humble upbringing.

'I shall now invite Miss Lola to drink this glass of the magical fluid,' announced the sword-swallower, when he could get a hearing. 'And then you must watch closely, for to see is to believe!'

Lola approached him and took her stance with particular care. Thackeray watched keenly. He already had an idea of how the disappearance might be effected. The drum-roll began. The sword-swallower made some spectacular movements with the cloak. The footlights and the side-lighting dimmed, leaving a single beam directed on the performers from the gallery. Lola held the glass high, lowered it and drank. Simultaneously the sword-swallower shielded her from the audience with the cloak. With a most convincing scream she dropped through the trap-door on which she was standing. The lights came on. The cloak was swept aside to show the disappearance accomplished. Gasps of amazement were heard from the auditorium.

'To see is to believe!' shouted the sword-swallower.

'And here I am!' a voice came from high in the gallery. Everyone turned to see. There she was in her spangles and little else, waving triumphantly. A thunder of applause greeted her. Few of those present could have realised, as Thackeray did, that they were not looking at Lola Pinkus, but her sister, Bella.

The sword-swallower extended a hand towards the gallery, bowed, took a step back, and bowed again. The curtain was rung down. As he made for the wings one of the stage-hands ran to meet him. He seemed to anticipate what was to be said. 'That scream . . .'

'That's right, sir,' said the stage-hand. 'We heard it too, from down below, a moment before she came through the trap. She was dying before she hit the mattress, sir. She wasn't conscious. She twitched once or twice and then went still.'

ELEVEN

The news from under the stage had an odd effect on Thackeray. Naturally, he was shocked by the sudden death of such a young and charming artiste. But, sad as it was, the passing from the scene of Lola Pinkus gave a significant lift to his morale. He now had a clear justification for being on the stage, and he could once again think and act as a simple policeman. And what a relief that was! His mortifying experiences as a stage-remover actually began to look like part of an inspired plan. Even that harrowing journey across the stage with Miss Tring took on a heroic quality. In fact, he could picture himself already in Number One Court listening to the Lord Chief Justice: *'It should not pass unrecorded that this case would never have been brought to trial but for the devotion to duty in the most unimaginable circumstances of a certain Detective Constable . . .'*

Once he had satisfied himself that Lola was undeniably dead — and by her expression and attitude the moment of death had been violent in the extreme — he realised that it was not, after all, going to be possible to carry out the duties of a

169

simple policeman. '*After the finding of a body,*' decreed the *Police Code* (which all self-respecting members of the Force knew by heart), '*the Coroner should be informed on the appropriate form.*' That was all right for the occasional corpse you found along the Embankment after an uncommonly cold night, but it didn't quite meet the present case. He mentally thumbed through the pages of the manual, searching for something more appropriate. '*When a dead body is found and there is no doubt that life is extinct . . .*' He peered closely at Lola's mortal remains—'*. . .it should never be touched until the arrival of a constable who should forthwith note carefully its appearance and all surrounding it.*' His hand went to the place where his notebook should have been. No reason to panic, though; he would commit the details to memory. *Countenance bluish and revealing unmistakable signs of pain. Eyes bolting open. Teeth bared and clenched. Body contorted, with legs bent unnaturally from the fall. Hands outspread but tensed, like claws. Body found on a straw mattress below the star trap. Pieces of broken glass scattered about nearby.* That would do for the present. Time was too precious to waste over details. What next? '*If he suspects that death was caused by violence he should not move the body or allow any part of the clothing or any article about it to be touched or moved by any person until the arrival of an Inspector, who should be sent for by messenger.*' Devilish difficult. Cribb would pass for an Inspector, of course. He was always telling everyone he carried all the responsibility without the rank. But contacting him through a messenger was next to impossible; the trap-man who had first reported Lola's death had gone away complaining of dizziness, leaving him alone with the body. What could he do by himself? Stop the show and ask 'Is there a detective sergeant in the house?' A question like that in this hall was liable to start a stampede for the exit.

So Thackeray decided to dispense with the messenger and fetch Cribb himself. That meant abandoning the body for a few minutes and taking the risk of someone interfering while he was gone, but really there was no other possibility. What disturbed him more was the prospect of venturing among the audience in his yellow livery.

He opened a door leading to the canteen. From the atmosphere of noisy gaiety it was clear that the news of Lola's death had not reached there. Girls of the chorus sat as usual on the knees of army officers, one hand waving a glass of gin, the other trifling with regimental whiskers. Thackeray threaded his way through, dreading that at any moment the red-headed Miss who had helped him with his scene-mounting would spring up from somewhere and fling herself upon him. However, he reached the other side unmolested and mounted the stairs leading to the auditorium.

Fortunately the turn in progress on the stage had the undivided concentration of the audience. A young woman he did not recognise was giving a male impersonation. The song was innocuous

171

enough; indeed, he had often hummed the melody himself as he pounded the streets of Bermondsey. But the emphasis the singer was giving to certain words quite distorted the original meaning but delighted the audience, ready by now to see innuendoes in anything. Thackeray could not hope to slip past the tables completely unnoticed in his satin, but at least the entertainment drew most eyes away. His main concern now was whether even Cribb was too caught up in the performance to notice him.

It was when he was almost mid-way through the cluster of tables that he first thought he recognised one of the audience. Bald head, aquiline profile, a good crop of whiskers. Yes, a face he knew from somewhere, though it was difficult to trace the connexion. No friend of his could afford champagne by the magnum and a courtesan dripping with diamonds. Not wishing to appear rude, he looked away — and spotted another face which he recognised at once. Two others at the table were familiar too, though not the female companions they had with them. He now knew all four men from a period he had once spent with B Division, Westminster. What had brought them here he did not like to contemplate, for they were Honourable Members of a quite different House, where music halls were spoken of as dens of iniquity.

When he reached the promenade Cribb was waiting for him, hands on hips, eyes aflame with all the fury of an officer confronting a deserter in the field of battle.

'Sarge, you've got your case,' Thackeray blurted out, 'and I think it may be murder.'

Within a minute they were entering the trap-floor, where someone was bending over Lola's body. Above their heads the boards thundered to the rhythm of the *cancan*.

'Step aside, if you please, Mr Plunkett. We are police officers.'

The manager was so startled that he almost tipped forward on to the mattress himself. *'You are what?'*

'If it's identification you require, I'll thank you to wait until I've examined this unfortunate young woman. Have you touched anything?' Without waiting for a reply Cribb put his face close to Lola's and sniffed at her mouth.

'I merely cleared away the pieces of glass,' said Plunkett.

'Glass?'

'Yes. She must have still been holding the tumbler as she came through the trap. It shattered on the floor.'

Cribb rounded on him. 'Where are the pieces?'

'Why I wrapped them in newspaper and put them on the ledge over there for safety.'

'If you please, Thackeray,' said Cribb.

The constable brought the package over. Cribb unwrapped it carefully, without touching the fragments. He sniffed several times at a circular piece that had formed the base of the tumbler. 'This will need to be analysed. The conjurer's fluid — what was it?'

173

'Water, with a dash of cochineal for effect,' answered Plunkett.

Cribb sniffed again. 'It's got a sickly sweet smell, for cochineal.'

Plunkett dipped his finger towards the glass. Cribb jerked it away. 'I wouldn't do that, sir.'

'Why ever not?'

'I'm no scientist, Mr Plunkett, but if I see a healthy young woman die in a matter of seconds and I can't find a sign of a bullet-hole I think of poisons. And when I see the centres of the eyes dilated as these are and the cheeks this bluish colour, I go through the list of symptoms I keep in my head, sir, and I come up with Prussic Acid. If that's what this is and you get a spot on your finger and lick it, we'll have two corpses for post mortem tomorrow morning, not one.'

The manager was plainly impressed. He thrust his hands immediately into his pockets. 'But I know you,' he told Cribb, 'and your friend. You were skulking at the back of my theatre during rehearsal yesterday, both of you. I sent you away to get some tickets, but that was for the first house, not this one. How the devil did you get in for this performance? And what is this person doing in the uniform of one of my staff?'

'Voluntary unpaid stage-remover,' explained Cribb. 'If he hadn't been here I shouldn't have known what was going on, should I? Your audience out there still don't know Miss Pinkus is dead.'

Plunkett's manner changed abruptly. He put a hand on Cribb's shoulder. 'No need for them ever to know, eh? We can handle things discreetly between us, can't we?' He pulled out his wallet. 'Dammit, this doesn't have to be a police matter, does it?'

'If you're suggesting what I think you are,' said Cribb, 'I ought to warn you that it's a criminal offence. We've our duty to do, sir, and we've every right to ask for your co-operation. That's not to say we'll stop the goings-on behind the footlights, even though I've serious doubts about 'em.'

'Come, come now,' said Plunkett. 'It's a private performance. Besides, there's nothing in my show that you can't see in other halls.' From his look of injured innocence he might have been staging a temperance concert.

Cribb nodded. 'I'll grant you that, sir. Such performances can sometimes be seen in penny gaffs in the backstreets of Cairo. But I ain't here to reminisce. Where's the conjurer this girl worked with?'

'Professor Virgo? I had him escorted to his dressing-room. He was more than a little upset, of course, and I didn't want a panic backstage. As it is, only a handful of people know about this, you see.'

'Who would they be?'

'Why, the two trap-men who work down here, yourselves, Professor Virgo and me.'

'What about the dead girl's sister?'

'Bella? Good Lord, I'd forgotten. Nobody's told her. She'll be down here looking—'

Cribb reacted quickly. 'That sheet, if you please, Thackeray. She'll be shaken enough at the news, without actually seeing the body. Will you tell her, Mr Plunkett, or shall I?'

'I'd rather you did, if you've no objection.'

'Very well. You'd better question Virgo, Thackeray. Find out what you can about the man himself, and then go over the performance with him step by step.' In case the responsibility went to his constable's head, he added, 'And get your jacket and trousers on. You look ridiculous.'

Nevertheless it was with a justifiable feeling of importance that Thackeray tapped on Professor Virgo's door a few minutes later. Constables capable of conducting important interviews were by no means thick on the ground in the Metropolitan area.

The Professor was sitting at a small dressing-table made from a tea-chest, a bottle of whiskey in his left hand, and a wand in his right, with which he was moodily prodding a fat white rabbit in a hutch. Thackeray cleared his throat in a business-like way. He knew all about questioning suspects. You had to be in control from the start, establish your official status and then keep the questions going like revolver shots. 'Detective Constable Thackeray, sir, of Scotland Yard. I have some questions for you.'

'Questions?' Professor Virgo twitched in surprise. So did the rabbit.

'Will you kindly tell me how long you've been on the bill at the Paragon, sir?' A good opening question, requiring a short statement of fact. Get them into the way of repeating facts and they'd be hard put to introduce evasions later.

There was a lengthy pause.

'You heard me, sir?'

Several seconds later, Virgo spoke: 'W-when I am nervous I develop an im-p-p—'

'—pediment?' God, what appalling luck! His first major interrogation and he had landed a stutterer.

'About six weeks is the answer to your qu-qu—'

'I believe you're a sword-swallower by training?'

Virgo nodded.

'And you had an accident?'

'At the Ti-Ti—'

'Tivoli Garden. Then what happened, sir?'

'S-s-sore—'

'—throat. Yes, I can believe that, sir. You was taken to Philbeach House in Kensington, wasn't you?' Putting words into their mouths was not the recommended procedure, but this interview was liable to last all night if he didn't.

Another nod.

'Someone there offered you an engagement at the Paragon. Am I correct? Good. Now who was that?'

'Mrs B-B—'

'Body. Thank you. Now where did you first meet the Pinkus sisters — at Philbeach House? Right. Did the suggestion that they worked with you come from them or from you?'

'From them.'

'I see. And when did you first appear with them at the Paragon?'

Virgo held up his fingers. 'Th-th—'

'Three days ago? No? Three weeks. Very good. Are you still feeling nervous? What's the name of your rabbit? Never mind. Look here, Professor Virgo, I need to hear your account of what happened tonight, from the moment you got to the theatre. Are you able to manage that? Have a drop of your whisky. Not for me, thanks. I'm on duty, you see.'

When he had upended the bottle for several seconds, Virgo seemed to recover some of his confidence. He was a decent-looking man, with regular features, but desperately thin. He wouldn't last long in Newgate, Thackeray reflected.

'G-got here about eleven. They didn't want us here while the other show was in p-p—'

'—progress.'

'I wasn't the first turn so I had some time to get my things ready. I put them outside the door here for the p-propman to collect and take downstairs.'

'That would be your swords,' recalled Thackeray, 'and your table, with the wand, your hat, gloves and the glass of magic fluid. What was in that fluid, sir?'

'W-water, and a little colouring.' Virgo produced a small bottle of cochineal.

'May I have it, sir? I'll see that it's returned. Now when were your props taken to the stage?'

'During the m-m—'

'Monologue. I see. Do you know who moved them?'

Virgo shook his head.

'So they was probably waiting in the wings about twenty minutes. That's a long time. Don't people ever tamper with a conjurer's tricks when they're lying about like that, sir?'

'Oh yes. You get lots of jokers in the theatre. That's what happened to my swords at the Ti-Ti—'

'Tivoli Gardens. Yes, sir. Then why did you allow your props to go down there so long before you did?'

Virgo raised his finger confidentially. 'Ah, there wasn't much they could do with those few things, was there? They could only add something to the magical fluid, and that's a chance you take. Why, my assistant once swallowed a glass of d-disappearing liquid and found later it was dosed with ca-ca-cas—'

'Cascara.' Both men smiled. 'So you came into the wings during the transformation scene,' Thackeray went on, 'and waited on the side opposite your table, which was brought on by er — a propman.'

'Yes. I went through the tricks as usual. The swords and the fire-eating. Then I introduced Miss Lola. It's odd you know. I never s-stutter during a per-per—'

'—formance,' said Thackeray. 'Did anything unusual happen?'

'Not really. I handed her the drink after she had taken off the cloak. Then I made sure that she — do you know the trick?'

'She stood on the trap,' said Thackeray in a superior way.

'Yes. She drank the water, I shielded her with the cloak and she dropped through the trap as usual.'

'But she screamed,' said Thackeray.

'Yes. That was the moment of her heart-attack, I suppose, poor child. She must have been terrified by the occasion. I don't think I've p-played to such a distinguished audience in my life, either.'

'What happened then?'

'I finished the act and when I came off, the man from the trap-floor told me she was dead. I was speechless.'

'I can believe that,' Thackeray assured him. 'A very tragical thing to happen, sir.'

'A choker,' said Virgo. 'I shall have to change my act now. That trick is impossible without twin s-sisters. And s-sword-swallowing isn't enough to keep a house like this one happy. They aren't content until there's a girl on the stage showing a plentiful amount of l-l—'

'Lower limb?' said Thackeray.

Virgo nodded. 'So you see I can't p-perform with Miss Bella on her own.' He tapped the wand on his forehead. 'Perhaps I could saw her in ha-ha—'

'I shouldn't,' said Thackeray hastily. 'There ain't much future in that sort of trick, sir. Well, I'm grateful for your answers to my inquiries. I must get back to my sergeant now. If he should want to speak to you, where will you be, sir?'

'In here for at least an hour,' said Virgo with a note of self-pity in his voice. 'I have to wait for the p-private omnibus to convey us all back to Philbeach H-H—'

'Thank you, sir.'

Finding the trap-floor deserted, Thackeray eventually tracked down his superior in the quick-change room. One of the scene-shifters was stationed at the door to repel intruders. For the rest of that evening quick changes would have to be performed in the wings, a contingency unlikely to cause embarrassment to anyone at the Paragon. Thackeray established his identity by flourishing his notebook — what a comfort to have it on one's person again! — and was admitted.

'There you are, Constable,' said Cribb. 'I was starting to wonder if you were lost in the dressing-rooms.'

Thackeray returned a sharp look. 'The questioning took longer than you'd think, Sergeant. The Professor had a defect of speech.'

'I'm not surprised. If *you* swallowed swords for a living you'd probably impair your faculties in time.'

'That's a risk I don't propose to take, Sarge,' said Thackeray firmly, now on his guard against any suggestion of Cribb's. He repeated Virgo's story, referring only briefly to his notes. 'So I can't believe he would deliberately poison Miss Pinkus,' he concluded, 'seeing that he'd only known the girl three weeks. Besides, she and Bella was needed for the disappearing act. It won't be easy finding replacements. And in case the thought had crossed your mind, Sarge,' he added, grinning, but still with a certain wariness, 'I don't happen to have a twin brother.'

'Even if you had, Thackeray, I can't picture him in spangles and tights,' Cribb reassured him. 'No, from what I gathered when I questioned our friend Plunkett, the Professor ain't likely to be looking for replacements. He's a pure-bred sword-swallower and fire eater. The disappearing trick was put in at the insistence of the management. The patrons don't take to any kind of turn, however excellent, without its provision of undraped female flesh. But Virgo only performed the disappearing trick under protest. When you're shoving swords down your own throat to impress an audience you don't like to sully your act with conjuring-tricks, or so Plunkett tells me.'

'That puts it in a new light, Sarge. Now you mention it, he didn't seem particularly put out that he wouldn't be able to do the trick again, but I didn't see no significance in it. I think I was too occupied trying to encourage him not to stutter. I'm rather short on experience of interviewing suspects, I'm afraid.'

It was Cribb's turn to grin. 'We'll remedy that, Constable. I must be off to report Miss Pinkus's death in the right quarter, but I want you to stay here and collect statements from everyone who was on that stage tonight up to the moment of Lola's death. You can tell 'em you're in the Force. Say you're carrying out routine investigations, consequent upon the sudden decease of Miss Pinkus. It'll take you most of the night, but don't let anyone go until you've questioned 'em. That'll give you some experience all right. Oh, and get statements from the orchestra as well, will you?'

TWELVE

Thackeray examined a faint blue stain on the coffee-cup he was holding. The heat of the cup had done what several minutes' assiduous scrubbing with carbolic soap had failed to do earlier: removed some of the residue of ink from his first and second fingers. The evidence of two laborious days' copying of statements was now neatly implanted on Great Scotland Yard porcelain, for he and Sergeant Cribb were seated on upright leather-upholstered chairs, being treated with unaccustomed hospitality by Inspector Jowett.

'From one's position here at headquarters one has to be constantly on one's guard against getting out of touch with — if you will forgive the phrase — the humble seekers after clues, the ferrets of the Force, in short, gentlemen, yourselves. Another digestive biscuit, Sergeant?'

The back of Cribb's neck had become noticeably pinker during Jowett's condescensions. He shook his head. Thackeray too felt a hotness around the collar and a curdling sensation in his stomach. Both their digestions would need something stronger after this than a biscuit. Each of them clearly remembered a time when Jowett was a detective sergeant competent only at sheering away from trouble. That ability, and certain family connexions, were said to have made his promotion inevitable. If Cribb and Thackeray were ferrets, Jowett was a pedigree rabbit, and much more acceptable in the Yard. In conversation his nose twitched distractingly.

'We at headquarters,' he continued, 'often envy you denizens of the underworld, you know. Unfortunately an efficient C.I.D. requires its planners, its co-ordinators, its intelligencers. So we remain bound to our chairs directing the efforts of worthy bobbies like yourselves, while the detectives within us cry out to be with you. For example, gentlemen, I have been reading with interest your report on the death of the young woman last Tuesday at that music hall.'

'The Paragon, sir.'

'Yes. Deuced unfortunate thing to happen. But what a splendid setting for an investigation! You have been to other music halls too, I gather?'

'Just the Grampian in Blackfriars Road, sir,' said Cribb. Curious as to Jowett's intentions, he added: 'Are you interested in variety entertainment yourself?'

'No, no. That's not my style of recreation at all. Hardly ever set foot inside such a place. Light opera is far more to my taste.'

'When constabulary duty's to be done, eh sir?' said Cribb.

'What?'

'*Pirates of Penzance,* sir.'

'Ah, yes. Quite so.' The allusion was plainly lost on Inspector Jowett. 'I like point-to-point meetings too.' He put down his cup and felt in his pocket for his tobacco. 'Your visit to the Paragon interests me, though. Tell me what you know about the place.'

'The Paragon? I think we've formed a pretty clear picture of what goes on there, sir. We've seen it for ourselves and we've documented the goings-on there in thirty or more statements.'

'Please enlighten me.'

'Well, sir, to most of the world it's a run of the mill music hall, a trifle more expensive than some of the halls, but offering the same kind of entertainment three nights a week as hundreds of others. It has its promenade, of course, and there's an element of license in that quarter, but otherwise the whole thing's as nice as ninepence — if you like music halls, that is.'

'I assure you that I don't, but go on.'

'The owner of the Paragon is the gin magnate, Sir Douglas Butterleigh. It seems he has an affection for the halls. He started a home for destitute performers in Kensington, Philbeach House. You may have heard of it. Now his idea was that artistes falling ill or suffering an accident could be rescued from the poor-house and put in the care of a certain Mrs Body at Philbeach House. When they were sufficiently restored they'd return to the stage at the Paragon. The manager there is a Mr

Plunkett, and I got his account of the Paragon from him the other evening. Now Plunkett's a hard-headed businessman, and in no time at all he saw Butterleigh's idea wasn't going to fill that music hall three nights a week.'

'Philanthropists rarely visualise their charity in commercial terms,' Jowett observed from the centre of a cloud of smoke.

'Well, Plunkett persisted for a few months, but the bill at the Paragon wasn't responding very well to charity. Three-quarters of the guests at Phil-beach House were singers — and poor ones at that. You can't recruit a music hall company from sing-ers alone. So importations were made and soon the Paragon was operating like any other hall, and attracting a regular audience. Sir Douglas Butter-leigh didn't know much about it because he was an invalid and out of the way. To salve his con-science, I suppose, Plunkett decided he would have to find something to occupy the dregs and lees at Philbeach House. He conceived the idea of a spe-cial performance just to show 'em they weren't for-gotten.'

'In addition to the regular show?'

'Exactly. But this was a quite different class of audience. Plunkett made it clear he was offering a charitable entertainment. He priced his tickets high, put Sir Douglas's name on them and then did the rounds of London society. He promised 'em a midnight show, strictly for a good cause, and every ticket was sold inside a week.'

'Really. I find that difficult to account for.'

187

'So did I, sir, until Plunkett told me what he told his customers: that since they were buying tickets for a private show they might expect something different in the way of entertainment. What he'd done, in fact, was to persuade a couple of lady vocalists to be transported across the stage with little more on 'em than a ray of limelight.'

''Pon my soul, what an extraordinary idea!'

'My sentiments entirely, sir, but there's no accounting for taste. Plunkett tells me the turn was a roaring success. The audience wouldn't let the show go on until those two had been pushed back and forth a dozen times, like the favourite frame in a magic lantern. And when the evening came to an end he was bombarded by requests for tickets for the next one. He realised he'd discovered a gold-mine. A secret music hall for the well-to-do, with certain additional attractions.'

'That's ingenious, by George.'

'Yes, sir,' said Cribb, 'but Plunkett was too smart a showman to believe it could continue very long like that. Even if he persuaded all the females in residence at Philbeach House to play the part of living statues — and most of 'em were sufficiently close to penury to do it — his customers were going to tire of the entertainment before long. Like any other bill, his midnight show needed variety. But he couldn't turn singers into sword-swallowers overnight. Nor did he want to recruit performers in the usual way, through their agents. That could only complicate his plans. No, the company for the midnight show had to come from Philbeach

House. Once a performer was sufficiently unfortunate to be living on charity he wasn't likely to argue over the kind of work you offered him. Plunkett's problem was that Mrs Body's guest-list didn't provide the variety he wanted. There wasn't a tightrope walker or a trapeze-artiste among 'em.'

'Singularly unfortunate,' said Jowett. 'Can I offer you some more coffee, gentlemen?'

'We never have a second cup, sir. Now it was about three weeks ago that I first began to be interested in a baffling series of accidents to music hall performers — a sword-swallower, a trapeze-act, a comedian, a conjurer and so on. I might not have investigated any further if someone hadn't warned me of an impending accident at a particular theatre — the Grampian, in Blackfriars Road. They put it in unduly strong terms. "Sensational Tragedy Tonight", the note said, and what we got was a strong man bitten in the leg by a bulldog, but that set me asking questions, sir. I began to look for similarities in the accidents. Was it just a joker at work, or was there more to it? Thackeray, tell the Inspector what we decided about the accidents.'

The constable jerked up in his chair. 'The accidents? Oh yes, Sarge. Well, sir, we was able to establish that they all happened at different theatres. And all the victims, if I may call 'em that, was put out of work. They all did quite different turns on the halls, too. And later on we learned they all got taken in at Philbeach House.'

'And one more thing,' said Cribb with an air of

significance. 'The nature of their accidents was such that none of 'em was likely to be hired again for a long time. The common factor was ridicule, sir. These unfortunate people were laughing-stocks — the comedian with the wrong words on his song-sheet, the sword-swallower who coughed, the trapeze-girls who collided with each other, the barrel-dancer who couldn't even stand on his barrels, the strong man who got bitten and fell through his platform, and the unfortunate girl on the swing.'

'What happened to her?' inquired Jowett.

'Words fail me, sir. Like all the rest, though, she's finished as a performer unless she changes her name and does a different turn. That ain't easy.'

Jowett drew heavily from his pipe and slowly exhaled. 'Let me get this clear, Sergeant. Are you suggesting that Mr Plunkett engineered all these accidents himself, in order to bring these people to Philbeach House?'

'I can't be sure of that yet, sir. He wouldn't admit that much to me. But six of 'em were performing at the Paragon the other evening, including the late Miss Lola Pinkus.'

'I will admit that you make it sound most plausible. How do you account for this young woman's death, however? Was it another accident that perhaps went wrong?'

'Emphatically not, sir. I've had the report on the post mortem. She died of Prussic Acid poisoning. Almost instantaneous. That was no accident.'

'Indeed!' Jowett's eyes narrowed to slits, the wrinkles creasing around them. All the indications were that he was about to make a profound observation. 'Then it was suicide. She killed herself. How very fortunate that the conjuring trick removed her from public view at the critical moment. The sudden demise of a performer must have a most unsettling effect upon an audience.'

'She screamed, sir,' said Cribb, 'but it was hardly heard above the drum-roll. The audience still don't know what happened. Most of 'em were taken in by the illusion and thought they were looking at Lola when Bella appeared in the gallery. Even if some of 'em guessed the secret they didn't know Lola was dying when she hit the mattress under the stage.'

'What a mercy! Tell me, Sergeant. What was the reaction of Miss Bella Pinkus?'

'She knew nothing until she came looking for Lola, sir. I broke the news to her myself. She refused to believe me at first. Couldn't see how the trick had worked so perfectly if it killed her sister. I had to show her the body to convince her. She took it well, though. They're practical people, these theatricals. There's a streak of toughness about 'em I wouldn't mind seeing in certain members of the Force, sir.' Cribb said this with such a bland expression that Jowett could not possibly take issue.

Even so, the inspector rose to take up a stance on the tiger-skin rug in front of the mantelpiece. A sepia photograph of himself in hunting-kit was displayed behind him. Thackeray reflected without much charity that the chair in the picture was identical to one he had seen in a studio in Bayswater.

'There is one thing that is not entirely clear to me, Sergeant. You implied that the patrons of these midnight performances were influential and wealthy members of London society.'

'The promenade was like Rotten Row at the height of the season, sir.'

'Kindly explain to me, in that case, how two common members of the Police Force gained admission.'

'They made the acquaintance of Mr Plunkett's daughter, sir,' said Cribb, as though that explained everything.

'I see,' said Jowett, frowning. 'And you mingled freely with the audience? Both of you?'

Thackeray's cup and saucer vibrated audibly in his hand.

'We separated to allay suspicion, sir,' said Cribb. 'I found myself a place in the pit. Thackeray was — er — more prominently placed.'

'Which must account for his being first on the scene when Miss Pinkus was found,' Jowett observed.

Thackeray nodded vigorously.

'Well, Sergeant,' said Jowett, straining to appear casual, 'I am confident that you can bring this squalid little affair to a summary conclusion. It should not be difficult to establish where Miss

Pinkus purchased the means of her self-destruction. It was acid, you say?'

'Prussic, sir. Just about the deadliest known. There was plenty of it, too. More than half of what was in that tumbler must have been pure acid.'

'Then we should have no difficulty. No chemist will have sold that amount of acid without making an entry in his poison-book.'

'I'm having the usual checks made, sir, but I ain't optimistic. There's too much of the stuff about already. It's used on rats, you know. The railway companies fumigate their carriages with it periodically. There's a devil of a lot of rats in ships' holds, too. God knows how much acid they use in the Port of London. Plunkett even thought they had a bottle at the Paragon but we haven't found it. After Tuesday night's display I can well understand that the hall wants fumigating regular, sir.'

Jowett rapped his pipe several times on the mantel-piece and started digging at the contents with a match-stick. 'Come, come, Sergeant. That sounds uncommonly like the outpourings one reads in the daily Press from retired schoolmasters who sign themselves "Father of Three Daughters" or "Pure in Heart". I can't believe there's a prude hiding under those side-whiskers of yours.'

Cribb accused of prudery? The sergeant wouldn't like that at all. Thackeray closed his eyes and waited for the explosion.

'Far be it from me to encourage wickedness,' the

193

inspector continued, 'but Heavens, man, there's worse sights in London than a few fillies in fleshings. You're old enough to have done a tour of duty at Kate Hamilton's in your time, aren't you?'

Somehow Cribb was keeping himself in check. 'But I can't see how that affects these shows at the Paragon. Why, there were people in the audience with names respected throughout the land, sir. Sitting there openly in the company of loose women — expensive courtesans, I admit, but no better for that in my opinion — and watching indecencies no music and dancing licence gives a music hall manager the right to exhibit. I certainly mean to see Plunkett get his deserts, irrespective of Miss Pinkus's death.'

'It was an indecent show, sir,' Thackeray confirmed. 'We'll get him under the Police Acts.'

'And fine him forty shillings for allowing an indecent song to be sung within view of a constable?' Jowett said scornfully. 'You can't hurt Plunkett like that. Let me give you some advice, gentlemen. On Tuesday night you contrived an entrance to an entertainment arranged for a class of audience accustomed to take its pleasures in private. You can be forgiven for mistakenly believing that what you saw might have a corrupting effect upon such people. But you were in no position to judge, nor should you set yourselves up as judges. They live on a different plane from yourselves, gentlemen, or from me.'

'Are you saying they're above the Law, sir?'

'Good gracious, no, Sergeant. But the Law takes

account of circumstances, and the circumstances into which you insinuated yourselves last Tuesday were quite foreign to your experience. Such private performances are not unknown in London. The patrons know what to expect when they attend, and we receive no complaints about the nature of the entertainment. If there is anything one learns at the Yard about administering the Law it is the importance of discretion. Discretion, gentlemen, discretion in everything.'

This was orthodox Jowett, now. Cribb passed Thackeray a knowing look, almost a wink. 'So you'd like us to concentrate our investigations on the death of Miss Pinkus, sir, and exercise our discretion over the matter of the midnight shows?'

The inspector nodded contentedly. 'Precisely, Sergeant. Devote your energies to the matter in hand. It shouldn't take you long to discover why she killed herself. There's a houseful of wagging tongues at Kensington ready to give you information. Gossip is part of the music hall tradition. You've already got your statements from the Paragon. No need to waste any more time there, eh?'

Cribb shook his head. 'Sorry, sir. Location of death. We'll be returning there, for sure.'

'Sergeant, Sergeant,' appealed Jowett, waving his pipe at Cribb, 'where's the discretion you agreed to exercise? Mr Plunkett has a reputation to keep up. He doesn't want detectives blundering about his stage.'

Cribb stood up decisively. 'If that's the way you see our work, sir . . .'

'For God's sake, Sergeant! Don't take umbrage, man. We're all members of the same Force, dammit. Surely we're not so confoundedly sensitive that we can't speak a few plain words to each other. I simply suggested that you concentrate your inquiries on Philbeach House and leave Mr Plunkett to—'

'Continue with his charitable work, sir? Yes, I understand you,' said Cribb, 'and if it's an order you're giving me to lay off Mr Plunkett I'll not defy it. But I'd be obliged if you'd give it to me as an order, because I'm apt to take suggestions for what they are, and set 'em aside if I don't see the logic in 'em.'

Jowett sighed. 'You're a difficult man, Cribb. Very well. I order you not to enter the Paragon again without consulting me.'

'Thank you, sir. And while we're exchanging plain words I'd like to make it clear that blundering about ain't an accurate description of the way your officers conduct 'emselves. I'm not sure what prompted that remark, sir, but if it's Constable Thackeray's part in last Tuesday's performance that's in question I should tell you that I take full responsibility. It was immaculate detective work, as discreet as you could wish and deserving of the highest commendation. That'll be in my report, sir.'

'I shall look forward to reading it, Sergeant,' said Jowett icily. 'The expression I used was a mere form of words. I was trying to see things from the point of view of Mr Plunkett. Nothing personal was intended. I have no more to say to you at this stage.' He indicated that the interview was over by walking to the window and looking out.

'There is one other matter, sir,' persisted Cribb. 'Woolston, the prisoner in Newgate. Stage-illusionist. Drove a sword through his assistant's leg, if you recall the case.'

'Dimly,' answered Jowett without looking round.

'He's innocent, sir, if our theories are correct. The charges should be dropped. He was almost certainly destined for Philbeach House and the Paragon. I've no doubt that Mr Plunkett—'

'I'll look into the matter. Good-day, gentlemen.'

As they emerged into the balm of a soft October drizzle Thackeray was moved to express his gratitude to Cribb. 'It was handsome of you, Sarge.'

'What was?'

'Speaking up for me like that. Immaculate detective-work and all that. I didn't look upon it as anything special myself.'

'Nor I,' said Cribb. 'But I'm damned if I'll accept insults from the likes of Jowett.'

They entered Whitehall in silence and stepped out briskly, indistinguishable in their bowlers from the Civil Servants hurrying from the Admiralty to secure early lunches in the pubs around Charing Cross.

'Do you really think it was suicide, Sarge?' Thackeray asked eventually.

'No,' said Cribb. 'Never said so either.'

'But the Inspector did, and you didn't take him up on it. He seemed to have made up his mind.'

'His mind stops at suicide,' said Cribb. 'Murder's unthinkable in his situation.'

'Why should that be, Sarge?'

'We've stirred up a hornet's nest, Constable, and there's some pretty big specimens in it.'

'Members of Parliament?'

'Yes, and others. There were a couple of faces at the Paragon the other night I couldn't place for the life of me. Heavily-built fellows with cropped hair and Prussian moustaches, sitting in a box feeding oysters to their doxies. I lost most of a night's sleep trying to remember where I'd seen 'em. It came to me quite sudden this morning — the Director's offices at the Yard.'

'Good Lord!'

'Now a murder's going to bring all manner of unwanted publicity to the Paragon if the Press get a sniff of it. It wouldn't do much for Jowett's career if the names of Tuesday's audience became known. Remember all that talk about discretion? So it's probably best if Jowett continues to think of Lola's death as suicide. If I mention murder, someone's liable to panic. You and I might find ourselves back on the beat.'

'It makes your blood run cold, Sarge.'

Two or three pints of half-and-half were found necessary at this juncture to revive the circulations of both detectives. 'Do we go to Philbeach House as the Inspector suggested, Sarge?' Thackeray asked, when he felt Cribb was ready to discuss the case again.

'I'd have gone there anyway. I need to find out more about the Pinkus sisters and how the other guests regarded 'em. In fact, I want a picture of what really goes on at Philbeach House.'

'But that'll take days, Sarge, questioning all them guests.'

'There's a short cut,' said Cribb. 'If you remember, I received an invitation to return there on a social call.'

'Mrs Body!'

'No-one's better placed to tell me what I need to know. There's nothing else for it, Thackeray. I'm going to take up Mrs Body's offer to inspect the box from the old Alhambra.'

'Her private room? She'll compromise you for sure. Don't consider it, Sarge. Why, it's moral suicide. The Yard hasn't any right to expect that of you. I'm damned sure Inspector Jowett wouldn't go.'

'Jowett hasn't had the invitation,' said Cribb. 'The Yard's got nothing to do with it. This is my decision absolutely. If I tell the truth, I'm rather looking forward to it.'

This was the man Jowett had labelled a prude . . . Thackeray walked to the bar to order a double whiskey.

THIRTEEN

Cribb's initiative suffered a temporary rebuff that afternoon at Philbeach House. The same battle-scarred manservant who had confronted the detectives on their first visit announced in a tone of finality that the Mistress was engaged. She was not to be disturbed. The visitor should return another afternoon. There the assignation would have foundered if Cribb had not thoughtfully placed his foot against the door. Did he have a visiting-card then? He had no card, but his C.I.D. identification was proof of respectability. Was this an official visit? No, social: Mrs Body had invited him to call. In that case he might wait inside, but there was no certainty she would see him. She could not be disturbed on any account before tea-time.

So he was admitted to a small anteroom furnished with upright chairs, a table and a whatnot neatly stacked with theatrical periodicals. A large marble timepiece on the mantelshelf ticked with an emphasis quite disproportionate to the size of the room. He selected a chair with its back to the clock and thumbed the pages of *The Bill of the Play* for 1880. Just as the journals in doctors' waiting-rooms were invariably filled with terrifying quack-medicine advertisements, so Mrs Body's literature was lavishly illustrated with embracing actors and actresses. When Cribb came to an advertisement depicting corsets he snapped the book shut.

The servant could not be blamed for having failed to recognise Cribb when he arrived at Philbeach House. Not only was he without his unforgettable assistant (who was biting his nails to shreds at Paradise Street Police Station); he was dressed in an altogether more flamboyant style, purple cravat with matching handkerchief, checkered Norfolk jacket and trousers, all topped with a Glengarry cap. And a yellow rose in his lapel. He kept his hat and umbrella with him, as etiquette demanded.

Presently there was another caller. The servant shuffled to the door. A woman's voice. Familiar. Cribb crossed to the door and listened. More footsteps and the swish of skirts barely gave him time to stand away when the door opened. She was ushered in without much grace and left there with Cribb.

'How d'you do, Miss Blake.'

'Sergeant! What a pleasant surprise.' Her face, dampened by rain, glowed pink under her velvet bonnet.

'Pleasure's all mine, Miss. You've come to call on Albert, I dare say.'

'That's right. It's a strange state of affairs when a lady calls on her young man, isn't it? But you know the circumstances here. None of the guests are allowed out except the Smee brothers.'

'The Undertakers?'

'Yes. And they're more staff than guests. So if I want to see Albert I have to call here myself. I'm allowed to converse with him in the drawing-room. Mrs Body is usually there as chaperon.'

'Very proper, Miss. How's Albert getting on?'

Ellen Blake's eyes glistened. 'He seems to be adjusting very well to the life here. He doesn't complain at all.'

'I believe it's a regular life of luxury, Miss. He's certain to enjoy it for a while, after his digs in Lambeth. He'll tire of it though, soon as he's fit enough to be back on the halls.'

'I pray that you're right in your opinion, Sergeant. There are things about this house, and some of the people in it, that make me fear for Albert. Why are you here? Has it anything to do with that tragic event at my father's music hall?'

Cribb shrugged his shoulders. 'Social call, Miss. Mrs Body invited me to come and see some of the architectural features.' He winked. 'She'll be too busy for chaperoning.'

'You were there the other night, weren't you, Sergeant? You stayed on for the second house. Father told me. He doesn't allow me to attend the benefit performances, but I have some notion of what goes on. The police are sure to put a stop to it all now, aren't they?'

'I couldn't say, Miss. That's someone else's concern.'

The door was thrust open again. The manservant's ugly countenance leered in. 'Mistress just called down on the speakin'-tube. Says she's free now. You can go up.'

Cribb picked up his cap and umbrella. 'My regards to Albert, Miss. I trust he'll soon be fit enough to leave this place.' He gave a slight bow and walked out to his meeting with Mrs Body with the *panache* of an Elizabethan nobleman going to the block.

'This way,' grunted the manservant, shambling ahead. He, in his turn, would have made a most convincing attendant at executions. They crossed the hall and passed through a door marked *Private* into a narrow carpeted passage. There was a spiral staircase at the end.

'Up them stairs, copper. 'Er room's at the top.' With that, Cribb's escort backed away and slammed the door shut.

He started up the stairs, gripping his umbrella as if it were a sword and keeping close to the curving wall on his left, where the footing was broadest. This was the interior of a turret-like extremity, just visible from the front of the building in Kensington Palace Gardens. Leaded slit-windows let in some illumination at intervals. The carpeting on the stairs muffled his tread.

More than midway up, he stopped. Rhythmic thuds above his head indicated for sure that someone was descending the stairs. A tread too deliberate for a woman. A man coming down from Mrs Body's private room? Cribb went down four steps and positioned himself in the shadow against the side, with a clear view of the shaft of light admitted by the window on the facing wall, some eight feet above him. Whoever was coming down would be clearly visible at that point. Presumably he knew that Cribb was on his way up, but he could not know how far he had got. If the sergeant kept his position, he had a momentary advantage. The steps continued to descend, though somewhat irregularly. Cribb watched, like a naturalist trapping a moth in a lantern-beam.

Then the face and figure were there, dressed in spectral white, a pale face with piercing blue eyes. And a crop of grey hair standing up like fresh lavender.

'Major Chick, by God!' said Cribb, running up to meet him.

'Scotland Yard late on the bloody scene, again, I notice,' mumbled the Major, his breath reeking of gin. He wore a rumpled white duck-suit, with the shreds of a red carnation in his buttonhole. His cravat was untied. So were his shoelaces. 'You've got to think ahead in this blasted job, Sergeant. No damned good messing about checking on poison-books by the hundred.' He tapped his forehead. ' 'Sintelligence that traps the criminal.'

Cribb held him by the shoulders, deciding whether it was safe to let him descend the rest of the way unaided.

'What's this?' demanded the Major, poking Cribb's buttonhole with his forefinger. 'I'd take it off if I were you, Sergeant. Look what happened to mine. She isn't interested in the blasted holly on top. It's the plum-pudding she wants.' With that he pushed Cribb aside and continued confidently down the stairs.

Shaking his head in disapproval, the sergeant watched the Major until he was out of sight. Then he directed his attention upwards. He climbed two steps, paused, frowning, removed the rose from his lapel and put it in his pocket, before tackling the rest of the stairs.

The small hinged door-knocker on the outside of Mrs Body's suite was cast in brass from a champagne-cork.

'That sounds suspiciously like the arrival of the detective department,' called Mrs Body from within. She opened the door. Cribb, two steps below her level, was still a head taller than she. 'What an agreeable surprise, Mr Cribb! I am delighted that you took my invitation seriously. Welcome to my little snuggery.'

'Charmed, Ma'am.'

He stepped into a modest-sized circular room lit by gas. Crimson curtains were draped from ceiling to carpet round two-thirds of the walls. To his right, built out from the remaining wall-space, was the box from the Alhambra, a magnificent wood and stucco construction in the baroque style, with gilt-painted muses as side-supports to a canopy of cherubs. Heavy silk drapes in gold were gathered to the sides in lush folds.

'Takes your breath away,' said Cribb.

'Not for long, I hope,' said Mrs Body. 'Come

and see the interior.' She led the way behind one of the muses into the box itself. It was furnished with total authenticity: two high-backed chairs with striped satin seats, a small table for drinks, the walls papered in an ornate red and gold design.

Cribb glanced at the lacquered door behind the chairs. 'Where does that lead to — the foyer?' he joked.

'No,' said Mrs Body. 'My bedroom. But I should warn you that there is a steep descent.'

'I shall bear that in mind, Ma'am.'

'Please sit down, and put your things on the table. I can draw the curtains if you find it cosier. I don't suppose these curtains were drawn in ten years before I bought them. What can I offer you to drink?'

There were no decanters in sight. Mystified, Cribb asked for gin.

'White satin?' said Mrs Body. 'There is plenty of that here. Butterleigh's, of course.'

'Naturally.'

She moved the curtain a fraction and put a speaking-tube to her mouth. 'Send up two gins, please.' Turning back to Cribb she asked, 'Did you meet the Rear-Admiral on your way upstairs?'

Cribb nodded. 'Ah. So that was who it was.'

'A personal friend of Sir Douglas. Strange for a nautical man to be affected by drink. Perhaps I should have offered him rum.' There was the sound of machinery from somewhere. 'Good. That will be our waiter.' She got up and opened a small door, impossible to detect in the intricate wall-decoration. Two glasses were waiting on a serving-lift. 'I am in contact with everyone, you see, but secure from intruders. Would you like to see my other contrivances?'

Cribb hesitated, half-looking at the door behind his chair.

'You're not nervous, Mr Cribb?' She pulled at a cord on her left, and the curtains on the wall facing them parted some six feet, revealing the bare, whitewashed wall. 'Now, if you will kindly turn down the gas above your head. Thank you. There!'

With the lowering of the light to a modest blue flame, a singular effect appeared on the white wall opposite, a coloured panorama with moving trees and minute figures in motion crossing green lawns.

'Kensington Gardens to the life!' said Cribb.

'A camera obscura,' explained Mrs Body. 'The camera is above our heads and looks out from the top of the tower. The image is projected on to the wall by an arrangement of mirrors and lenses. By working a lever I can turn the camera through the full sweep of landscape visible from the tower, including my neighbours' houses and gardens. Sometimes it can provide diverting entertainment.'

'That I can believe,' said Cribb. 'I was wondering how you passed the time, sitting in a box like this, staring at a blank wall. It's most ingenious. Scotland Yard could do with some of them, mounted on the higher landmarks of London.'

'Ah yes. What a pity Mr Body has gone over to the majority. He could have worked miracles for Scotland Yard. He was a man of science, you know. I have a weakness for men with inventive minds. Why, there is a room downstairs still filled with his contraptions and chemicals. I have a magic lantern he made. I show the pictures on the wall here. There are several melodramas in sets of frames, and some whimsical figure-studies which you may care to see later, after more drinks. My gentlemen-friends usually—'

'You won't mind my addressing myself to you in a personal way, Ma'am?' Cribb suddenly said.

'Not in the least, my dear.' Mrs Body drew her chair closer to Cribb's. She was wearing black satin that rustled each time she moved.

'Seeing that you've been so friendly as to show me your boudoir here, Ma'am—'

'That is my pleasure, Mr Cribb.'

Cribb coughed over his gin. 'Quite so. I thought it right to warn you that certain complications could arise from something that happened at the Paragon music hall last Tuesday.'

'The accident to Lola Pinkus?'

'No accident, Ma'am. Murder, almost certainly. The manager there, Mr Plunkett, could find himself in a deal of trouble. In a statement he made to the police he mentioned a connexion with you—'

'Outrageous! My reputation is beyond reproach.'

'Nothing of an indelicate nature, Ma'am,' Cribb hastened to add. 'No-one would suggest anything of that sort. May I turn up the light a fraction? No, the connexion in question is purely of a business nature, Ma'am. I believe the artistes at Mr Plunkett's midnight shows are conveyed to the Paragon from Philbeach House in a private omnibus.'

'God forgive me, yes.' Mrs Body picked up a large fan and fluttered it in a frenzied way. 'It is the only time they leave the house. They have all agreed not to step outside these walls. They have every convenience here.'

'What would happen if one disobeyed the rules, Ma'am?'

'He would be asked to leave. But my guests are not foolish, Mr Cribb. They are here because they are unemployable. They would starve if they left.'

'So they have no choice.'

Mrs Body called into the speaking-tube, 'More gin, if you please. Send up the bottle.'

'It sounds rather institutional, Ma'am — to an outsider, I mean.'

'Not at all. The guests come here of their own volition. I am paid to see that they are well looked after and there are no complaints. They are given work by Mr Plunkett. I even permit visitors to come, if they are respectable. Ah, here's the gin. Let me fill your glass.'

'I suppose you wouldn't have much knowledge of the benefit performances at the Paragon?' said Cribb.

'No knowledge at all, Mr Cribb, beyond what I overhear being rehearsed downstairs. Is there anything irregular in the shows?'

'I'd rather not comment, Ma'am. You've never attended any of the performances, then?'

209

'My duties keep me here, you see. George and Bertie, the Undertakers, escort the artistes to the Paragon. I really know nothing of what goes on there.'

'You've nothing to fear then, Mrs Body. You can still help me, though. Tell me what sort of girl young Lola Pinkus was. Did she get along with the other guests? Was she a good mixer, would you say?'

Mrs Body giggled slightly. 'Pardon my amusement, Mr Cribb. Lola's achievements as a mixer are unparalleled in my experience.'

'You mean that she . . .'

'Flirted outrageously, Mr Cribb. One hesitates to speak uncharitably of the departed, but, frankly, all members of the opposite sex were like curtain-calls to Lola, every one a fresh delight. Sam Fagan, Bellotti, Professor Virgo, almost the entire orchestra of the Paragon. It led to some bitterness here, I assure you. She and her sister had promised Bellotti they would assist him in his barrel-dancing act. You may imagine the poor boy's disappointment when Lola took up with the Professor instead.'

'Ah,' said Cribb. 'He was jealous, then.'

'It quite ruined Bellotti's act. A man on barrels isn't much of an attraction without a pretty assistant, is he? I believe they pelted him with champagne-corks at the Paragon.'

'Did he argue with Virgo over the girls?'

'No, no,' said Mrs Body. 'Bellotti knew that the Professor hadn't taken the girls from him. How they wheedled their way into the sword-swallowing act I do not like to speculate, but the trick they made the Professor do was quite out of keeping with the rest of his act. He is an orthodox sword-swallower and fire-eater, not a conjurer. The poor man was thoroughly miserable about it, but Lola had some way of compelling him to co-operate, I'm sure of that.'

'You're sure it wasn't Bella who persuaded him?'

Mrs Body shook her head emphatically. 'Bella had no initiative whatsoever. She was entirely dominated by her sister. Oh, they had arguments enough, and bitter ones, too. Such language, Mr Cribb! But Lola always had the last word. There was just one occasion when she met her match and that was last Monday.'

'How was that?'

'Did you meet my new guests, Albert, the strong man, and his mother? They arrived on Sunday, bringing their bulldog with them. I do not usually encourage pets, but as Beaconsfield has trodden the boards like the rest of us and was a working member of the troupe, I made an exception. The lady is extremely attached to the animal, you understand, and she asked me whether it could recline at her feet under the table at dinner on Monday evening. I had no objection myself, because it looked a placid beast, but naturally I said that if any of my guests objected, Beaconsfield would have to leave the dining-room. I was thinking of Professor Virgo, a man of nervous sensibilities, you know.'

'So I believe.'

'Well I made sure Beaconsfield was installed under the table before I sounded the gong. All credit to that animal; it did not make a sound. I suppose it must have fallen asleep. The Professor took his seat — naturally Lola had reserved a place for herself next to him — and all went perfectly until we got to the final course, the fruit and meringues. Then Lola must have been afflicted by some muscular spasm, for her meringue jumped from her plate and rolled under the table. "Oh," she said. "My meringue!" Professor Virgo — a gentleman through and through — ducked beneath the tablecloth to retrieve it. It all happened before any of us had time to think. We heard a yelp from the dog and an expression of surprise from the Professor, followed by a bump as he endeavoured to stand up. Man and dog were agitated beyond belief, Mr Cribb, and Lola was laughing like a child at the pantomime.'

'Most regrettable.'

'But Albert's mother was more incommoded than anybody. She plainly believed Lola had cold-bloodedly set the meringue rolling in Beaconsfield's direction. If people couldn't bring a decently-behaved pet into a dining-room without some vicious girl shying meringues at it, she said, she intended to take her meals in her room in future and she advised everyone else to do the same. Whereupon Lola retorted that a dining-room was not the place for — pardon me, Mr Cribb — stinking animals. In that case, said Albert's mother,

Lola herself should leave the room, for Beacons-field at least had a fortnightly bath. It was the only time I ever saw Lola lost for a reply. Somehow one knew that whatever she said would be bettered by Albert's mother.'

'A formidable lady,' agreed Cribb. 'I don't think they use her to the best advantage at the Paragon, swinging her about in a balloon-basket. She's a rare sight as Britannia, when Albert's lifting his dumbbells.'

'I have good news for you, Mr Cribb. She will soon be accompanying her son again in a new series of tableaux, arranged specially for the Paragon. His leg has improved beyond all expectation with the help of a whisky rub and he is already lifting again.' He should certainly be fit for next Tuesday.'

'Tuesday?' queried Cribb.

Mrs Body placed her hand on Cribb's knee. 'My, Scotland Yard is slow this afternoon. The next benefit at the Paragon, you dilatory detective! You know all about that, surely?'

Cribb was open-mouthed. 'Do you mean that they're continuing with these exhibitions, Ma'am?'

She laughed aloud. 'Well, they'd find it difficult to cancel Tuesday's engagement, wouldn't they?'

Cribb stood up. 'I don't know what you mean, Ma'am. A young woman murdered on the stage, and they're callously planning the next perfor-mance! That's a cool way of going on, in my view.'

'Perhaps it seems like that to you, Mr Cribb, but really there is no choice. The show was arranged before Lola's untimely death. My information is that the Paragon is to receive a visit from a most distinguished patron next Tuesday night. He cannot possibly be disappointed. It is, in effect, a command performance.'

Cribb paled. 'My Lord! Not the . . .'

'He is quite old enough to have a mind of his own, Mr Cribb. If he chooses to take an interest in the Paragon we must not disappoint him. That is why Albert has made such efforts to be fit. The honour, you see. What on earth are you doing, Mr Cribb?'

'Climbing over the edge of your box, Ma'am. I can't stay, I'm afraid. Urgent matters to attend to, by Heaven!'

'Send me another bottle of gin,' called Mrs Body plaintively into the speaking-tube, when Cribb's footsteps had receded altogether.

FOURTEEN

Saturday morning found Cribb and Thackeray seated in an omnibus bound for Kensington High Street. It was a joyless journey. The first fog of winter quite obscured the interesting activity along the pavements. The passengers could see only what passed within six feet of the window: the bobbing heads of cab-horses, flickering coach-lamps and brash advertisements for cocoa and safety matches on the sides of passing buses. Thackeray sat forward, elbows resting on his knees, feet idly manoeuvring a cigarette packet through the straw provided on the floor. He was shrewd enough to know when conversation with Cribb was inadvisable, so he let the sergeant's monologue continue, making token responses at decent intervals.

'I don't ask for much, Thackeray. I'm not particular about the hours I work or the cases I'm put on, or the company I have to rub shoulders with. You've never found me a difficult man, have you? There's malcontents enough in the Force, but I've never counted myself one of 'em, though I've had more cause for complaint than most. But an officer's entitled to look to his superiors for support, ain't he? Superiors, my hat! D'you know where I ran him to earth eventually, after I'd spent an hour and a half convincing Scotland Yard it was important enough to disturb him when he was off duty? Where d'you think?'

'I don't know, Sarge. His club?'

'The Westminster Aquarium, goggling at a bloody fish-tank. "Ah," he says to me, "I didn't know you were an icthyologist, Sergeant." You and I run around like lunatics trying to prevent a national catastrophe while Inspector Jowett studies the habits of gold-fish! "Most awfully sorry to invade your privacy," says I, "but it's a matter of over-riding importance that we stop the next show at the Paragon." Then I tell him what I learned from Mrs Body, and what do you think he says when he's heard it all? "Oh," says he, still pressing his nose against the glass, "I know all about that. No need to agitate yourself, Sergeant. You get back to your questioning of chorus-girls and leave affairs of State to those that understand 'em." I don't believe he's any intention of stopping that show, Thackeray.'

'You've done your loyal duty, anyway, Sarge. Can't do more than that, unless you can charge Plunkett with murder before Tuesday.'

'Maybe I'm becoming a cynic,' said Cribb, 'but I've a feeling in my bones there ain't any future in charging Mr Plunkett with anything. He's one of the bigger fish that Jowett keeps his eye on. You and I are minnows, Constable. Ah, you can build a pretty strong case against Plunkett. As manager he had every opportunity of poisoning Lola Pinkus. No-one would question his appearing in the wings or touching the props. He knew the order of the acts perfectly, and Virgo's routine. The poison was available on the premises. And the staging of the murder was damned professional, wasn't it? Didn't interfere in the least with the performance. He was one of the first on the scene afterwards, too.'

'But why should he want to poison the girl, Sarge?'

'Plunkett's got plenty of money and plenty of things he'd rather keep to himself. Could be that Lola was trying to blackmail him. A man of his sort isn't going to let a chit of a show-girl stand in his way. So he removes her from the scene in the neatest possible way. If we hadn't been there he'd have put the whole thing down to heart failure and had the girl buried next day.'

'Monstrous!'

'That's only theorising, of course. We'd need to be sure of the motive. But while we're under orders to keep away from Plunkett we're not likely to find one, are we?'

'It makes you feel completely impotent, Sarge.'

For the first time that morning the gleam returned to Cribb's eye. 'Hadn't affected me quite as bad as that, Constable. However, there's a possibility in my mind, just a possibility. If the Law can't approach Mr Plunkett, that don't prevent a private agent from approaching him.'

'Major Chick! That's why we're going to call on him, is it?'

'That's one reason, Thackeray. There's several things I'd like to know from the Major. Besides, I've never seen a private investigator at home, have you?'

Major Chick's address was a matter of two minutes' walk from the bus-stop, a set of rooms on the first floor of a large house overlooking Holland Park. A housekeeper admitted them and escorted them upstairs, asking, 'Was you expected?' rather nervously before she tapped on Chick's door. It was pulled briskly open.

'Good Lord! Never thought I'd see the day when . . . Come in, gentlemen,' said Major Chick. He was in shirtsleeves and waistcoat; the first time, Thackeray reflected, they had seen him out of disguise.

If the Major's apparel lacked interest on this occasion, the novelty of his living-room made up for it. Entry was a matter of sidling round two sides of a vast table, at least nine feet square. It was completely covered by a map of London, with the Thames, blue-tinted and six inches broad in parts, sinuously disposed across the centre like a basking boa-constrictor. Chessmen ingeniously marked points of interest: a queen for the Palace, bishops for the Abbey and St Paul's, a knight for the Horse Guards, a castle for the Tower; and (less happily) pawns for Scotland Yard and the various Divisional Headquarters. There were also up to a hundred champagne-corks, neatly trimmed for stability.

'Music halls,' answered the Major to the inquiry in Thackeray's puckered brow.

'Speaks volumes for your standard of living,' commented Cribb, with undisguised envy.

The end of the room was occupied by the fire-place, an unbelievably tidy desk, square to the wall, and three chairs in rigid rank on the opposite side. Over the mantelpiece was a portrait of Her Majesty, flanked by the Union Jack and the colours (presumably) of the 8th Hussars.

'Sleeping quarters through there,' said the Major, indicating a door beside the desk, 'and ablutions on the left. Not quite what I've been used to, but it suffices. I was working on my diary when you knocked. No Orderly Room Sergeant here, you see. The housekeeper cleans my bed-space daily and that's all the batting I get. Kindly sit down there and tell me what your business is.' He briskly rotated the revolving chair at his desk and sat with arms folded and legs crossed, facing his visitors.

'You're looking in very good fettle, sir, if I may say so,' began Cribb. 'I thought you might be laid up this morning, after Mrs Body's hospitality.'

'Not at all,' said the Major. 'Never had problems over liquor. Got a first-rate pick-me-up. Two-thirds brandy, one-third cayenne pepper. Strongly recommended.'

'I'll remember that. Good of you to receive us unexpected like this, even so. Major, you ain't a man to mince words and nor am I. May I put some blunt questions to you?'

'If you don't object to blunt answers.'

'Very good. Since we met at the Grampian on the night of Albert's accident, Thackeray and I

219

have seen you on four other occasions. We were led to understand at the Grampian that it was the manager there, Mr Goodly, who had engaged your services. Was that correct?'

'Absolutely.'

'You were there in a precautionary capacity, in addition to the usual police patrols?'

'Yes.'

'And you investigated the circumstances of Albert's accident, and traced him to Philbeach House?'

'Yes.'

'What happened after that, sir?'

'I was given the sack. I told Goodly what was happening at Philbeach House from my observations there, but once the blighter knew there wasn't likely to be another accident at the Grampian he didn't need my services any more. I was demobilised quicker than a coolie with cholera.'

'Yet you're keeping up your interest in the case,' said Cribb. 'Has anyone else engaged you?'

'No such luck,' said the Major. 'But if the Yard wants assistance, I'm open to offers.'

Cribb smiled. 'Well if no-one's paying you, where's the profit in continuing with your inquiries?'

'God, you've got a mercenary mind, Sergeant. Take a look in that corner behind you.'

Cribb glanced over his shoulder. Two piles of newspapers, painstakingly folded and stacked to a height of three or four feet, rested on a small table there.

'*The Times* and *The Morning Post*,' said the

Major. 'I'm a man of method, and when I planned to set myself up as a private investigator I went to see an old army colleague who had made something of a study of detective methods. "How do I start?" I said. "Study the personal columns every morning," he told me. So I have, for eight months. And you'd be surprised at the knowledge I've acquired, Sergeant. I know every patent remedy for rheumatism there is. I can tell you when your old boys' association are having their A.G.M. Interesting information, you understand, but it isn't yielding dividends yet.'

'You haven't had many matters to investigate, sir?'

'Two. The first was the whereabouts of the newspaper delivery boy the week he went down with mumps. The second was Mr Goodly's assignment. Now do you understand my reluctance to give up the case? I've had enough of reading newspapers. I want some action. And by Jove, this case is providing it! When I set up my campaign headquarters here I wasn't anticipating a murder inquiry.'

'Well, we've got one now, sir, and a very urgent inquiry it's become, as you'll no doubt appreciate.'

'Indeed I do! What's going to happen next Tuesday night at the Paragon if there's a murderer loose in the house? The consequences could be appalling! Dammit, Sergeant, I'm a commissioned officer . . . oath of loyalty and so forth. There was a time when I was determined to solve this case alone, but I know where my duty lies. I'm putting my resources at your disposal, gentlemen.'

'That's uncommon generous of you, Major,' said Cribb, entering into the spirit of the offer. 'Shall we discuss strategy at the table?'

Thackeray watched incredulously as the sergeant picked up a swagger-stick from the mantelpiece and approached the map of London in a business-like manner. Was he actually going to play soldiers with the Major? Maps and tactical discussions were about as relevant to Cribb's methods of detection as a manual of etiquette.

The Major provided more illumination by lighting a paraffin-lamp suspended over the table. Thackeray took up a position at Woolwich, where the Thames reached its limit.

'We shall need something to mark Philbeach House,' said Cribb. 'The stopper of that bottle on the shelf behind you, if you please, Thackeray.'

Major Chick held up a restraining hand. 'A most appropriate emblem, Sergeant, but I don't think Prussic Acid fumes would help our deliberations.'

'Prussic . . .?' Thackeray peered at the label on the bottle. 'That's what it says, Sarge.'

'There isn't much left,' said the Major, 'but enough to blight three promising careers if we stayed here long enough with the stopper out.'

'What do you keep it for?' asked Cribb, as casually as if he were inquiring about a household pet.

The Major slapped his thigh and laughed uproariously. 'You think that I . . .? Good Lord, I wouldn't keep the blasted bottle on my shelf if I had! No, Sergeant, I picked it up yesterday afternoon at Philbeach House. The late Mr Body was a bit of a scientist, you know. There's a roomful of his paraphernalia there, optical instruments, electrical dynamos, magnets, photographic apparatus and several shelves loaded with chemicals. This bottle was among 'em.'

'Available to any of the guests at Philbeach House?' queried Cribb.

'Readily available. The room wasn't locked.' The Major handed the bottle to Cribb. 'Scrutinise it carefully, Sergeant. Do you notice the lines that have formed on the inside, showing the various levels of the acid as it was used? Do you see how clear the glass is between the last mark and the small amount remaining? Must be three inches at least. That indicates to me that the last person to take acid from that bottle took a deuced large amount. I think this may be important evidence. Don't you agree?'

'It's a valuable find, Major,' said Cribb, 'and I'd like to express my gratitude to you for handing it over to the proper authorities in this way. We'll get someone at the Yard to test your theories about the encrustment on the inside. You've a decent-sized overcoat pocket, there, Thackeray. See if you can get it inside, will you? Did you pick up any other evidence, Major?'

If the Major had, he was not saying so.

'In that case, let's plan our troop emplacements,' continued Cribb, his object achieved. 'We'll use this halfpenny for Philbeach House. It seems to me that there are two points at which we should concentrate our forces.' He tapped the halfpenny and one of the champagne corks. 'Mrs Body's establishment, and Mr Plunkett's. Any comments, Major?'

'Seems reasonable,' said the Major, with a sniff.

'Good. Now it's sound strategy, I suggest, to dispose our forces according to the platoon strength. Wouldn't you agree, Major?'

A nod from the Major.

'So that the platoon with the greater number of personnel concentrates on the point on the map where the enemy are ranged in the greater strength.' Cribb tapped the halfpenny again.

'You and the constable go to Philbeach House. I take the Paragon,' said the Major.

'Thank you, sir. That's a handsome offer,' said Cribb, tucking the swagger-stick under his armpit. 'We're all in agreement, then. Any questions, gentlemen?'

'Yes,' said the Major. 'What shall I say to Plunkett?'

Cribb locked his hands behind his back and patrolled his side of the table, about-turning each time he reached the corner. It seemed to Thackeray that he was enjoying himself. 'It's the devil of an assignment, I know, Major, but I think you're the only man who can handle it. We need to discover whether there can possibly have been a reason for Plunkett murdering Miss Pinkus. Blackmail seems the likeliest motive, but we need facts. I suppose we can't rule out passion either. Unrequited love—'

'But you don't think Plunkett did it himself?' said the Major. 'It's obvious who murdered Miss Pinkus.'

'Who's that?'

'Mrs Body. Dammit, Sergeant, she had her husband's bottle of acid to hand. She detested Lola Pinkus; the girl was making life impossible at Philbeach House. Didn't you talk to Mrs Body? There were dreadful scenes. Open fights on occasions. Lola made trouble whenever she could, insulting the ladies and flirting with the men. She even set out to seduce poor old Virgo out of sheer malice — you know Mrs Body's sweet on Virgo, don't you?'

'No,' said Cribb. 'I didn't think Mrs B. was more partial to *one* man than any other.'

'Ah, there's a type she goes for,' said the Major affirmatively. 'She picks out the fellows with an obvious weakness, like an old lioness at the waterhole looking for a lame buffalo.'

Cribb shot a menacing look in Thackeray's direction, almost daring him to infer anything from the Major's remark. 'I suppose you mean that her late husband couldn't see without his spectacles and Professor Virgo has a stammer.'

'Exactly,' said Major Chick. 'She wasn't very interested in me when I tried the sentimental approach yesterday afternoon. Had to drink myself into a stupor before she'd even let me sit in her confounded box. It's the runt of the litter that lady fancies, I can tell you.'

'You were telling us why you suspect her,' Cribb reminded him acidly. 'You think she was jealous of Lola's friendship with Professor Virgo.'

'Lola did it out of spite, of course,' said the Major. 'She wasn't a bit interested in Virgo. Young Bellotti was far more attractive to a girl like that, but, you know, she took an impish pleasure in jilting him for the older man. She was tormenting Bellotti and Mrs Body at the same time, you see. Hussy like that doesn't get much sympathy from me when someone feeds poison to her.'

'How did Mrs Body manage to administer the poison when she wasn't even at the Paragon?' said Cribb.

'How do you know she wasn't there, Sergeant? You've got her word for it, and that's all. Everyone else was there, so there was nobody to provide an alibi for her at Philbeach House. I think she saw the others off in the bus and then took a cab to the theatre herself. She knew the order of the acts as well as Plunkett himself, so it was easy to judge the moment to transfer the acid to the tumbler. Poison's a woman's way, Sergeant.'

'I could name you a dozen men who swung for using it, Major,' said Cribb.

'Well, that's my opinion, blast it. Crime of passion. Why, you can't deny that Virgo's act was chosen for the murder. That's significant, in my view. Like taking revenge at the moment of unfaithfulness. These theatrical wallahs are apt to arrange things with an eye to dramatic effect, you know. That's their weakness.'

For a second, Cribb eyed the Major, standing over his map with the lamplight accentuating his features, like a tableau of Wellington on the eve of Waterloo. He passed no comment.

'All right, Sergeant. In spite of all my theories, you still want me to question Plunkett,' said the Major, in a resigned tone.

'You're quite a mind-reader, sir. Yes, it's a plausible case you've made out against Mrs Body, and you may be sure Thackeray and I will put some strong questions to the lady. I still want to know about Plunkett and his possible links with Miss Pinkus though. You'll have to put your questions delicately, of course.'

'I'll do the best I can. Shall I say I'm from the Yard? He doesn't know me, you see.'

'Better not, sir,' said Cribb hastily. 'It's never advisable to impersonate the police. I think you'll find him quite talkative if you lead him to believe you're acting in a legal capacity, trying to establish the beneficiaries of Miss Pinkus's estate.'

'Did she have one?'

'I doubt it, sir, but money talks with Mr Plunkett. He'll be ready to believe she left a fortune if you hint at it.'

'You're a shrewd old devil, Sergeant.'

'Thank you, Major. It's time we started though. May we rendezvous here again at two? Thank you. Thackeray, sound the advance, will you?'

FIFTEEN

Thackeray was dumbfounded. Not by the deception Cribb had practised on Major Chick; it was obvious (to a man of Thackeray's insight) that the elaborate charade in the Major's rooms was staged solely to get the Major to the Paragon. No surprise at all that when the Major had marched away on his mission and been swallowed by the fog, Cribb suggested a glass of ale at the nearest pub. And really to be expected that Cribb should then announce he had no intention of spending the rest of the morning at Philbeach House. Nor did Thackeray turn a whisker when the sergeant plunged into a two hour analysis of the whole inquiry, event by event, culminating, several glasses later, in a review of the murder suspects. Cribb didn't usually do such things, but the man was only human and probably wanted to try his theories on an intelligent ear. What finally shattered Thackeray's composure was the climax of Cribb's disquisition. As brisk and positive as a turnstile-man, the sergeant took the suspects one by one, examined them and allowed them to pass out of reckoning. One was left. Only one who could have murdered Lola Pinkus.

'I can't believe it, Sarge.'

'D'you mean I've been wasting my time?'

'Lord, no, it makes sense enough. Couldn't really have been anyone else from the start, though I didn't see it myself. It's the coolness of it that takes my breath away. Fancy thinking that by causing Lola's death . . . It's abominable, Sarge!'

'What murder isn't? There's no point in agitating yourself, Constable. If you want to fret about something, give a thought to next Tuesday night. That, at least, ought to be preventable, though I'm damned if I see how.'

'The Yard won't intervene, Sarge, and it's more than our jobs are worth to try and stop the show ourselves.'

Cribb took out his watch. 'Time we moved. Can't be late for our rendezvous with the Major. When we get there I want you to leave the talking to me and don't look surprised at anything I suggest. Got that?'

Thackeray sighed as he followed Cribb into the street. Was he really as transparent as that?

When they knocked, the Major flung open his door so abruptly that he must have been standing there waiting.

'We're not late, are we?' asked Cribb.

'Late? No, no. I got back early. Had time to mess out in Knightsbridge.' The Major pointed out the location on his map.

'Ah, well done. You concluded your interview with Plunkett quite quickly then.'

'Too blasted quickly. Had me guns spiked, in fact. The fellow wasn't prepared to talk at all. He was too damned worried about his daughter. Couldn't put his mind to anything, he said. She went to call on her young man yesterday — odd behaviour for any girl, in my view — and hasn't been heard of since.'

'Miss Blake?'

'No, Plunkett's daughter, I said.'

'But that *is* Miss Blake, Major. Ellen Blake, the friend of Albert, the strong man. She went to call on Albert at Philbeach House. I spoke to her myself. We must get over there at once! This is appalling. I hope to God it's not too late.'

Finding a four-wheeler in the fog was so unlikely that the detectives started out for Kensington Palace Gardens on foot, Cribb setting the pace at a brisk jog, the Major, light of step and obviously quite fit, matching his strides, while the third member of the party laboured to keep the others within earshot, privately cursing Cribb and his liquid lunches. For all that, he was not long in rejoining them when they reached Philbeach House, hats, coats and eyebrows white with freezing fog.

Cribb's knock was masterful. So was his entry, growling the word 'Police' as he shouldered aside the door and the ugly manservant and strode through the hall with the others at his heels.

'Who is there?' A woman's voice from the drawing-room. Not Mrs Body's.

They entered that eccentric room of faces. In

Mrs Body's chair, like a monstrous cuckoo, was Albert's mother.

'What's this — the police?' she boomed, so loudly that Beaconsfield, prone at her feet, opened one eye to survey them. 'I didn't send for the police.'

'Where's the lady of the house, Ma'am?' demanded Cribb.

'Are you being offensive?' asked Albert's mother, moving her hand to the bulldog's collar.

'Mrs Body. We must see Mrs Body.'

'*Must?*' repeated Albert's mother. 'That is no way to request an audience with a lady. She is unable to see you, anyway. She is indisposed. I have accordingly taken charge as housekeeper. I shall be writing to Sir Douglas—'

'Indisposed, you say. What's the matter with her?'

'She has an attack of the vapours and will not leave her room. Somebody had to take charge, so I—'

'The *vapours,*' said Cribb. 'Better get up there at once, Major! Thackeray, sound the gong in the hall. I want everyone out of their rooms and down here.' He turned back to Albert's mother, who was visibly outraged at such liberties. 'Your son, madam. He's in the house, I hope? I shall need to question him.'

'You have no authority—'

'Madam, I'm investigating one murder and trying to prevent another. I hope you wouldn't contemplate obstructing me in the execution of my duty. If it's authority that's wanted I'll remind you that I'm acting in the name of a lady with authority

231

extending a good deal further than yours or Mrs Body's — over an Empire, in fact.'

'Officer,' said Albert's mother, in a voice quaking with emotion, 'that gracious lady has no two subjects more loyal than Dizzie' — her palm sought the comfort of Beaconsfield's tongue — 'and me. If you had any knowledge at all of the halls you would know that our careers are *dedicated* to the red, white and blue. There is no need to remind us where our duty lies.'

'Thank you, Ma'am,' said Cribb tersely. 'Then you'll do that lady a very good service by helping to instil a co-operative spirit among the other guests when my constable has—'

Thackeray had found the gong, and was plainly infected by his sergeant's sense of urgency. Startled residents came running from many points in the house.

'In here, if you please,' called Cribb, when he could make himself heard. 'Is anyone out this morning?' he inquired of Albert's mother over the heads of those streaming in.

'We are all permanently at home. It is a rule of the house.'

Thackeray began to make a mental roll-call. Quite soon everyone he could recall having seen there before had crowded into the drawing-room, except Mrs Body. Albert, flushed from recent exercise and wearing a dressing-gown, was one of the first; he stayed near the door, away from his mother. Professor Virgo peered in and prepared to bolt away again, but Cribb extended an arm to him in a way that was part invitation, part coercion. Sam Fagan, Bellotti and the Undertakers arrived together, making their entrance with the aplomb of well-established residents. Soon it was impossible to keep a tally, for others, members of the Paragon chorus or orchestra perhaps, or servants, were entering through the second door. Bella Pinkus, in black crepe, came last, supported quite superflously by Miss Tring; Professor Virgo, twitching through the length of his body each time his eyes met anyone else's, looked far more ready to collapse.

'We'll give Mrs Body a few minutes,' Cribb announced.

'You can give her all day and next week as well, mate,' said Sam Fagan. 'A dinner-gong ain't going to fetch that one out, when she can get her food sent up in the lift. She's got no intention of coming down here. Been there since yesterday afternoon and refused to have anything to do with us. Fortunately for all of us we've got a new housekeeper now.'

The new housekeeper bestowed an unctuous smile on Sam Fagan. Albert glanced sharply at his mother and longer and more speculatively at Fagan. Thackeray felt a small rush of sympathy for the strong man.

The Major reappeared, shaking his head. Mrs Body would not be making an appearance. 'Can't get a word out of the woman,' he said, 'but I heard movements in there all right. Blasted place is built to withstand a siege. Only way of getting her out, in my opinion, is to send the bulldog up in the serving-lift.'

Albert's mother caught her breath in horror.

'Shame!' said Sam Fagan, a fraction too late to be convincing.

'Ladies and gentlemen,' announced Cribb, mounted suddenly on the very chair used by W. G. Ross when he sang the *Ballad of Sam Hall,* 'I'm most obliged to you for responding to my call so promptly. Many of you know that I am an officer in the Criminal Investigation Department of the Metropolitan Police. My assistants and I are making inquiries into the sudden decease — if you'll forgive me, Miss Pinkus — of one of your number. Now it's not my wish to alarm you, so I shall count it as a particular favour if you listen calmly to what I've got to say. We have reason to believe that a second young lady — not one of your company, I promise you — is in some danger.'

There were stifled gasps all round.

'The lady in question is Miss Blake, the daughter of Mr Sam Plunkett, known, I believe, to all of you as the manager of the Paragon music hall. Miss Blake visited this house yesterday afternoon and has not been seen since.'

There was a short interruption while Miss Tring, who had fainted in Bella's arms, was deposited in an arm-chair.

'Depend upon it, we shall spare no efforts in finding her,' continued Cribb, 'and I hope you will appreciate the necessity of what I have to tell you now — that I propose searching this house room by room. While my assistants are conducting the search I must insist that the rest of you remain here or in the rehearsal room next door. And with your further co-operation I should like to ask any lady or gentlemen who saw Miss Blake at any time yesterday or this morning to come forward and give me a full account of the circumstances. That is all I have to say for the present. Rest assured that my colleagues will show the utmost respect for your property. I hope we shall not inconvenience you very long.'

The impression Cribb's statement had made was clear from the din of excited — even hysterical — conversation that began before he stood down. Several ladies converged on him, not to give information about Miss Blake, but to seek it. He extricated himself at the first opportunity, sought out the Undertakers and asked them to stand guard at each door. Then he took Albert's arm and guided him outside and into the small waiting-room across the hall.

'I was watching you as I made my announcement in there,' Cribb said, when they were seated on either side of the table. 'You took the news of Miss Blake's disappearance most manfully.'

'That was because I knew of it already,' Albert said. 'Mr Plunkett was here before breakfast this morning, asking if we'd seen her. Mama and I were the only ones about at that time; I rise early for fitness, you see, and Mama was attending to the housekeeping arrangements. We didn't say anything to the other guests because they aren't aware that Ellen is Mr Plunkett's daughter. She is known here simply as Miss Blake. If they knew who she was, some of 'em might take it amiss, you see, Mr Plunkett holding the position he does.'

'You mean they could be jealous of you walking out with the manager's daughter?'

'Well, yes, except that walking out is the one thing nobody can do here.'

'Ah yes. Rules of the house.' Cribb took a turn round the small room and came to rest with his elbows on the chair where Ellen Blake had sat the previous afternoon. 'Well, they all know her identity now, thanks to my announcement. Unavoidable. There won't be bad feeling, will there?'

'Finding Ellen is more important to me than a pack of tongue-waggers.'

'Glad you think so, lad. Well let's concentrate on that. D'you think she's here somewhere?'

Albert shook his head. 'I showed her out myself yesterday at ten past four. She turned right at the gates as she usually does to walk to the cab-shelter in Kensington High Street. Ellen wouldn't have come back, Sergeant. I'm sure of that.'

'How long did she spend here?'

'Three-quarters of an hour, I should think. Mama was there as chaperon.'

'Can you recall your conversation with Miss Blake?'

Albert toyed reflectively with the ends of his moustache. 'We talked of my injury and I informed her that I was almost fully recovered. I told her of my training and my efforts to achieve a state of fitness in time for next Tuesday. That's an occasion I don't intend to miss, Sergeant. The honour, you understand.'

'You weren't at the Paragon last Tuesday then.'

'Why do you say that? No, I wasn't, Sergeant.

Mama went with Beaconsfield, but I remained here, taking hot baths to reduce the stiffness in my injured leg. Of course I heard the tragic news of Miss Lola's death when they all returned.'

'I see. You were telling me about Miss Blake, though. She was happy to see you fit again, I dare say?'

'Less happy than I expected,' said Albert, with a trace of chagrin. 'I've always cut a shine with the ladies, you know, having a well-developed torso, but I'm damned if I understand 'em. Last time Ellen came she was beside herself with concern for my injury. Advised me to take hot baths and brought some embrocation for me. Yesterday when I told her I was fully recovered and lifting, she refused to believe it. Told me I ought to get a doctor's opinion. I suppose she doesn't want me to come to grief a second time, but I told her there's no trace of pain in the leg.'

'Did you part on good terms?'

'Oh yes. You can ask Mama. We arranged that Ellen should come again next Friday. That's why I'm sure she didn't return.' He shuffled in his chair. 'How shall I put it? There's never been anything clandestine in my friendship with Ellen, Sergeant. She's a most high-minded young woman. Not at all the sort who'd linger in the road outside and then creep back in through a window, if that's what you suspect. It's unthinkable that she should spend a night away from home. I can understand the state her father's in. She won't even stay for dressing-room parties for fear of upsetting him by

237

being home late. It's a very good thing this has become a police matter, I assure you.'

'She didn't mention any other appointment when she was with you?'

'I understood she was going straight home, Sergeant. Of course if she did take it into her head to visit some aunt or cousin in the suburbs, the fog may have delayed her return. It was already coming down at ten o'clock last night.'

'I think she'd have started for home before then,' said Cribb. 'If there's nothing else of any significance I'll be obliged if you'll return to the others, then. I'll see your mother if you'll kindly invite her to step over.'

But it was not to be. The next person to enter, in a small flurry of black lace and tossing curls, was Mrs Body. The vapours had clearly intensified to a point where thunder was imminent. 'Mr Cribb! I propose to register the strongest possible protest at the manner in which I have been treated. Not content with hammering upon my door for a full five minutes, you sink to the shabbiest of stratagems to evict me, a poor wilting woman, from my bed. A bouquet, the voice assured me, a dozen red roses, freshly purchased from the florist outside Paradise Street Police Station, at the express instructions of a detective sergeant who wished to remain anonymous. But when I unbolted my door and opened it, I was brushed aside by that bearded barbarian who accompanies you. There was not a rose to be seen. And when I taxed him with ungentlemanly conduct do you know what he told me?'

'I've no idea, Ma'am.'

'He was sorry but it was his job to *winkle* me out. Well, Mr Cribb, winkled out I may have been, but I am not the defenceless widow you take me for. The Home Secretary shall hear of this!'

'It was unforgivable, Ma'am,' said Cribb. 'You mean that he didn't deliver those roses? That constable shall answer for this.' On an impulse he thrust his hand into his jacket pocket and pulled out a rather tired yellow bloom. 'In the meantime, if I may be so bold . . .'

Mrs Body melted. 'Mr Cribb, I hadn't realised. I was disposed to think after yesterday . . . Oh, you gallant man!'

It is likely that the sergeant would have found himself embosomed in black lace if Albert's mother had not chosen that instant to enter.

'What do you want?' demanded Mrs Body.

'I had an appointment with the sergeant. You seem to have made a spectacular recovery, my dear. Shall I withdraw?'

'No, no,' Cribb hastened to say. 'Mrs Body was merely inquiring about the search. Now that her rooms have been seen she must get back to bed. Can't take a chance with the vapours.'

With a simper and a sigh Mrs Body pulled her peignoir about her and withdrew. Cribb closed the door after her and stood with his back resting against it for several seconds.

'It's a scandal,' said Albert's mother, depositing Beaconsfield on a chair.

'What's that, Ma'am?'

'Why, that bold-faced hussy masquerading as

housekeeper. She has no notion at all how to cater for people of taste. She is a charlatan, Sergeant. If the owner of this house knew what was going on here in his name, she would soon be back on the streets where she belongs. The vapours! Did she look as though there was the *least* thing wrong with her?'

'Perhaps she was a trifle feverish,' said Cribb.

'Over-rouged. She's no more ill than you or I. Her curiosity got the better of her when she heard the commotion downstairs. Now that she's satisfied, she won't be down again for days. I shall be obliged to carry out her duties.'

'That's very handsome of you, Ma'am. Must be appreciated by the other residents. But the experience won't be wasted, I dare say.'

'What do you mean?'

'Well, Ma'am, I was reflecting that if Mrs Body lost her position for any reason, and you were carrying out the duties so capably — as Mr Fagan appeared to imply — it would seem prudent on the part of Sir Douglas Butterleigh to offer you the position.'

'Really?' Albert's mother beamed altruistically at Cribb. 'The thought had not occurred to me. But there must come a time, of course, when I shall have to consider retiring from the boards. A widowed woman must think of her future.'

'Naturally,' said Cribb. 'Come to think of it, Mr Plunkett might be disposed to put in a word on your behalf. That's if his daughter hasn't come to any harm, of course. You saw Miss Blake when she visited Albert yesterday, I believe?'

Albert's mother blinked at the sudden swerve in the conversation. 'Er — yes, I did.'

'She seemed quite well, did she?'

'Oh yes. She is quite attached to my Albert, I fancy.'

'Sounds like it, Ma'am. She's shown a lot of concern about his injury, I understand, bringing him embrocation and the like.'

'That's quite correct, Sergeant. Miss Blake will make a very agreeable wife, don't you think?'

'If she's still alive, Ma'am,' said Cribb. 'Did you hear her say anything that might help us to find her — whether she had anyone else to visit, for example?'

'I'm afraid I can't help at all. The two young people met in the drawing-room, and you know how large that is. I was there as chaperon — a rule of the house — and I remained at the opposite end, out of earshot, mending a pair of Albert's tights. One observes decorum, but one tries not to intrude, you understand. The only words I heard from Miss Blake were the formalities at the beginning and end of the visit. She left soon after four o'clock. You don't really believe this is connected with the death of Lola Pinkus, do you?'

'Why shouldn't I?' asked Cribb.

'Lola was a totally different class of person, as brazen as any I've met on the halls, Sergeant. As a cheap figurante, I've no doubt she performed a useful function, but she was good for nothing else. Her behaviour here was unpardonable. You could tell the Sergeant, couldn't you, Dizzie?'

241

Beaconsfield, panting rhythmically on his chair, almost appeared to nod.

'I expect you're referring to the incident with the meringue, Ma'am,' ventured Cribb.

'You heard about that? She was a Jezebel, Sergeant,' continued Albert's mother, inspired to more vituperative flights, 'a mischief-maker and a trifler with men's affections, too. Oh, I've a lot of sympathy for the poor wretch who took it upon himself to put an end to that young woman's capers.'

Cribb got up to answer a tap on the door. Thackeray and Major Chick were there. From the state of their clothes the search had left nothing unturned.

'We've been right through the house, Sarge. Basement to attic, including Mrs Body's rooms.'

'So I understand.'

'And the outbuildings. We found no-one, Sarge. I'm sure she ain't here.'

'No evidence of recent digging in the garden, either, so far as I could make out in the blasted fog,' said the Major, ruefully.

'But I told you that she left here yesterday afternoon,' insisted Albert's mother. 'If you would listen—'

She was interrupted by a loud ringing at the front door.

'Answer that, Thackeray,' ordered Cribb. He asked the Major to escort Albert's mother back to the drawing-room.

The visitor was Plunkett, ashen-faced. He sank into a chair without removing his coat.

'What can we do for you, sir?' asked Cribb.

'I must speak to Albert, the strong man — in private. It is a matter of the gravest urgency.'

'The gravest urgency?' Cribb tucked his thumbs into his waistcoat pockets in the manner of a farmer assessing a pen of sheep. 'What would that be, then — something pertaining to your daughter's disappearance?'

'It's no concern of yours.'

Cribb shook his head slowly. 'This time it is, sir. You can see Albert if you wish, but I'll be present, and Constable Thackeray. I've reason to believe what's happened to your daughter is closely connected with the case I'm conducting at present, into the death of Miss Lola Pinkus.'

Plunkett started at the name. 'What? You believe that the murderer of that girl—'

'I believe it so strongly, Mr Plunkett, that I demand to hear what you've got to say to Albert, and I don't mind if you protest to my Inspector or the Chief Superintendent or the Director of Criminal Investigations himself. Charitable peep-shows may be out of the law's reach, but killers of young women are not. Fetch Albert,' he told Thackeray, 'and keep all the others out, including the Major.'

Plunkett wheeled round in his chair as though to stop Thackeray, but found no words. Instead, he turned back to the table and slumped over it, his fingers clawing at his hair.

'I won't mince words,' said Cribb. 'I've little sympathy for you, Mr Plunkett. I went to a deal of trouble to learn about the methods you employ to stock your music hall with performers. In the end I got enough to paper the walls of the Paragon with charge-sheets. But, by God, those walls are protected, aren't they? All I got for my trouble was a sizeable flea in my ear from Scotland Yard. But it's a queer sort of world, ain't it? You're going to have my help in finding your daughter, whether you want it or not. Now that's altruism, ain't it? Better not waste any more time, then. It's a letter you've got, is it?'

A murmur from Plunkett confirmed that it was.

Thackeray returned with Albert, clearly nervous at the prospect of a second interrogation. He and Plunkett exchanged nods.

'Now, sir,' said Cribb.

Plunkett swore violently, more at his own predicament than Cribb's intransigence. Then he took a letter from his breast-pocket. 'This came by the second post. You had better read it.' After a pause, he added, 'All of you.'

Albert spread the two sheets of writing-paper on the table so that their contents were clear to all:

Friday

My dearest Papa,

—By now you will know that after my visit to Albert this afternoon I did not reach home. The reason is that I have been abducted and am being held captive until arrangements can be made for my release. I want to assure you, Papa, that I am unharmed so far, and have been treated with civility. As proof, I am permitted to write this letter to you, sections of which I am allowed to say will be dictated for me to write in my own

244

hand. A lock of my hair is to be included with the letter as further evidence of my identity.

My safe release rests with you. If you wish me returned unharmed, you must follow meticulously the instructions I give you.

You are to place five hundred pounds in used bank-notes of any denomination in a leather valise. At a quarter to midnight tonight, after the house at the Paragon has dispersed, no doors are to be bolted. The valise is to be carried to the centre of the stage by Albert (this is at my suggestion, for I fear for your heart), who must gain leave from Philbeach House on some pretext. You are to arrange for a beam of limelight from the wings to illuminate the place where Albert is to leave the valise, but the rest of the hall must be in darkness, and *no person other than Albert is to be in the building*. When he has placed it in position he is to withdraw and return to Philbeach House. The money will be collected, taken away and counted, and if all is in order I shall be released within the hour, to meet you outside the Paragon at the main entrance. Any failure in carrying out these instructions, or any attempt to communicate with the police, or to try to follow the person who collects the money, will have consequences which must cause you lasting distress. I repeat that no-one but the courier (Albert) is to be inside the hall. The night-watchman is to be instructed to lock the doors at one o'clock, by which time,

God willing, I shall be restored to you. Please do not fail me, Papa. I am mortally afraid.

> Your ever-loving,
> Ellen

'You see now why I couldn't tell you about the letter,' said Plunkett. 'Already I may have condemned my daughter to death. Oh, God, have I done that?'

'I doubt it, sir,' said Cribb. 'No-one outside this house knows the Yard is here. We came on foot, you see, through the fog. The four of us in this room are the only living souls who know of this meeting.'

'Well, what am I to do?' Plunkett appealed.

'What were you planning to do, sir?'

'Precisely what they want. Heavens, my daughter's worth five hundred to me! I was coming to tell Albert about his part in the proceedings.'

'Well, Albert,' said Cribb. 'Are you game?'

The strong man's chin tilted to its most intrepid angle. 'I'll do whatever I can to help Ellen, Sergeant.'

'Good man. Do you have this amount of money, Mr Plunkett?'

'I've several hundred in the safe. After tonight's performance I'll have enough.'

'Capital. I'll provide the valise,' said Cribb, 'and then we'll all have made a contribution. Oh, and one more thing, Albert. I'd like to borrow Beaconsfield. He'll come to no harm, but we won't alarm your mother, eh? Tell her you're both required by Mr Plunkett for a secret rehearsal for next Tuesday.'

'He's not a very good guard-dog, Sergeant.'

'He'll do for my purposes,' said Cribb.

SIXTEEN

Several times that evening, as they sat in the pit at the Paragon, Thackeray found himself speculating on the strategy of his sergeant. Was it really necessary to their investigation to spend three hours watching the entire bill, including every turn they had seen the previous Tuesday? It would go into the report, he supposed, as 'The proceedings were kept under continuous observation': justification enough for studying the chorus-line through opera glasses, but questionable as an explanation of Cribb's lusty singing of the chorus of *Slap Bang, Here we are Again.*

For Thackeray himself, the evening was an ordeal. Music hall had never held much appeal for him, but until the present inquiry he had at least been able to sit through an assorted programme of clog-dancing, contortionists, serio comics and buffo vocalists without intimations of distress. This evening he found that certain turns, the monologist and the ballet, revived sensations of acute embarrassment, while throughout the rest of the bill he could not forbear from gripping the edge of his seat in anticipation of some fresh calamity. It would be a long time before he would voluntarily enter a music hall again.

Mercifully the moment arrived, soon before eleven, when the patrons rose, swaying, to render the final chorus, the National Anthem, before streaming to the exits and the public houses. This was the hour when lady promenaders still without an escort cast about in desperation, and might even settle on a middle-aged detective constable with symptoms of nervous exhaustion. He was glad to follow Cribb's rapid movement to the vestibule. Was this to be some rendezvous with Plunkett to arrange a secret vantage-point from which to witness the collecting of the ransom? No. Cribb's object was to secure a penny copy of *Slap Bang, Here we are Again*.

They had not seen Plunkett during the performance, but that was not surprising. Forward-looking halls like the Paragon had dispensed with the chairman seated among the audience; he was part of the tradition of sanded floors and spittoons that had until quite recently limited the patronage to the lower levels of society. Instead, he was positioned prominently in the vestibule, beside a bill advertising the following Tuesday's entertainment, raising his silk hat assiduously to the classes of customer he wished to encourage. The small army of vendors of pies, nuts, oranges and matches had been persuaded to mount their attack on the steps outside, so that an air of refinement was preserved within.

'Come along,' said Cribb, tucking his song-sheet

into an inside pocket. 'We don't want to be left here.'

Thackeray frowned. His impression was that the reason for attending the music hall was to be installed there when the hand-over of the five hundred pounds took place. With a nod in Plunkett's direction, he followed Cribb between the groups making their farewells under the portico, past the line of cabs outside and into the enveloping fog. In the thick of the dispersing audience he had to keep a sharp eye on the sergeant's bowler ahead. He only hoped Cribb planned an arrest inside the hall. In these conditions pursuit through the streets would be next to impossible. He pulled his muffler over his mouth and caught up with Cribb at the next street lamp.

Some fifty yards along Victoria Street they turned into a public house almost as dense with tobacco-smoke as the fog outside. Saturday night was being celebrated in style around the piano, and in the skittle-alley in the cellars below, from the rumpus penetrating upwards.

'What's your tipple?' Cribb asked.

'The usual, if you please, Sarge.'

'Three pints of East India, landlord. Did my friend arrive?'

'Waitin' in the back room, guv. Over there behind the money-changin' machines.'

They discovered Albert seated in isolation in the intimacy of the private room, beneath a framed text reading, *Women and wine should life employ. Is there aught else on earth desirous?* A vase of chrysanthemums had been provided on the table.

'Good. You're quite ready then. Where's the dog?' said Cribb all in one breath, as he placed the drinks on the table.

'Beaconsfield? He's tied up in the yard,' said Albert. 'The landlord wouldn't allow him in. Said the customers mightn't take kindly to a dog barking. Have you ever heard Beaconsfield bark, Sergeant? There's ten or more brats in that public bar squawking fit to deafen you, and poor old Beaconsfield has to sit out there in the fog. He didn't think much of that, I can tell you. I just hope nobody trips over him.'

'Are you still quite prepared to go through with this?'

Albert seemed surprised at the question. 'Naturally. I've given my word. There's no danger, is there? You will be watching from somewhere, won't you?'

'Not exactly,' said Cribb. 'We can't afford to take risks where Miss Blake's concerned, can we? Best carry out the instructions implicitly. We'll be outside the hall.'

'Outside?'

'We won't be spotted in the fog, you see. Now are you quite clear about your part in the proceedings?'

Half an hour later they collected the shivering bulldog and made their way back towards the Paragon. The lights at the front and in the foyer had been turned off. The last of the street-vendors had left.

Plunkett was waiting for them in a shop doorway opposite, valise in hand. The genial mask of an hour before had vanished; lines of anxiety creased his face.

'Capital show tonight, Mr Plunkett,' said Cribb, with the warmth of a genuine enthusiast.

'What? Oh, yes.'

'The money's all in the bag, is it? No mistake?'

'I checked it twice. And I've left the single lime-light on in the hall.'

'Very good, sir. Let's look at the time, then. Three minutes to go, according to me.'

Plunkett was peering hard into the fog. 'Where are the others, then?'

'The others?' queried Cribb.

'The uniformed police. I thought you'd have the hall surrounded.'

Cribb shook his head. 'Wouldn't be wise, sir. Might put our kidnapper off. Now I'd like you to do one more thing for me, Mr Plunkett. This poor perishing animal plainly wants a brisk walk round the streets. Would you do it that kindness, sir? By the time you come back, Albert should have done his job and we won't have long to wait for your daughter.'

Beaconsfield's short leash was put into Plunkett's hand. Before he had time to protest, the manager's arm was yanked in the direction of the next street-lamp.

'We shall require the bag, sir,' Cribb reminded Plunkett. He dropped it for the sergeant to retrieve before Beaconsfield hauled him away.

'Sixteen minutes to midnight, Albert,' said Cribb, handing him the valise.

'Are there *really* no policemen about?'

'Thackeray and me. How many more d'you want? We've got to think of Miss Blake, Albert. What was that phrase in the letter? "Lasting distress." Sounded ugly to me. On your way, lad.'

The strong man nodded manfully, took a deep breath, crossed the road and disappeared into the Paragon.

'It shouldn't take him long, Sarge, should it?' inquired Thackeray, feeling an upsurge of sympathy for the young man. The prospect of venturing into that darkened hall would have made an experienced constable hesitate.

'Ten minutes,' said Cribb. 'It just occured to me, though, that Albert's the only one of us who's never set foot in the Paragon before. It'd be a crying shame if he lost his way. We'll give him fifteen minutes and then you can go in after him.'

But there was no need. In a very short time the strong man emerged looking distinctly happier. 'I put the bag exactly in the centre,' he told them. 'Shall we see Ellen soon?'

'Quite soon, if the letter's anything to go by,' said Cribb. 'Did you hear any movements in there?'

'No. It was perfectly quiet, but I had a strong impression I was not alone.'

'I hope you weren't,' said Cribb, 'or we're all wasting our time.'

The three of them lapsed into silence, all attention directed to the double doors across the road. Their line of vision was intermittently blocked by nocturnal traffic, cabs mostly, with bells jingling, a few late omnibuses and one police van, the horse led by a safety-conscious constable, lamp in hand.

Cribb touched Thackeray's arm. 'That figure, approaching from the right. Watch.'

It was devilish difficult identifying anything at all in the conditions. Thackeray squinted in the general direction, watching for some movement. Sure enough, a figure in a long coat, muffled to the eyes, passed in front of the lighted confectioner's. Was there a certain stealth about the walk, a hunching of the shoulders, or was that the wishful thinking of a constable desirous of a quick arrest and back to Paradise Street for cocoa? Ah! No question about it: the fellow had mounted the steps of the Paragon and was at the doors trying the handle.

'Grab him, Thackeray!'

Action at last! No time to look out for traffic. Just a dash across the street, arms going like piston-rods, footfalls oddly muffled in the fog.

The suspect had no chance at all. One second he was stepping cautiously into the darkened vestibule, the next hauled out again, his arm locked agonisingly behind his back, a nutmeg-grater of a beard thrust against his cheek and neck.

'Let's have a look at you then,' panted Thackeray, yanking away the rest of the muffler. 'Blimey! Not you!'

'Pursuing my lawful occupation,' groaned Major Chick. 'Let go, man. You're breaking my blasted arm!'

'Not till I've got you across the road.'

'Neat work, Constable,' said Cribb, when Thackeray had brought his prisoner to the shop-entrance. 'Better let go now. Well, Major, what are you doing out in weather like this?'

The Major massaged his arm. 'Following a suspicious person, dammit. Trailed the blighter all the way from Kensington and then lost him up the street there. Didn't need much deduction to tell me he was making for the Paragon, though. I see you've apprehended him, Sergeant.'

Cribb gave a contemptuous sniff. 'Albert? He's assisting us. And *you* precious near sprung the trap, Major. I might have known we couldn't throw you off as easy as that.'

'I think he's got a firearm in his pocket, Sarge,' cautioned Thackeray. 'I felt it as we crossed the road.'

'You're a bit late in telling me,' snapped Cribb. 'He could have filled the three of us with lead by now, if he'd a mind to.'

'Well, Sarge, seeing as you told me you don't suspect the Major . . .'

'That's irrelevant. I could have been wrong. I'll trouble you for that gun just the same, Major. This ain't the weather for shooting-practice.'

Major Chick delved into his pocket. 'Merely a pair of opera-glasses, Sergeant. A present from Mrs Body. You can take them if you like, but they're no damned use at all in the fog.'

Cribb glared at Thackeray, but immediately wheeled round at the sound of footsteps accompanied by the most stertorous breathing imaginable. Beaconsfield had brought back Mr Plunkett.

'Have you been in there?' the manager anxiously asked Albert.

255

'Yes, sir. I carried out the instructions absolutely.'

Plunkett turned to Cribb. 'What now, then? Can we all go in?'

Cribb shook his head. 'That wouldn't do at all, sir. We're working to the arrangements in the letter, if you remember. Let me take the dog now, and you can wait for your daughter across the road. Don't go inside, mind. We'll watch from here.'

As Plunkett obeyed, it took all Cribb's strength to keep Beaconsfield from following. The animal seemed to sense the drama ahead.

For more than fifteen minutes the only action was Plunkett's nervous pacing back and forth along the steps of his music hall. Even the traffic had come to a halt.

Then he paused, rubbed at the glass on one of the doors, and put his face to it. He opened it and someone came out and fell into his arms, weeping. A mass of flaxen curls nestled on his shoulder.

'Ellen!' shouted Albert and sprinted across the road, with the others at his heels.

'Are you quite unhurt?' her father was asking. 'Are you safe, Ellen?'

'Quite safe now, Papa dear.' She lifted her face, cruelly strained by her experience. She smiled through her tears at Albert. 'When they had counted the money, they got out through the prop-room window. There was a carriage waiting there.'

'Escaped!' declared the Major.

'Who were they?' asked Cribb.

'I still don't know. A man and a woman. They

kept me in darkness all the time, blindfolding me when they wanted to move me. They gave me a light to write the letter and that was all. Even then they stood behind me, out of sight.'

'You've no idea where you were kept?'

'It cannot have been more than a mile from here, Sergeant, allowing for the time the carriage took. I think I was in a cellar of some description. They didn't ill-treat me, but I was so terrified, Papa. Please take me home now.'

'Try to help the Sergeant, Ellen,' Plunkett appealed. 'Did you recognise either of their voices?'

'I couldn't, Papa, except to say that one was a woman.'

'Sergeant,' said Major Chick suddenly, 'can you hear anything?'

'What do you mean?'

'From inside the hall.' The Major pushed open the door. 'Curious sort of smell, too. I'm going to look inside.'

'Go with him, Thackeray.'

They crossed the vestibule together. The noise was clearer there, and certainly coming from the hall itself. To Thackeray it sounded like someone trying to wrap a small present in a huge sheet of brown paper. He opened the door leading to the hall. Smoke billowed out.

'My God! The place is on fire!'

Like the monstrous creation of some demented scene-designer, the stage was ablaze from end to end. Huge yellow flames leapt to the full height of the proscenium, achieving a brilliance quite beyond the powers of gas and lime. One of the main curtains crashed downwards in a shower of sparks.

'My hall!' shouted Plunkett, suddenly with them.

'The Major's gone to sound the street fire alarm at the corner,' said Cribb from behind. 'There's nothing you or I can do with a fire like this, sir. It's a job for Captain Shaw and his men. Albert's clearing the buildings on each side. Come away, sir. We'll meet the Brigade at the door.'

They persuaded the manager to sit on the marble steps, with Ellen comforting him. 'Next Tuesday would have been the greatest honour of my life,' he was moaning. 'To have that snatched away like this — it's unendurable. Who could have done this to me?'

'It must have been the limelight, Papa. It was unattended for so long. You've always said they are dangerous. There was probably an explosion in the limetank.'

Albert rejoined them. 'There's nobody in either of the adjoining buildings, Sergeant. There shouldn't be any casualties, even if there's a lot of damage to property. You're quite sure there's no one in the Paragon, Mr Plunkett? It's a large building and — ' He stopped and turned to Cribb. 'What's happened to Beaconsfield?'

The sergeant was dangling the leash absent-mindedly in one hand. 'The dog?' He glanced into the vestibule, thick with smoke. 'He shouldn't be long.'

Albert turned on Cribb in horror. 'He's in there, you mean? You let him go into that inferno?'

'It was before we knew the place was on fire —

when Miss Blake came out, in fact. He was curious to have a look inside so I slipped him off the leash.'

'That doesn't sound like Beaconsfield to me,' said Albert bitterly. 'Poor old animal must have been burned alive. How shall I tell Mama? She'll call you every name she can lay her tongue to.'

'You can tell her he was assisting the police in the execution of their duty,' said Cribb starchily. 'Just a moment. Take a look through here.'

He pulled the double doors fully open. Through the suffocating smoke wreathing hideously ahead of them it was just possible to distinguish something small and white coming towards them in jerking movements. Beaconsfield's rump. He was struggling heroically to drag something held firmly between his jaws. Cribb ran to assist him. Man and dog gripped the valise together and brought it to the steps outside.

'Well done, Beaconsfield! A trifle singed about the ears, and in need of a good bath, but none the worse for your escapade.' Cribb opened the valise, brought out something and handed it to the grateful bulldog. 'Aniseed. A powerful attraction to any of the canine species, even a lethargic old beast like this one. Now what's this also in the bag? A monkey, Mr Plunkett. In other words, your five hundred.'

Plunkett shook his head in bewilderment. 'But I thought the man and woman who kidnapped Ellen had taken it.'

Cribb patted Beaconsfield's back. 'And but for the efforts of my slightly scorched assistant here, I'd have found it difficult to prove they hadn't.'

'But why did they go to so much trouble if they didn't take the money, for God's sake?'

Cribb opened his hands like a conjurer at the end of a trick. 'Because they never existed. Your daughter, Miss Blake, invented 'em, didn't you, Miss? Nobody kidnapped her. She's been as free as you or I this twenty-four hours. Wrote that letter in some comfortable lodging-house, I dare say.'

Ellen Blake plunged her face into her hands.

'That's an infamous suggestion!' said Plunkett to Cribb. 'Why should Ellen do a thing like that to me?'

'That's a question only the lady can answer, sir, but I fancy it has something to do with Albert.'

'Me, Sergeant?'

'You see what she's achieved, gentlemen: the Paragon in flames and likely to be gutted unless the Brigade gets here soon, Tuesday's performance cancelled and Albert's honour saved. If I weren't about to arrest her she'd be making plans to marry you, I reckon, Albert.'

'Arrest Ellen? On what charge, for Heaven's sake?'

'Take your choice, sir. Obtaining money by false pretences. Arson. Or murder. The murder of Miss Lola Pinkus by administering poison. I've got a police van waiting at the end of the road, Miss, and I'll be obliged if you'll accompany me to the nearest police station.'

Plunkett placed an arm protectively in front of his daughter. 'This is madness, Sergeant. I'll have you cashiered. I've got friends at Scotland Yard,

260

you know. You can't make accusations like this without—'

For the first time, Ellen spoke, in a voice of studied calm. 'Father, at least do me the kindness of letting me face what is to come with dignity. Can't you see that your intrigues brought me to this? I want no more of them. Stay here and watch your music hall burn, and pray that the flames will purify your soul. Albert, my dearest, my poor innocent, if you ever come to understand my actions, believe that there was nothing you could have done to alter them. You will visit me if they allow it, won't you? I can hear the fire-engine, Sergeant. I am ready to go with you.'

'I have been perusing your report, Sergeant,' said Inspector Jowett at the Yard the following Monday. 'Miss Blake has made a full confession, you say?'

'That's correct, sir. Appendix One.'

'Ah yes. What makes a young woman as vicious as that, do you think?'

'A strong streak of Puritanism,' said Cribb. 'And infatuation for a young man. A powerful combination, sir.'

'Puritanism — in a music hall singer?'

'Her songs were strictly respectable, sir. She disapproved most strongly of the ditties they sang at the midnight shows. And she took a pretty poor view of her father's method of recruiting performers.'

'The accidents?'

'Yes. When an accident was planned for the hall

where Albert was appearing she became most upset. Didn't want the young man she admired to come to grief, you see, so she sent an anonymous message to us.'

'Thinking that the police would prevent the accident?'

'Possibly, sir. We'd be on the stage as soon as it happened, at any rate, and so we were. That's when we first met the young woman. Later, when we'd tracked Albert to Philbeach House and found the connexion with the Paragon she did a queer thing, sir.'

'What was that?'

'She knew we were police officers when she sold us tickets for the show — the regular show, not the midnight one. But she didn't warn her father who we were. And she actually offered to take us behind the scenes, and left us there to go off to her turn at the Grampian. That was almost like throwing a clue in our faces, sir. Naturally we looked about a bit and discovered Bellotti's barrels, the second positive link with Philbeach House. We'd seen Beaconsfield's basket arrive when we bought the tickets, if you remember. That was when I first began to be suspicious about Miss Blake. It was plain from her conversation that night that she disapproved strongly of her father.'

'But you didn't realise then, presumably, that she would come back from the Grampian to the midnight music hall to poison Miss Pinkus.'

'No, sir,' said Cribb. 'But she could do it in plenty of time. She could pass unnoticed in the Paragon, as long as she kept out of her father's way. She took the acid kept for fumigating the hall and tipped enough into the glass to kill Lola.'

'Whatever for, though? Where was the motive, Sergeant?'

'Lola meant nothing to Ellen Blake, it's true, except as a possible rival for Albert's affections, remembering that Lola was inclined to be flirtatious, sir. I think by this time Miss Blake was desperate to save Albert's reputation. It was likely to be her last chance to do something that would close the hall. A sudden death — whether it was diagnosed as an accident or suicide or even murder — seemed the best plan. She had the deadly poison available, and this suggested the method to her. There was only one act in which she could use it and that was the magician's. So Lola had to be the victim. Cold logic. There's the single-minded way of the murderess, sir. The despatching of one vulgar little showgirl was nothing compared with the sullying of Albert's reputation. Ellen Blake was a fanatic, you see. She had to deter Plunkett from going on with his show, and violence was the likeliest way of stopping him. What she hadn't reckoned with was the er — over-riding reason why next Tuesday's performance had to go on.'

'We won't go into that again,' said Jowett, shifting in his chair. 'I recall that I sent you to Philbeach House to investigate the death. What did you discover there?'

'Enough to eliminate several other suspects, sir. Albert's mother I knew couldn't have administered the poison, because she was already up in her balloon when the conjurer's table was brought to the wings. Albert and Mrs Body were keeping each other company at Philbeach House that evening, so I doubted whether either of 'em could escape the other to get over to Victoria. The Major was playing in the orchestra, where I kept an eye on him. That left me with Plunkett and Miss Blake, and I couldn't see Plunkett killing the girl in his own hall, even if he had a motive. It would have put everything at risk.'

'So you reasoned that Miss Blake was your murderess.'

'No doubt about it, sir. I needed evidence, though, and I couldn't get that without visiting the Paragon again to question her. That would have been contrary to orders, sir. I'm no fool.'

'I know that, Sergeant.'

'I reckoned that as soon as Miss Blake thought the pack was on the scent, she'd make a break for freedom. Ten to one she'd run to Albert first, and I'd be waiting there at Philbeach House to meet her.'

'*That* was why you sent the Major to question Plunkett — merely to strike panic into his daughter so that she'd run into your trap.'

'That's right, sir, but she'd already gone when he got there. Outsmarted us. I feared at first that she'd got clean away on the night train to Dover and was already in France. My only recourse was to get to Philbeach House at once and see if Albert was still there. Oddly enough, he was, and he hadn't seen hide nor hair of the young woman. It was quite a relief when Plunkett arrived there with the ransom-note, I can tell you. I knew when I saw it that she'd devised a plan to draw suspicion away from herself. At the same time she was making Albert the instrument of her rescue, and a hero in her father's eyes. She was going to hide the ransom-money in the Paragon and later use it to give Albert the wherewithal to quit Philbeach House and marry her.'

'So you decided to allow the ransom to be collected.'

'Yes, sir. But I smeared the valise with aniseed and put some more inside and employed Beaconsfield to sniff it out. I didn't allow for the fire, though.'

'Did she set the hall ablaze deliberately?'

'Yes sir. The firing of the Paragon answered her purposes better than the original plan, you see. Albert would be saved from performing next Tuesday, the valise would be destroyed in the blaze, so that she could say it was taken by the kidnappers, and her father couldn't put on any more vulgar shows. Five hundred of his money wasn't much to go up in smoke in the cause of decency. Fortunately, the bulldog did its work well and rescued the lot. That's a ridiculous animal, that Beaconsfield, but I've a certain regard for it. When I saw smoke coming out of the hall I was almost more concerned about the dog than the evidence.'

Jowett rose, came round the desk and put a hand on Cribb's arm, a most uncharacteristic display of warmth. It would have made anyone suspicious. 'You're a sentimental fellow at heart, I do believe, Sergeant. You've done well, though. First class investigation. Won't be forgotten.'

'Thank you, sir.'

'There's one thing I ought to mention, though. A case like this one has ramifications in other places, you know. Those little entertainments at the Paragon had quite a following in certain circles.'

'I'm aware of that, sir.'

'Splendid. Then you'll understand the disappointment that's going to be felt at the cancellation of next Tuesday's performance. Ah' — Inspector Jowett raised his hand to silence Cribb before he could utter a word — 'I know the burning of the Paragon wasn't your fault. How could you have anticipated such a catastrophe? But I rather fear, even so, that when certain patrons of the midnight shows read their newspapers they will mistakenly assume that you stood by while the hall burned down.'

'I sent for the Brigade at once, sir,' protested Cribb.

'Quite so, Sergeant. Exemplary conduct on your part throughout the investigation. No fault of yours that the place is now a charred ruin. I stand firm on that point, whatever anyone else might suggest. But you do appreciate, I hope, that the Yard wouldn't want to over-emphasise its part in these events.'

Cribb gave a qualified nod.

'In short, Sergeant, I advised the gentlemen of the Press, when they called, that the apprehension of Miss Blake and, indeed the initiative throughout this investigation must be credited to that private detective, the military chappie, er—'

'Major Chick.'

'The very man. *The Times* wrote an excellent piece on him for this morning's edition. Have you seen it yet? He was, after all, closely concerned in all the events you describe in your report. A notice like that should help his practice immeasurably.'

'I don't doubt it, sir.'

'That's not to say your part in the investigation will go unnoticed, of course. Heavens, yes, we like to give praise where it's due, and that's why I called you in, Sergeant. If you never hear another word from this office about your sterling work, don't imagine that I've simply locked your report in a drawer and forgotten about it, will you? As a matter of fact, the Yard has decided to show its recognition of your admirable handling of this delicate affair.'

'Thank you, sir.'

Jowett opened a drawer in his desk. 'The public sometimes send tokens of appreciation to the Yard for our handling of difficult cases. We received this from a grateful music hall manager. We have decided to present it to you.'

Cribb accepted it with good grace. Only when he was outside in Whitehall Place did he open the envelope and examine the slip of paper inside. It was a year's free admission to the Middlesex. He took it to the Embankment, made a small boat of it and dropped it into the river, watching thoughtfully as it drifted away on the tide.